# LION OF HEARTS

## A MEDIEVAL ROMANCE
### SONS OF CHRISTOPHER DE LOHR
### PART OF THE DE LOHR DYNASTY

## BY KATHRYN LE VEQUE

KATHRYN LE VEQUE
NOVELS

## ARE YOU SIGNED UP FOR KATHRYN'S BLOG?

You'll get the latest news and information on exclusive giveaways, exclusive excerpts, coming releases, sales, free books, cover reveals and more.

Kathryn's blog followers get it all first. No spam, no junk.

Get the latest info from the reigning Queen of English Medieval Romance!

**Sign Up Here**

kathrynleveque.com

**What happens to a man who has fallen for the wrong woman when the right woman comes along?**

**Myles de Lohr is about to find out.**

As the humorless, sometimes taciturn middle de Lohr brother, Myles is all knight, all the time. The man couldn't crack a smile to save his life, and something like romance is completely out of his wheelhouse. Love has never crossed his mind until he meets a woman who sweeps him off his feet.

Or so he thinks.

Unfamiliar with the difference between love and lust, Myles is convinced he is in love with Lady Aviara, an epic flirt. Enter Myles' cousin, Oliver de Grey. As the Earl of Ilchester, Oliver views Aviara as a prize and steals her out from under Myles' nose. As Aviara becomes Lady Ilchester, Myles is convinced his life is over and he has lost everything.

Until he meets Veronica de Wolviston.

Veronica's father was a much-sought-after cartographer and a vassal of Myles' father, Christopher de Lohr. When Edgar de Wolviston passes away, he leaves a note asking Christopher to escort his daughter to her betrothed. With Myles in turmoil after losing the lady he lusted after, Christopher orders his muddled son to take Veronica north and deliver her to her betrothed, hoping the trip will clear his son's head.

Surely no two people in this history of the world have ever made more miserable traveling companions.

And that is the start of an unexpected—but eye-opening—revelation for Myles when it comes to the bookish, brilliant Veronica. Join the star-crossed couple on a journey for the ages, where the understanding of friendship and love are something both of them must learn from one another, where loyalty and honor mean more than lust and instant gratification, and where the growth of true and deep love is something that comes from the very soul. None of that is more evident when Myles is unexpectedly presented with the choice between the woman he lusted after and Veronica. Then he has an epiphany.

It's a decision that only his heart can make... when the heart of a lion is the biggest heart of all.

# House of de Lohr motto

*Deus et Honora*
God and Honor

# AUTHOR'S NOTE

And we're off and running with Myles' book!

Myles is named after Myles de Lohr, who made his appearance in *While Angels Slept*. Myles married the sister of the hero in that book, and—BAM—our baby de Lohrs were born. So, Myles is the name of Christopher de Lohr's father. I really, really loved the character of Myles de Lohr in *While Angels Slept*—he was a seasoned, responsible warrior with great patience, which he had to have because he wanted to marry Val du Reims, who was a warrior woman with zero interest in marriage. Therefore, Christopher and David come from warrior stock because both of their parents were seasoned veterans.

Now, let's talk about Myles (our hero) a little bit. Be advised that he's different from the start. When I write about heroes, I always give them traits that I like in men (humor, passion, etc). Not that Myles doesn't have these traits, but he's also a little sharp at times. Blunt. It takes him a little while to warm up in this tale, but this tale is about the growth of a man. He's different from his father and brothers. He just has to find the right woman to discover that about himself. I think it's an exciting journey for him.

And our heroine? She's amazing. Strong, bright, logical, but she's found herself in a bad situation when Myles comes into her life. I love watching them figure it all out together.

As I usually do in the de Lohr books, here's a quick family tree on who all of the children of Christopher and Dustin de Lohr are and whom they're married to. It gets updated with each successive book in the series. A very helpful family list!

- Peter (The Splendid Hour) Lord Pembridge, eventually Earl of Farringdon. Garrison commander Ludlow Castle
- Christin (A Time of End) Married to Alexander de Sherrington, Garrison commander of Wigmore Castle
- Brielle (The Dark Conqueror)
- Curtis (Lion of War) Earl of Leominster (heir apparent to the larger Earldom of Hereford and Worcester), Baron Ivington
- Richard "Roi" (Lion of Twilight) Earl of Cheltenham
- Myles (Lion of Hearts) Lord Monnington of Monnington Castle, a Marcher lordship—Lordship of Doré
- Rebecca
- Douglas (Lion of Steel)
- Westley (whose middle name is Henry and he was sometimes referred to as "Henry" when he was young) (Lion of Thunder)
- Olivia Charlotte (the future Honey de Shera from the Lords of Thunder series)

I like to say that the de Lohrs are my favorite secondary characters. They pop up in a lot of novels. The de Lohr sons first make an appearance, as secondary characters, in *The Dark Conqueror*, which is their sister, Brielle's, story. They're very young—and silly—and it has been fun rereading that book to get a feel for their dynamics, as I wrote it a few years ago. Clearly, they're adults now, so things are different, but *The Dark Conqueror* is one of my favorite de Lohr stories. It's fun to read about Curtis, Richard, Myles, Douglas, and Westley before I really started to develop their characters. I do want to say that in that story, I made a note about Douglas, which I need to clarify (and will clarify in his story again).

The case of two Douglas de Lohrs...

Douglas de Lohr made an appearance in *Tender is the Knight* and, as it ended up, he was the antagonist. He was also killed. I had always intended that he should be Christopher's son, but as it worked out, he would have only been around seventeen years old at the time—and the Douglas de Lohr in the story was much older. So—Douglas de Lohr, son of Christopher, got a second chance at life, and I'm so pleased. He's been a great character so far. The "other" Douglas? He's a distant cousin with the same name. And that's how he'll be remembered. When you have a universe as big as mine, sometimes things get twisted up a bit. What I'd intended for a character ten years ago is not what I intend for him now. That's the beauty of fiction. But I can always—and usually—logically clarify the characters and their relationships.

And now, the usual pronunciation guide:

Myles—Miles, like the name (or the distance), just a
    different spelling.
Doré—Door-AY

And with that, we're ready to roll with Myles and Veronica's story—so hang on and enjoy the ride!

Happy reading!

# PROLOGUE

*Year of Our Lord 1235*
*Tidworth Castle*
*Wessex*

S HE'D BEEN FLIRTING with him all night.
Myles de Lohr was convinced that he was the only one she'd been flirting with, a beautiful and alluring vixen with a golden cap on her head and golden tassels that brushed against her shoulders when she moved. She had dark hair curling out from underneath the cap and pale, flashing eyes that had been sending him titillating glances from the moment he walked into the great hall of Tidworth.

And why not? Myles was what his brothers referred to as a beauteous lad. With flowing blond hair, a square jaw, and eyes the color of the sky, he was a prime male specimen. Most of his brothers had the blond good looks and their father's soaring height, too, but with Myles, it was taken a step further.

He was a god.

Gods had their pick of women, and tonight would be no different for Myles—although in his case, the pick of women had nothing to do with romance or even wooing. It had everything to do with conquest. Cold, unfeeling conquest.

Myles was a conqueror.

He was also on a mission.

As one of the senior operatives of a covert group of agents known as the Executioner Knights, he was at Tidworth Castle for a purpose, and that purpose wasn't to flirt with the lady in the golden cap, although he knew her well and had for some time. Lady Aviara de Serreaux was the daughter of a friend of his father's, a lass who lived at Aldsworth Castle in Gloucestershire and who had fostered with Myles' youngest sister. She'd probably been in love with Myles for that long, or at least in lust with him, so seeing her at this feast given by a de Lohr ally wasn't unusual.

But it was… unwanted.

Myles didn't need the distraction.

"Stay away from her." The voice in his ear was soft, deep. "I know she's been eyeing you all night, Myles, but stay away from her. I need you on task."

Myles recognized the voice of his eldest brother, Peter de Lohr. Also known as the Earl of Farringdon, he was in command of the Executioner Knights. Control of England's most elite group of spies had been passed down to Peter when the Earl of Pembroke, Ansel Marshal, passed away. Ansel was the son of the man that many referred to as England's greatest knight, William Marshal, who had formed the Executioner Knights during the days of King Richard's reign, using some of the greatest warriors in the world. These days, the Executioner Knights were formed of legacy members, meaning their fathers—or mothers—had once been part of the contingent. There was a mighty group of spies in the hall as a result.

And they were on the hunt.

"I *am* on task," Myles said after a moment, his eyes on the hall. "Why would you think I am not?"

Peter stood next to his brother, his gaze on the same people that Myles was looking at. "I will say this only once," he said with quiet authority. "We are in a brittle situation, Myles, and I need your focus. I realize your young woman is seated near the dais, in conversation with her giddy friends, and I further realize she is quite aware of your presence. She is also aware of Oliver's presence."

That was the magic name, as far as Myles was concerned, and not in a good way. He knew very well that his brother was referring to a distant de Lohr cousin, Oliver de Grey, who was also in attendance at the feast—and when Peter mentioned the name, it was like throwing water on a fire.

Myles struggled not to feel doused.

"That makes no difference," he insisted. "Oliver is immaterial to my life or pursuits."

Peter looked at him. "Then you are the only one in England who does not know that Lady Aviara de Serreaux has been pitting you against Oliver for months," he hissed. "Hell, she's been doing it for at least two years that I can recall, and possibly longer than that. Are you truly so dense, Myles? Your aloof and apathetic behavior is believable only so far. Do you really not know what she is doing?"

"Clearly, I am not as stupid as you think I am."

"I never said you were stupid. I asked if you were dense when it came to a woman."

"I'm offended that you would even ask that question."

He meant it. Myles was not a good-natured man. Taciturn was where he began. Where he ended, no one knew, because he wasn't congenial or jovial or even particularly likable—until one got him drunk, and then all of that suppressed personality came out. But in fairness, he had his good qualities—he was loyal to the bone, brave as few men were, and morally just in all situations. Myles was a man of honor, a man of good character, but the warmth that his brothers had, including Peter, was sorely lacking in him. Simply put, Myles was indeed cold and aloof and, at times, quite emotionless, although no one could figure out why. It wasn't as if he'd had a brutal childhood or been raised by barbarians. He'd been raised by loving parents in a loving family. But one would have never known it based solely on his behavior.

Myles de Lohr was as cold as ice.

An attribute that made him one of the better Executioner Knights, however, if not *the* best. If there was something down, dirty, and deep that needed to be done, Myles would do it without question. He wasn't swayed by tears or begging, nor pleading. He would complete his task no matter what. Peter knew that, but he also knew that Aviara had been taunting his cold brother for months now, drawing him in with her flirting and giggling and then playing him against his rival, Oliver de Grey.

That distant cousin he'd spoken of.

Truth be told, Oliver wasn't a terrible person. Quite the opposite. He was cousin to the House of de Lohr on their paternal grandfather's side, and Myles considered him a friend. At least, he had at one time. But that was before Lady Aviara began her campaign of flirtatious bombardment, pitting the beauteous but cold Myles against the charming but not-quite-as-beauteous Oliver.

Peter didn't want any part of that woman's plans to interfere with his own.

"Then I am sorry if you are offended, but I have a job to do," Peter muttered after a moment. "So do you. I must make sure that you are on task and not falling for that woman's obvious traps."

Myles' patience finally left him, and he looked at his brother, scowling. "Be plain, Peter," he growled. "What has you harping on me like an old fishwife?"

Peter cocked an eyebrow. "If I was harping on you, I would be much more obvious than this," he said. "All I know is that more than a year ago, Lady Aviara and her father stopped at Lioncross Abbey to break their journey from Liverpool. Bertrand de Serreaux is a friend of Papa's, that is true, and Olivia fostered with Aviara, so they knew her. It was, by all accounts, an innocuous visit, until Aviara decided that she had to have your attention. All of it. Worse still, Oliver was visiting because Papa had some business with his father, and Lady Aviara discovered that she had two knights to pit against one another for her affections. This is the story I got from Papa, so if it is a lie, then you can tell him to his face. *Is* it a lie, Myles?"

Myles was unhappy with the turn the conversation had taken. "That is Papa's opinion," he said. "It was not mine. Peter, I can focus on my task with or without Lady Aviara. Do you really think I would fail? I've not failed you yet."

Peter backed down a little. "Nay, you've never failed me," he said. "But this is an important gathering. We have a courtier who is sending information to the French king on Henry's movements. Every time the king makes a decision to move men, or he devises political plans, Louis finds out. With the tension between Henry and Louis right now, that puts Louis at an advantage, but more than that, it is dangerous. Louis is planning on going on crusade, and the pope himself has promised to protect the man's lands while he is away. That puts Henry in peril should he move against France, because he and Louis are verging on war. Henry would be fighting the pope."

Myles sighed softly. "I know."

"Then you also know that Henry would call upon Papa and you and me, and we would all be fighting the church."

"I understand."

"That would be a disaster for us, Myles."

Myles was well aware. This situation was more than the need to support the king, because this situation, in particular, had far-reaching implications for Henry's allies and their relationship with the Catholic Church. If Henry went to war against France, which would be under the pope's protection, it would be a mess that the English warlords would likely not soon recover from.

God may be forgiving, but the pope wasn't.

"Papa sent word to the man we know who is passing secrets to Louis," Myles said in a low voice. "He summoned him to Tidworth's gathering under the pretext of meeting with him. No one refuses a summons from the great Christopher de Lohr."

Peter nodded. "Indeed not," he said, looking around the hall. His gaze fell on a tall, young nobleman near the dais in conversation with a few men. "But the truth is that there is a spy from Louis here tonight who is preparing to connect with the courtier. In fact, I see that courtier now. Seabourne St. Albans has always been a congenial man, and well liked by Henry. A pity he is a traitor."

Myles' gaze moved to St. Albans, who was taller than most of the men in the hall, with receding blond hair that hardly covered his scalp as it reflected the candles from the chandeliers overhead. He had an impeccable pedigree hiding a mountain of debt, something Louis was more than happy to pay for in exchange for a little information.

That was the crux of the situation.

"And the French spy?" Myles asked softly.

Peter turned away, looking at his brother again. "We have paid a good deal of money to discover that he is posing as a servant and will be serving Lord Tidworth personally. He will make contact with Henry's courtier at that time, and when the courier excuses himself from Tidworth's table, we will follow him. We must intercept him and the spy before the exchange can be made. You, Myles, will be charged with watching St. Albans. Never let the man out of your sight. If he moves, you move."

Myles nodded firmly. "Aye, my lord."

"The other agents will move when you do. You are our lead."

Again, Myles nodded. He was usually the man to make the first move in situations like this because he was so infallible. He knew the operation rested on him.

He preferred it that way.

"Who else is in the hall?" he asked. "I've only seen Broden."

He was referring to another cousin, Broden du Reims, a man to whom he was close. Unlike Oliver, Broden and Myles had been close since childhood, and Broden was a likeable man. Son of the Earl of East Anglia, he was auburn-haired and quick-tempered, and he and Myles had bonded over their mutually cold temperament.

But he wasn't the only one in the hall.

Peter gestured toward the entry.

"Andrew and Madoc are over by the door," he said. "They

are dressed in the regalia of a Tidworth knight. Do you recognize them?"

Myles had to look hard, something he didn't really want to do, because anyone watching him would want to see what he was looking at, but it was necessary. He spied his nephew, Andrew, son of his older sister, Christin, a tall and muscular lad who looked just like his black-haired, black-eyed father, Alexander. But it took him a moment to identify Madoc of Loxbeare, son of one of the original Executioner Knights. Madoc had more the look of his mother, with pale hair and brown eyes, but he was built like a bull, as his father was. When a knight near the entry shoved back some revelers who had come to crash the party, Myles immediately realized it was the heavy-handed Madoc.

"Aye," he finally said. "I see them. Peter, if you put Madoc of Loxbeare in charge of admitting guests, he is going to kill people who are not to his liking."

Peter fought off a grin. "Or start a war."

Myles rolled his eyes. "He's just like Maxton," he mumbled. "Just like his father. Maxton was a brute."

Peter smirked. "That is Papa talking."

"Papa was right."

That comment had Peter breaking down into soft laughter. "Papa and Maxton were never what you would call friends," he said. "I think they were just far too similar. But they would have died, or killed, for one another. They were the true heart of what an ally should be."

Myles couldn't dispute that. The dislike between Christopher de Lohr and Maxton of Loxbeare was legendary in the annals of the Executioner Knights, but Peter was right—either one of them would have killed, or died, for the other. Such were allies at times, knowing they needed one another in spite of their personal opinions of one another.

Some wondered if, deep down, they really did like each other.

"Mayhap," Myles said after a moment. "Papa and Maxton aside, however, I'm still not sure I agree with your putting Madoc at that post. But he is there and we must make the best of it. Who else is in the hall?"

Peter dipped his head toward the eastern side of the hall, where many were gathered around a table that had been laid out with elaborate food creations for the guests to admire. There were also never-ending pitchers of wine and boiled fruit juice for those who couldn't tolerate the strong drink. Dozens of people were picking over the table, with hovering servants nearby, and it took Myles a moment to recognize Corey MacRohan and Bowie Forbes, finely dressed as guests.

Corey was the son of Bric MacRohan, England's greatest Irish legacy knight, while Bowie was the son of the great Gart Forbes. In battle, no man had been Gart's equal, and he'd served the House of de Lohr flawlessly for many years. Both families were allied with Tidworth, so their disguises as guests were completely appropriate. No one would think it odd to see them. But as Myles watched, Bowie reached for something on the table, and a serving wench standing nearby slapped him on the hand. He withdrew the appendage sharply and wandered away.

Myles struggled not to react.

"Did I just see Alis de Dere slap her husband?" he said incredulously.

Peter had been watching the same thing. "You did," he said. "Alis is posing as a servant to glean what information she can from those who serve Tidworth. It also gives her an opportunity to keep an eye on St. Albans. But she is clearly trying to keep Bowie from the wine. The man needs to be clearheaded tonight."

Myles couldn't help but grin at Alis, tough as nails and a Blackchurch-trained warrior just like her mother, married to Bowie Forbes, who was quite possibly one of the most congenial and likable men in England. But he had his father's vicious temperament when provoked, making him one of the deadlier men as well. When Alis slapped, Bowie obediently slinked away, properly rebuked by his lovely but formidable wife. Myles always thought Bowie and Alis' marriage was one of the better matches he'd encountered.

And he was glad to have the pair here in the hall.

The Executioner Knights had come prepared.

"What will you do now?" Myles asked his brother. "And where do you want me?"

Peter gestured toward the dais. "I will attach myself to Tidworth," he said. "You find MacRohan, and the two of you will watch St. Albans like a hawk. And I'll be watching you in case you move."

"Aye, my lord," Myles said. But then he seemed to look around as if searching for something. "I see everyone else, but where is Broden?"

"I've put him outside in the bailey," Peter said. "If St. Albans or the spy escapes us, he is the net. They will not get past him."

"Understood."

"Go forth, brother."

With that, they separated, heading into the smoky, fragrant hall and mingling with the crowd that was growing by the moment. It seemed that several houses arrived at the same time, so Madoc and Andrew were admitting people, though holding off those who were heavily armed. Tidworth had requested that arms be left outside the hall, which didn't go over well with some of the attendees, so Madoc found himself frequently posturing in a threatening manner until those protesting were forced to bend.

Much like his father, he'd always enjoyed that part of his profession.

Making others bend.

But Myles had missed most of it because he was fixed on Corey, who was over by the table laden with food. As he walked up, the big knight was shoving stuffed eggs into his face, and, with his mouth so full he could hardly chew, he caught sight of Myles. He tried to grin, but that revealed the big, white side of the hardboiled egg only. It looked like the man had egg for teeth.

Myles shook his head reproachfully.

"God's Bones, MacRohan," he said. "You are going to choke if you continue to eat like that."

Corey, big and blond and quite handsome, struggled to chew and managed to swallow some of it before speaking. "I grew up with brothers who would steal food out from underneath me," he said. "My father would encourage us to take what we wanted, when we wanted, but my mother admonished us to show manners and thoughtfulness. Quite confusing for a gang of half-Irish lads who all possessed that wild streak."

Myles fought off a smile. "I adore your father," he said. "How is Bric these days?"

"Just as he always is," Corey said. "He is big and powerful and beloved by all."

"Still at Narborough Castle?"

"Still. He'll never leave."

"And your mother?"

"She has my father falling at her feet, as usual."

"And her children, too, I would imagine."

"Of course. Eiselle MacRohan is our rock."

Myles understood that because he had a mother who was much the same. Formidable and greatly loved, Dustin de Lohr was the beating heart of their family. He reached down and collected one of those eggs Corey seemed to be so fond of, realizing they were stuffed with meat and quite delicious. He took a couple.

"You have your orders, do you not?" he asked Corey, his mouth full.

Corey took another egg because he didn't want Myles getting all of them. "I am to support you."

"And so you shall."

With that, they pretended to be just like any other guest, eating everything they could get their hands on. The stuffed eggs were only the beginning. But when it came to the wine, they took the boiled juice instead. As Corey found a braided loaf of bread to tear apart, Myles was caught off guard by a vision in silk in his periphery. Before he could turn around, a soft voice arose.

"I should be very angry with you, Myles de Lohr."

Lady Aviara had snuck up on him, and Myles silently cursed himself for being stupid enough to have let her. He caught a faint whiff of perfume—undoubtedly very expensive—that assaulted his nose to the point of his having to shake off a sneeze. His eyes were watering as he focused on the beautiful young woman in the gold cap.

"Good eve, my lady," he said evenly. "What dastardly thing have I done to cause you such fury?"

She batted her eyelashes at him in a practiced gesture. "You did not greet me when you entered," she said. "You went to the other side of the hall, and I saw you speaking to your brother. He does not like me, you know. He never has. He must have poisoned you against me."

Myles lifted a blond eyebrow. "What a thing to say," he said. "No one could poison me against you. And I did not come to you directly because I had a message for Peter from our mother. That is something I could not delay."

It was a lie, but she had no reason to believe otherwise. Her features relaxed and she smiled.

"Then I forgive you," she said, looping her hands through the crook of his elbow affectionately. "And how is Lady de Lohr getting on?"

"Remarkably, as always. I shall tell her you asked after her health."

"Please do," Aviara said. "And Olivia?"

"She is very well."

"I am glad to hear it." Aviara still had him with one hand as she turned to the table and pointed. "Would you fetch me some wine? I am parched."

Myles dutifully grasped the pitcher with the wine, made difficult by the fact that Aviara was clinging to his left arm. But he managed to pour her a cup, handing it to her. She let go of him long enough to grasp the drink, but their fingers brushed during the hand-off, and she smiled alluringly at him as she sipped the tart, strong wine.

"It has been a few weeks since we last saw one another," she said.

Myles smiled faintly. "Six weeks, three days, and about twelve hours," he said. "Had I not made the journey into

Gloucester for my father back in the spring, we would not have seen one another at all. It was quite fortuitous."

Her smile faded. "I know," she said. "Myles… I hope I can speak freely."

"Absolutely."

"I cannot go the rest of my life hoping we will see one another from time to time."

"What do you mean?"

She sighed sharply. "Must I explain myself?"

Myles was at a loss. "I suppose you must. Am I being dense?"

She frowned. "You are," she said. "Terribly dense. You have been terribly dense for the past two years, and I cannot depend on good fortune or God or whatever winds of fate you believe in to put us in the right place at the right time so that we may see one another. I have done everything I can to ensure we were at the same place at the same time, the same feasts, the same gatherings, but I cannot continue that indefinitely."

He was waiting for her to continue, but she stopped, so he looked at her, eyes narrowed, trying to figure out what she was attempting to say.

"Are you asking to know my plans?" he said. "Things I am to do during the course of my duties so that you can be where I am? Because I do not know everything, my lady. I—"

She cut him off with a frustrated grunt. "God, you truly *are* dense," she said. "It is a good thing you are handsome, Myles de Lohr, because you are as dumb as a sack of rocks. I am trying to tell you that I wish for there to be something more between us, but since you've not brought it up, it appears I must be the one to finally present the subject, and I refuse to wait any longer."

"What subject?"

"I want you to court me."

Myles' eyebrows shot up. "*Court* you?" he said, suddenly feeling uneasy and, frankly, a little nervous. "I… Is that what this is about? You want to… to be married?"

His clear reluctance wasn't what Aviara wanted to hear. Her mouth popped open in outrage. "You've not even *considered* it?" she nearly shouted. "How, in God's name, can you say that? You mean all of the sweet words we've spoken between us have meant nothing to you?"

Faced with an angry woman, Myles struggled to come up with an answer. "In fairness, *you* spoke the sweet words," he said. "I merely let you."

Aviara slammed the cup down, splashing wine onto the table. "Is that so?" she said angrily. "And what about the kisses at Lioncross back in January when my father and I visited? I seem to recall that *you* kissed *me*."

"And you let me."

"I am coming to see that I should not have!"

Myles wasn't quite sure why she was so angry, but deep down, he suspected he knew. He'd indeed been dense, and he'd let a pretty woman flatter him. But she wanted something in return. Truth be told, she was pretty enough to marry, and would more than likely give him strong sons. That was reason enough to marry, wasn't it? Good breeding? And he liked her fire—it was a great contrast to his coldness. Aye, he liked her well enough.

However, he was in no position for a romantic conversation.

He had a task to complete this night, and he was dangerously close to losing his focus. He didn't want Aviara angry at him, but the truth was that he wasn't very good with women. He never seemed to say the right thing. He knew what she wanted—he'd always known—and perhaps someday he *would* court her, but not now. He wasn't in any hurry. He was frankly astonished that she would be so bold about it, so unless he wanted to lose her attention, he would have to make amends.

Truth be told, he had no idea how, but he had to try.

"Aviara, you know I am not very good when it comes to flattery," he said. "You must forgive me for being... dense. Of course I would like to speak to you further, but not now. Not in a hall full of people. I would rather do it when we are alone, with no distractions. I... I do not wish to share your attention with anyone."

The flame of anger in Aviara's eyes dimmed, but it didn't go out completely. "That is what I want to hear," she said. "You do not have to behave so evasively, Myles."

"I am not deliberately trying to be evasive."

She softened further. Finally, she grinned because she knew Myles very well. "I know," she said. "You are simply being what you always are—a rock. A cold, immovable, dense rock."

He smiled weakly. "I suppose it is my nature."

"It is," she said, her eyes twinkling. "But you are one rock I wish to warm. We've had this conversation before."

He was glad that she didn't seem so angry. He may not have wanted to marry her tomorrow, but that didn't mean he wanted her angry with him. "I know," he said, shrugging. "What more can I say? It is simply the way I am."

Aviara's smile grew. "And it is maddening," she said. "But will you at least try to behave as if you like me? It would make me feel as if this is not such a one-sided venture."

His smile grew. "I *do* like you," he said softly. "Better than any other lady I know. But you must give me time to show it."

"I will be old and gray before that happens," she said, rolling her eyes. "And next time I bring up the subject of courtship and romance, you do not have to pretend not to know what I am speaking of. That is insulting."

"I did not mean to insult you, truly."

"Whom did you insult, Myles?"

The question came from behind, and Myles turned to see Oliver coming up alongside him, smiling directly at Aviara. Charming, amiable Oliver with hair the color of dirty straw and a big gap between his front teeth. Before Myles could reply, Oliver spoke in that smooth way he was so capable of.

"Well?" he said to Aviara. "What did my cousin say to you that was so terribly insulting?"

Aviara wasn't in a particularly forgiving mood. Besides, she'd become quite practiced at pitting Myles against Oliver to stroke her feminine ego.

"Myles does not seem to want to court me at the moment," she said. "What do you think, Ollie? *Am* I worth courting?"

Oliver didn't hesitate. He reached out and took her hand in a genteel manner. "Of course you are, my lady," he said sweetly. "In fact, I should ask to court you this very moment if I thought you would accept. Myles may not appreciate you, but I certainly do."

Myles watched with growing displeasure as Oliver kissed Aviara's hand. She turned her charm to Oliver, smiling at him, clearly intent on making Myles jealous, but he hadn't the time to react because someone was hissing in his ear.

"Myles," came the voice. "*Myles!*"

It was Corey. Myles was forced to turn away from Aviara and Oliver, snapping his head around as Corey indicated St. Albans, now moving up beside Tidworth at the same time several servants approached the dais with food in their hands. Immediately, Myles moved away from Aviara and Oliver, his hawklike focus on St. Albans as the man stood next to Tidworth, engaging him in conversation. As Myles and Corey watched, a small man with dark hair, bearing a Tidworth tunic, brought a trencher and a knife to Tidworth. He set the trencher down, but St. Albans reached out to politely take the knife by the hilt, and then carefully set it down next to Tidworth's trencher.

But he had something in his hand.

Something had been attached to the hilt of the knife, but neither Myles nor Corey could see what it was. They simply knew it *was* there by the way St. Albans was clutching a fist. The servant quickly left the dais, only to be followed by Alis, in her servant's garb, and then eventually by Bowie, who followed his wife casually from the hall. Myles and Corey were focused on St. Albans, however, and they continued to watch him as he spoke amiably to Tidworth and another lord at the table, before glancing at his hand, pausing, and then casually moving away from the dais.

Myles and Corey went in pursuit.

"Myles!"

Aviara was following. Myles ignored her, moving after St. Albans as the man headed for the main entry of the hall, but Aviara ran up behind him and grabbed him by the arm.

"Myles de Lohr!" she said furiously. "Where are you going?"

Corey was still following St. Albans, but Myles had been forced to come to a halt. Having no patience for interference, even from Aviara, he yanked his hand away from her.

"Out," he said. "I will find you later."

He turned to move away again, but she charged after him.

"Don't you dare leave," she said. "We are not finished with our conversation!"

Myles didn't have time for her tantrums. In fact, he could see Peter closing in quickly on them, and he hastened to get rid of Aviara. "We are finished for the moment," he said to the woman, fearful of what his brother might say to her. "I will seek you later and we will continue our conversation, but for now, I must go."

"You," Peter spat at Aviara, pulling her away by the arm. "Go back to your father and leave my brother alone."

Seeing that it was Peter, a man who had historically been impervious to her charms, Aviara turned on him viciously. "You cannot order me about," she said angrily. "I do not care if you are the Earl of Farringdon. My business is with Myles and not you!"

Peter's eyes narrowed at her as his patience vanished. He didn't much like her as it was, and her insolence displeased him greatly. "You've been teasing and taunting my brother for some time now," he said. "You pit him against de Grey in the competition for your affections, and do not deny it. We've all seen you do it. You use the tricks of a harlot, so if you do not want me to think of you as one, I would suggest you return to your father and stop tormenting my brother. Your games are unbecoming a lady of your breeding."

Aviara's mouth popped open in utter rage, but before she could reply, Peter was moving away from her, blowing past his brother as he headed for the door. Myles knew that he had no choice but to follow, and he did, leaving Aviara standing where they'd left her, insulted and enraged.

But he couldn't think about that now.

He had a job to do.

Once outside the hall, Myles rushed past his brother, pursuing Corey to the bailey outside, where St. Albans seemed to be heading for the outbuildings that housed the smithy and wheelwright, among others. St. Albans didn't seem to be aware of his surroundings because he wasn't looking around to see if he was being followed or observed, but even so, Myles caught up with Corey and pulled the man into the shadows. As they stood in the darkness of the gateway that led into the smithy yard, Peter came up on the other side of the gate, watching St. Albans as well.

For several long and tense moments, they simply watched.

And waited.

But they didn't have to wait long.

This part of the yard was connected to the stables, which was a large, L-shaped block. Part of it contained a corral with a roof over it. The smell of horses and hay was heavy in the air as St. Albans came to a halt in the middle of the yard, clearly waiting for something. Or someone. He kept looking to the stable, and as Myles and the others watched, they saw the man flinch as if he'd heard something. Then he flinched again as a pair of men came barreling through the stable door, spilling out into the smithy yard. Fists were flying as Bowie, in combat with the French spy, landed in the midst of the yard.

But that wasn't the only fight going on.

Chaos was instant.

Inside the stable, Alis was in a fight of her own against two more men, but neither Myles nor Peter nor Corey could see it. They could hear it, however, and realizing there was mortal danger to two of the Executioner Knights, they came out of the shadows. Myles bolted for the stables along with Corey, and Peter headed for Bowie. While Bowie's opponent was subdued quickly once Peter entered the fight, the battle in the stables was another matter.

It was bloody from the onset.

Alis had done her best against two opponents. She'd held them admirably, which both confused and infuriated them. No one had known that the French spy had other men with him, spies that had come along for support, so Alis had been attacked from behind by one of them and ended up with a dagger in her shoulder. But she wore a broadsword underneath her peasant skirts, and even with the injured shoulder, she was still managing to hold off two men. However, her wound was bleeding and she was quickly tiring as a vicious fight ensued. As Myles rushed into the stable, he pulled the sword from her grip and assumed her fight. Normally, Alis would have slugged him for such a thing, but she was in pain and weary.

She let Myles take charge.

As Alis moved aside, heading out into the smithy yard to see how her husband fared, Myles and Corey went after the two French opponents with a vengeance. No one survived against a de Lohr and a MacRohan for long, and in little time, the Frenchmen realized they were in trouble. Both Myles and Corey were fresh and in full health, and they managed to quickly beat back the Frenchmen, who weren't giving up without a fight. But that changed when Broden rushed in through the main stable entry, coming up behind the Frenchmen and lifting his broadsword, taking off the head of one of them right away.

The dynamics instantly changed.

The man who was left realized he would be killed if he didn't surrender, so he immediately dropped his sword and fell to his knees, holding up his hands in supplication.

"*Ne me tue pas!*" he cried. "*Montrer de la pitié!*"

Myles bent over the man and grabbed him around the neck with a hand the size of a trencher. "I will consider it," he growled. "Tell me if there are any more French bastards here. Did you bring more men with you?"

The Frenchman was clearly terrified. "I do not know what you mean," he said. "The lady attacked us. We were fighting for our lives!"

Myles cocked an eyebrow. "Lie to me again and I will ensure your death is as painful as possible," he said. "I will ask again. Did you bring more men with you?"

The Frenchman faltered, and when he did, Myles squeezed so that the man's face turned purple. He was struggling to breathe, finally fighting back against Myles' iron grip. Myles responded by balling a fist and hitting the man squarely in the face. Bones cracked and teeth broke as the man ended up on the ground of the stable, bleeding profusely.

"I will ask once more," Myles said unemotionally. "Did you bring more men with you?"

The Frenchman was bleeding all over the place. He sat up unsteadily, spitting out blood and trying to wipe it from his mouth. "*Non,*" he finally said, muffled by his pummeled mouth. "No more men."

Myles considered him for a moment before turning to Corey. "Take him to the gatehouse and release him," he said, quietly enough that the Frenchman couldn't hear him. "Follow him and see if he leads you to more French spies."

Corey looked at him with suspicion. "You do not believe him?"

"I do not."

"Nor do I."

"Then go forth."

Corey nodded, reaching down to pull the man to his feet. As he dragged the injured Frenchman from the stable, Broden came to stand with Myles, watching MacRohan with his injured prisoner.

"What do you think?" Broden asked quietly. "Do you think there are more?"

Myles shrugged. "If there are, surely he will lead us to them," he said. "Mayhap he is more valuable alive."

"Who is more valuable?"

Peter came up behind them, a streak of blood across his face that wasn't his. He saw the headless body on the ground and pointed.

"Who is this?" he asked.

Myles didn't answer. He was looking at the body, so Broden spoke up. "One of the men fighting Myles and Corey," he said.

Peter looked at him. "Where is the other one?"

Broden gestured toward the gatehouse. "Corey is releasing the man," he said, wondering why Myles wasn't speaking up. "Myles thought it would be better not to kill him, but to release him and then have Corey follow him to see if he joins up with other Frenchmen."

Peter looked at his brother. "There are others," he said. "The spy just confessed that there are others waiting in the village. If the spy you just released gets to them and tells them what he knows, then they will scatter back to France."

Myles wouldn't look at him. "I doubt he knows anything," he said. "The meeting between St. Albans and the spy was never made. Words were never exchanged."

"That you know of," Peter said, increasingly frustrated. "Do not let that man leave, Myles. Go and get him now."

It was a command, not meant to be disobeyed. Myles didn't

say a word as he headed out of the stable, eventually breaking into a run to catch Corey and the Frenchman just as they reached the gatehouse. He managed to grab the Frenchman by the hair and drag the man all the way back to the stable where Peter was waiting. He practically threw him at his brother's feet and then stood there while Peter interrogated the man.

It was a nasty business.

It was also a long activity that went well into the night. When Peter was finally certain that the Frenchman didn't know anything at all about St. Albans or the exchange of information, he sent him off with Broden to be imprisoned in Tidworth's vault until they could decide what to do with him. Two out of the three French spies were dead, St. Albans was imprisoned for transport back to London to face Henry's wrath, and the Executioner Knights had prevented yet another potentially catastrophic happening against Henry's reign.

But something else catastrophic had happened that night.

When Myles returned to the hall later that night to find Aviara and apologize for Peter's harsh words, he was told in no uncertain terms that the lady didn't wish to speak to him—by Aviara's father, no less. Bertrand de Serreaux was a kind man with a good deal of wealth and a daughter who would make someone very rich through marriage. He had been hoping that man would be Myles de Lohr, but Aviara had tales of being horribly insulted by the Earl of Farringdon, and that brought her father's wrath.

It was something that could affect the alliance with Christopher de Lohr, too.

Unfortunately, Myles had never been a good negotiator. He was all business, all the time, and in battle, there was no one finer. In an interrogation, Myles could extract information when no one else could. He was a man of few words, but those few words were important. Therefore, he was at a loss as to how to soothe Bertrand, a valuable ally, so all he could do was apologize for his brother's boorish behavior. He couldn't even explain it away because he couldn't think of a lie that would be convincing enough. But when Peter entered the hall some time later, Myles had a few choice words for his brother.

*Fix it.*

For the alliance with Christopher, Peter tried. But for anything to do with Aviara, he couldn't.

*Wouldn't.*

And Myles knew it.

# CHAPTER ONE

*Year of Our Lord 1236*
*Lioncross Abbey Castle, Herefordshire*
*The Month of March*

"I SAW THE messenger from de Serreaux," Myles said with as much anxiety as his stone façade would allow. "Is it for me?"

He'd burst into his father's grand solar, a chamber that had an enormous vaulted ceiling, hides on the floor, and rich furnishings befitting the Earl of Hereford and Worcester. The walls of that old chamber had seen much history transacted by some of the most important men in England. It had also seen its share of tragedies.

Christopher was thinking this would be one of those times.

Seated behind an enormous table with a carved lion's head on each corner and legs fashioned to look like lion legs and clawed feet, Christopher de Lohr, a man once known as the Lion's Claw, among other monikers, glanced up at his son. He heard the hope in the man's question and wasn't quite sure how to answer him.

Something odd had happened to Myles over the past several

months.

Ever since the incident at Tidworth Castle back in the summer of the previous year, Myles had changed. The unfriendly man became unfriendlier. Once, there had been some warmth in him, especially when it came to his family, but even that had faded. Myles became nothing more than a knight who lived and breathed his profession, with time for nothing else. He was the first man on watch, the last man to leave, and managed Lioncross' legions of men at arms with strict but fair efficiency. But there was no connection to anyone beyond that. Not even his beloved older brothers, Curtis and Roi, could break through to him. As his mother had said, somewhere on that fateful night at Tidworth, Myles had lost his humanity.

Something had happened to him, indeed.

Peter was the only one with the answers. He'd told his father what had happened, how the Executioner Knights had been on an operation and how Aviara de Serreaux had greatly distracted Myles with her leading ways. Peter admitted to insulting the woman, but it was deserved, in his opinion. Christopher understood because he knew how Lady Aviara had taunted Myles, who truly didn't understand or appreciate the games men and women sometimes played. Lady Aviara was an epic flirt, pitting herself against a man who didn't have a romantic bone in his body. But Myles had liked the attention and, according to Peter, had been considering asking to court the woman. That was, until Peter said what he'd said.

Now, Lady Aviara was gone, and the de Serreaux alliance wasn't as strong as it had been.

Quite honestly... Christopher didn't care.

Not much, anyway.

But now, he had a problem. A very big problem. Looking at

Myles' face, which held as much emotion as he'd seen from the man in months, he knew he needed help. Trying not to show how concerned he was, he waved his hand casually toward the door.

"Send your mother to me, please," he said. "I have need of her."

Myles' brow furrowed. "I will," he said. "But... what about the missive? Was it for me?"

"It was not."

That wasn't the answer Myles had been hoping for. In fact, he was quite puzzled. "Then who was it for?"

Christopher grunted with some exasperation at the questioning. "I have an alliance with Bertrand," he said. "Did you stop to think that it could have been for me?"

Myles clearly hadn't, but he paused, nodded his head, and lowered his gaze. A cloud of disappointment settled over him. Christopher watched his son as the man headed out of the chamber in search of his mother, and after he left, Christopher read the missive from de Serreaux again. And again. Setting it back on the table, he rubbed a weary hand over his face.

This day was not going to get any better.

He only hoped it would not get worse.

As he was lost in thoughts of what the future held, it was some time before his wife appeared. She rushed into the chamber without knocking and, suddenly, was standing before him, her face flushed and a dirty apron around her waist.

She didn't look pleased that he'd summoned her.

"What is it?" Dustin said impatiently. "Myles said that you wished to speak with me."

Christopher frowned as he looked at her. "Why are your cheeks so pink?" he said. "And what are you covered in? Dust?"

Dustin lifted a well-shaped eyebrow. "I've been in the kitchens, if you must know," she said. "One of the cook's servants hurt herself when an oven caught fire, and now we're trying to ensure there is enough bread for the evening meal. We're down one oven, and I have a thousand men to feed. Truly, Chris, I have little time. If it is nothing urgent, then it will have to wait."

A smile licked his lips as his gaze lingered on her face, a face he'd loved for decades. His marriage to Dustin Barringdon had been an arranged one, and after an extremely turbulent beginning, he'd fallen for the woman. He'd loved her more every day of their marriage. She was a fiery lass who wasn't afraid to help when an oven broke down or dress in her finest and be the very definition of a countess. Dustin de Lohr was a woman with many facets, and he adored every one of them.

At the moment, he was seeking one particular facet.

He needed her wisdom.

"It is urgent, I am afraid," he said quietly. "Where is Myles?"

Dustin brushed her hands off on the apron. "I am not entirely certain," she said. "I thought he followed me from the kitchens, but I do not know where he has gone."

Christopher tilted his head in the direction of the chamber door. "Make sure he is not lingering outside," he said. "I do not want him to hear what we must discuss."

Dustin's manner moved from hurried to curious as she went back to the door and peered into the corridor beyond. After a moment, she shut the panel and bolted it.

"He is not out there," she said, coming toward Christopher. "Why? What is it?"

Christopher indicated another chair, pulled up against the table. "Sit," he commanded softly. "I believe we have a problem."

Dustin sat down, with some relief because she'd been on her feet all morning. "What problem?" she said. "Has something happened?"

Christopher's answer was to hand her the missive from Bertrand de Serreaux. She took it with puzzlement, opening it and carefully reading the scripted letters written with red ink. Dustin could read, and write, and she was quite intelligent, but she had to read the missive twice before she finally lifted her eyes to her husband.

"He didn't," she said.

Christopher nodded slowly. "It seems that he did."

Curiosity on Dustin's part now turned to concern. "God's Bones," she murmured. "Does Myles know?"

Christopher shook his head. "Nay," he said. "That is why I wanted to speak to you first. I do not know how we are going to tell him that the missive from de Serreaux is an announcement of Lady Aviara's marriage. To Oliver de Grey, no less."

Dustin put a hand to her forehead, a gesture of disbelief and perhaps even a little horror. "Somehow, Oliver was able to wrest a betrothal out of Bertrand," she said. "We were well aware that Lady Aviara was pitting Myles against Oliver, but we were also well aware that Bertrand preferred Myles. He never seemed enthusiastic for Oliver, not ever."

Christopher sat back in his chair. "Nay, he did not," he said. "Mayhap Peter's rebuke of the lady was worse than we thought."

Dustin pursed her lips irritably. "She deserved it," she said. "She deserved everything Peter said to her. I am sorry that it cost Myles a wife, but to be perfectly honest, I wouldn't want her for Myles. She would torment him for the rest of his life."

Christopher couldn't disagree. "But the result of Peter's

action is that the lady is irrevocably insulted, as is her father, and she married Oliver," he said. "I think Myles was hoping that, with time, she would forgive and forget, but it seems that is not the case."

"Unless this is another ploy to make Myles jealous," Dustin said. "I would not be surprised if it was. Mayhap this is the *only* announcement of the wedding, and once Myles flies to the lady's side to fight for her, there will be no marriage at all."

Christopher wasn't so sure. "You believe this is just a ruse, then?"

Dustin shrugged. "Truthfully, who knows?" she said. "All I am saying is that I would not be surprised if it was."

Christopher considered that, taking the missive from her and looking at it again. "But it has Bertrand's seal on it," he finally said. "I cannot believe that he would be a party to his daughter's games."

Dustin shook her head in disagreement. "The man would do anything for his daughter, and you know it," she said. "I would not be surprised if she had manipulated him, too."

"You do not think very highly of Lady Aviara."

"It is worse than that. I think she is a—"

He cut her off. "Do not say it," he said. "I know what you mean."

Dustin fought off a grin. "I was going to call her a scheming cat."

"You were going to call her a raging cock-whore."

Dustin burst out laughing. "What if I was?" she said. "Would I be wrong?"

Christopher shook his head. "You would not," he said. "But I do not want to hear those words coming out of your mouth. It is beneath you."

Dustin was greatly humored, rolling her eyes at him. "You've heard worse coming out of my mouth," she said. But she quickly sobered. "Whatever she is, she is creating a problem with Myles, and he is the son we do not need any more trouble with. He has always been rather humorless and cold, worse since he returned from Tidworth."

"That is true," Christopher said. "And this wedding announcement is not going to help matters."

It wasn't. They both knew that. But Dustin had something more on her mind to that regard, at least as far as Myles' behavior was concerned.

"Do you want to know what I think about this situation?" she asked.

Christopher nodded. "I do."

Dustin was thoughtful as she spoke. "You want to know how to tell Myles that the lady he wished to marry has married another," she said. "Given Myles' behavior as of late, it is a valid concern. But I never thought he was in love with her."

Christopher frowned. "Of course he is."

But Dustin stood her ground. "I do not think so," she said. "I think it is more complicated than love. If it was only love, then it might be easier to deal with, but Myles has never fallen for a woman in his life. I honestly do not know if he is capable of loving a woman as we know love. I think he viewed Lady Aviara as a prize."

Christopher's frown deepened. "You do?"

Dustin nodded. "I do," she said. "Myles has three older brothers that he has always been in competition with," she said. "You know it and I know it. Everything Peter or Curt or Roi did, Myles had to do better. Or, at least, as well as they did it. He grew up always feeling as if his older brothers were always exceeding him in their accomplishments, and that ate at him. He is driven and he is a man who seeks victory, in all things. You know I'm right."

She was. Christopher nodded his head. "So you think Lady Aviara was just another accomplishment for him?"

Dustin nodded seriously. "I do," she said. "Peter married for love. So did Curt and Roi. They all married fine, lovely women. Lady Aviara comes along and throws all of her attention on Myles, and in her, I believe he saw something to equal what his brothers had—a beautiful wife. An heiress. It is a competition all over again, made worse with Ollie's interference. That's when Myles started looking at her as more than a prize, I think. He looked at her as a conquest. Something to use to defeat Ollie and to show his brothers that anything they can do, he can do, too."

She made sense. Christopher well remembered the younger brother, the middle son, who was constantly striving for perfection. Anything to be as good as his brothers. Anything to be noticed. He sighed heavily as he leaned back in his chair.

"Then you do not think he ever loved her?" he asked.

Dustin shook her head. "I do not," she said. "In spite of the fact that we have set a good example for Myles, and his older siblings have also, I do not think he understands the concept of how a man loves a woman. He does not understand that kind of selfless emotion, not yet."

"Why not?"

"Because the right woman hasn't come along yet. He's not had the chance to learn it."

Christopher smiled faintly. "You are optimistic that there *is* a right woman," he said. "We are talking about Myles, after all. He has a heart of stone."

"So did you," she said pointedly. "As I recall, you were quite hardened when we first met, so he gets it from you. But even the mighty Defender of the Realm learned how to love."

Christopher's grin broadened. "I did, indeed," he said. "Then I suppose there his hope for him, too."

Dustin nodded. "There is," she said. "But I think this missive is going to be more trouble than we know."

"Why?"

"Because of the fact that Myles viewed Lady Aviara as a conquest," she said. "I fear that Myles views the woman as a victory, not as a woman of flesh and bone. Now, Ollie will achieve the victory, not Myles, and that is going to be an enormous blow to his pride. He will not let it go easily."

Christopher's smile faded. "I suppose not," he said. "I fear he may even want to confront the newlyweds simply to make a statement, and that would be a disaster."

"Agreed," Dustin said. "He must not go anywhere near Ollie or the de Serreaux stronghold. It will not end well if he does, because now, his honor is involved. He will see it that way."

"I think you are correct."

"Of course I am," Dustin said. "But we must not be petty about it. We must send word to congratulate them. Mayhap we should even go and visit them. I do not want them to think we are bitter because she did not marry our son. We want to keep family harmony, considering Ollie is your aunt's grandson."

Christopher didn't appear too keen on that. "I do *not* want to visit them," he said frankly. "I am afraid of what I might say other than congratulations."

Dustin understood. But, as she'd said, she felt that they should at least try to present the picture of good losers. "I suppose I cannot disagree with you," she said. "But I do think it is important to at least maintain the illusion of being unconcerned that Myles lost a wife."

"Then you visit them. But I will not."

Dustin shook her head. "My concern is that it would appear as if I was more relieved than grieved," she said. "Can you imagine my congratulating them and then cheering when their back was turned that it was not my son who married the harlot? Nay, I cannot go. In any case, we do not want Myles heading off to confront his cousin, or worse, create a scene. We need to keep him busy. Is there anywhere you can send him? Do you need him to deliver a missive to the north, or mayhap there is business he can conduct for you in London? Anything to keep him away from Ollie and his new bride."

"Keep him distracted?"

"Exactly. He will have to accept the marriage and forget about Aviara, but he needs time."

"Do you think it is really that simple?"

"I think it will be worse if we do nothing at all."

Christopher's gaze lingered on her a moment before he turned to the clutter on his desk and began hunting for something. He picked up a few pieces of vellum, glancing at the contents before setting them aside, until he finally came to the one he was looking for. Picking it up, he glanced at his wife.

"Do you remember Edgar de Wolviston?" he asked.

Dustin nodded. "The scholar?"

"The cartographer."

The light of recognition went on in her eyes. "Of course," she said. "He creates those beautiful maps you use. The man is an artist."

Christopher extended the missive to her. "He *was* an artist," he said. "It seems that he died a few months ago. That missive is from his brother, who manages his estate."

"Oh?" Dustin said as she took the missive from him. "I am sorry to hear of his passing, though I did not know much about him. I only met him once or twice when he came to deliver his commissions."

Christopher watched her as she began to read. "As I recall, he told me that he came from a wealthy family and was highly educated, but rather than follow the family profession, he chose to become a priest instead," he said. "I do not know what happened, or why he decided a life of celibacy was not for him, but he told me that he used to copy manuscripts and Bibles when he was a priest because he had a talent for artful writing. That somehow became cartography. His maps were so in demand that when I would commission one from him, it would take almost a year for him to complete it. He had a talent few do."

Dustin was listening, but she was also reading. "And he has a daughter who is betrothed, according to this message," she said as she finished the missive. "He asks for your help in escorting his daughter to her intended."

"It would seem it was Edgar's wish."

"But does he not have his own men for that?"

Christopher shrugged. "Other than a few servants working for him, I do not think he had any men at arms that served him," he said. "No men at arms for protection, which was odd. He lived over in Worcester, a rather large manse I visited once. But for a rich man, he lived simply."

Dustin understood, sort of. "So he asks his liege to provide an armed escort for his daughter?"

"That is what his brother says," he said. "He does not have

any armed men, so I suppose that it is natural that he would ask me. It will be a long journey to Manchester, and a journey such as that will require armed men. Men who will be gone several weeks, at least."

Dustin suddenly caught on to his thought processes. She glanced at the missive again. "An armed escort to a betrothed that lives in Manchester," she said pensively. "If Myles were to lead the escort, it would take him north for quite some time."

"And away from Gloucestershire."

"But what happens when he comes back in a month?"

"Then I send him to Croft Castle. I've just acquired it, and it needs a commander."

Dustin sighed with some relief. "Perfect," she said, handing the missive back to him. "We send Myles north with the de Wolviston lass, and by the time he returns, we'll send him on to his own command. That should keep his focus away from the little minx who teased him into a frenzy. Or, at the very least, the time away will take the edge off the sting of defeat."

Christopher grinned. "What a brilliant plan, Lady Hereford," he said. "I knew I could count on you to come up with an unfailing scheme."

Dustin laughed softly. "You would not be able to breathe without me," she said, standing up from the chair. "I do not know why you think you could possibly plan something so devious without me."

Christopher reached out to take her hand, bringing it to his lips as he'd done a thousand times before, with a thousand different reasons, each one of them more important than the last. Sometimes, he kissed her hand for no reason at all.

Those were the best of all.

"I cannot live without you," he said, brushing his beard

affectionately against her hand. "That is why I needed you here to discuss the situation. Above all, I want Myles to be protected. He is a different breed from the rest of our children, and I will admit that I worry for him more than the others. I fear… I fear he may not find himself. I fear he may wander for the rest of his life."

"Wander how?"

He thought on her question. "Peter and Curt and Roi have all married," he said quietly. "Douglas and Westley love women. Westley in particular has a special gift with them. There is no question that they will marry, too, someday. But Myles… There is something hard in him. You know that. I've heard women say that he is the most handsome of our sons, but he's also the biggest puzzle. I fear he may wander and never find happiness because of that hardness he has. That is why I fear the situation with Lady Aviara may truly upset him. At least if he married her, he would have a wife and some chance at a family and happiness."

Dustin was looking at him dubiously. "Even if I do not like her."

"You would not be the one marrying her."

Dustin sighed faintly at an answer she did not like, truthful as it may be. "That hardness you speak of," she said. "I believe it hides a tender heart, one he is afraid to show. One he is afraid may be more powerful than his reason is."

Christopher rubbed her hand against his beard again, thinking on her words. "I remember when he was a lad, he seemed to want to show love and compassion, but he could never quite manage it," he said. "He seemed to pull back when others were unafraid."

Dustin nodded. "I know," she said. "That is what I mean by

him hiding a tender heart. Once it is unleashed, there would be no way for him to contain it. Myles is, above all, a man of control. He is afraid of losing control."

"I would agree with that."

"I've always believed he has a tender side. We've simply not seen it yet."

Christopher kissed her hand once more before releasing it. "I hope you are right," he said, wearily rising. "Meanwhile, I must tell him of the marriage."

"Must you?"

He looked at her. "Why would you say that? I thought that was why we were sending him away? To ease the pain of the news."

She shrugged, averting her gaze. "I do not know," she said. "The more I think on it, the more I wonder if that is wise. I mean, what will it accomplish? It will upset him. Mayhap we should simply send him north and then tell him when he has returned. When everything is over with and he can do nothing about it."

He could see her reasoning, but he was uncertain. "I suppose it would make the journey easier for him."

"I think so," Dustin said honestly. "I am not advocating that we never tell him, of course, but the timing… Mayhap it is most important that the timing be right. You will have to decide if the time is now."

Christopher took that under advisement. Now, he, too, was wondering if they should tell Myles before he headed off on an escort mission. What *would* it accomplish? He looked at the de Wolviston missive one last time before heading out of his solar, moving stiffly and with a slowness that had come with age. He was an enormous man, six and a half feet tall, with a body that had seen much abuse over the years. Christopher had been active in battle since he was seventeen years of age, so the decades of strain had taken their toll. He could still fight better than almost anyone in England, but he had a wife who wouldn't let him. He let his sons do the fighting these days.

Christopher de Lohr had earned the rest in his later years.

Dustin smiled at him as he moved past her, and he reached out, gently touching her cheek, before heading into the foyer and the keep entry beyond. The sooner he dealt with Myles, the sooner he could get him out of Lioncross and away from Gloucester. It all seemed simple enough, but both Dustin and Christopher knew that it was not.

Myles was not going to have an easy time of it.

The conqueror didn't like to lose.

They'd soon find out just how badly.

# CHAPTER TWO

"**I** SAW THE de Serreaux rider. What did old Bernard have to say to you?"

Myles heard the question, turning to see his younger brother, Douglas, as the man found him on the wall walk. Myles had been on the western side of the wall, away from the gatehouse and the men at arms who knew about the de Serreaux rider who had come through bearing a missive. Of course, the news spread like wildfire, and Douglas, who had been with some new army recruits in the stable yard, had come to find him. Myles loved his brother, but he wasn't sure he wanted to discuss the subject with him.

He wasn't sure how he felt about anything at the moment.

"There is nothing to say," he said, leaning on the wall, his gaze on the mountains to the west. "The missive was not for me."

Douglas, a big lad with the handsome de Lohr traits, looked at his brother in surprise. "*Not* for you?" he repeated. "That does not sound possible. It should have been for you. It should have been Aviara's apology for treating you so poorly."

Myles shook his head. "Papa said it was not for me," he said.

41

"Though you are correct. It *should* have been for me. I sent her a groveling apology months ago, pleading forgiveness and criticizing Peter for what he said to her. I practically slandered my own brother in an apology so she would know that I did not agree with what he said to her. But... she has sent no reply to me. I am certain she is just trying to make me suffer."

Douglas leaned against the wall next to him. "If that is true, then she should be begging for *your* forgiveness."

"Women like Aviara do not beg for forgiveness."

"I am coming to see that."

"What did the missive say, Myles?"

Another shout filled their conversation from afar. Myles and Douglas turned to see Westley and Broden coming toward them across the stones of the dusty wall walk. They, too, had seen the de Serreaux rider, and as Myles returned his attention to the misty mountains to the west, Douglas silently told his youngest brother and his cousin to stop asking questions. Gestures were made, and facial expressions conveyed the fact that Myles didn't want to talk about any of it.

Westley and Broden took the hint.

"There are traveling minstrels in Leominster," Westley said in a complete change of subject. "I saw them when I was in town earlier. They have an entire troupe of women who dance, and I've heard it's quite vulgar, so I was hoping to go back tonight and see them perform. Come with me, Myles. We'll drink and watch women behave badly."

Douglas hissed at him, waving his hand at him behind Myles' back to shut him up, but Westley had no idea he'd said anything wrong. At twenty years and two, he was always ready for anything vulgar or scandalous. Three years older, Douglas had more maturity, but he wasn't beyond gaping at the same things Westley gaped at. Myles, however, had never been that sort. He was nine years older than Westley, and as his mother once said, he was born old.

He didn't appreciate naughty ladies.

Or, at least, he wouldn't admit it.

"I think not," Myles said. "But you go. And try to stay out of trouble."

Westley leaned against the wall, looking at his older brother. "Then come with us and we'll gamble at The Fish and the Fowl. That tavern is always good for strong drinks and a few laughs. Please say you'll come."

Myles looked at Westley. "Nay," he said, more firmly. "Go and enjoy yourself, but if you lose too much money, you'll need to make excuses to Papa."

"What excuses?"

Another man joined their group. Alexander de Sherrington emerged from the tower nearest where they were all gathered. Father of Andrew de Sherrington, who was already a highly skilled Executioner Knight, Alexander—or Sherry, as he was known—was legendary. He'd gone on King Richard's crusade forty years earlier as a young man, but he'd been a knight who made a name for himself as a skilled spy and an even more skilled assassin. That had been Alexander's lot in life for several years before he joined the Executioner Knights and subsequently met his wife, who happened to be Christopher and Dustin's eldest daughter. Christin de Lohr was a legend, as well, and the two of them had made an unlikely, but extremely happy, couple. Marriage and children had settled them both down considerably.

But there was still something about Alexander that terrified even the bravest heart.

That went for Christopher's sons, as well. They loved and respected Alexander, but there wasn't one of them that didn't have a healthy respect for the man, even at his advancing age. In his youth, he'd had black hair to match his black eyes, but these days, the hair had mostly gone silver.

But the mind and the skills were just as sharp.

"Greetings, Sherry," Douglas said. "West was trying to convince Myles to go into town and watch some naked women dance around."

Alexander's eyebrows lifted. "Naked women?" he repeated. "Where?"

Myles snorted. "He'll not tell you because you'll tell Cissy, and she'll tell Mother, and then they'll ride into town like Valkyries and chase the women away," he said, referring to his sister by the family nickname. "More than that, if Cissy believes you might want to see them yourself, you risk your very life. I do not think you wish to do that."

Alexander fought off a grin. "Very true," he said, pretending to be serious. "Sage advice, Myles."

They glanced at one another, the reluctant grins coming forth, but Westley was defiant. "If I want to go, I will go," he said firmly. "Two old women are not going to prevent me from doing what I want to do."

Myles hung his head, trying not to laugh at his brother's declaration, as Alexander let out a low whistle. "You take your life in your hands referring to your mother and sister as old women," he said. "Those two old women would take you to task, and there would be nothing any of us could do to help you. Moreover, your sister is not old. She's just the right age."

Westley shrugged, looking to Douglas and Broden for support, but neither one seemed inclined to support his slander against his mother or his sister as far as their age. In fact, Broden put up his hands in surrender.

"I'll not say a word about Lady Dustin," he said. "She is a lovely woman, as is Lady de Sherrington. You should be ashamed of yourself, West."

Westley rolled his eyes. "Cowards, all of you," he said. "*I* am going into Leominster tonight, and I am going to watch those women dance. You can come with me or not. I do not care."

With that, he leaned on the wall and looked off into the distance, pretending to ignore his traitorous relatives as they smirked at his behavior. Westley was the family entertainment—young, rash, emotional, and dramatic—and it made for great fun at times. But he was also hell on the field of battle, because that passion and unrestraint translated into a knight of uncommon valor. Westley was very much his mother's son with her strong personality, but he was also very much his father's son with his skill as a knight, and every man there knew it. Westley would always be Westley. As he pouted, Broden and Douglas converged on Myles.

"Are you certain that missive was not for you?" Broden asked, watching Douglas frown at him as the delicate subject was once again raised. "I know you do not wish to discuss this, but I was there the last time you saw Lady Aviara. I know what happened. My only concern is for you, Myles. I will help if I can."

Douglas rolled his eyes and tried to speak for Myles, to tell Broden it was not a welcome topic, but Myles put up a hand to still his brother. "I am not troubled speaking about it," he told him before looking to Broden. "Nay, the missive was not for me. It was for my father."

Broden frowned. "I simply cannot believe Lady Aviara

would not have contacted you by now," he said. "I saw her on that night. I saw how much she wanted your attention."

Myles grunted. "Until Peter told her to leave me alone."

Broden shook his head. "Since when has Lady Aviara ever done anything she was told?" he said. "Do not forget that I know her, too. She is like a dog with a bone when it comes to you. Nothing short of death could stop her from her pursuit."

Myles shrugged. "I think she is trying to teach me a lesson," he said. "She is trying to make it so I will forgive her anything and fall at her feet the next time I see her."

Alexander had joined the conversation at this point. He knew the entire story of Aviara de Serreaux and Myles de Lohr. When he heard Myles' comment, he clapped the man on the shoulder.

"This is like the songs the poets used to sing," he said with some irony. "A romance that never comes to fruition because neither the man nor the woman know anything about the other one, and they pine their lives away hoping one of them will come to their senses."

Myles, Douglas, and Broden looked at him. "You're the great expert, then," Myles said sarcastically. "*You* tell me what she is doing."

Alexander shrugged. "I could not tell you," he said. "But what I do not think she is doing is punishing you. It is quite possible the lady has simply moved on."

Myles frowned. "Do you truly think so?"

Alexander lifted his hands in a gesture of uncertainty. "Would *you* want to marry into a family where one of your husband's brothers thinks so poorly of you?"

That had Myles frowning further. "Are you suggesting I have Peter apologize to her?"

Alexander laughed, but it was humorless. "As if he would," he said. "Peter would cut his own manhood off before apologizing to the likes of Aviara. The great Earl of Farringdon does not apologize for things when he is in the right."

That had Myles stiffening. "Then you think he was right to say those things to her?"

Alexander fixed him in the eye. "You've never asked me that question," he said. "Ever since you returned from Tidworth and I heard what happened. I hope you know I would never lie to you, and I further hope you know that anything Peter does, or I do—or any of the men in the family do—is to help or protect you. You do understand that, do you not?"

The conversation took a serious turn as Myles stood up from leaning over the wall and faced Alexander.

"I know that," he said. "I trust you, and everyone else, with my life."

"Then understand me plainly, Myles. Peter was not wrong. If you think he was, then *you* are wrong."

Myles didn't have much to say to that. He adored Alexander, as they all did, and he knew the man would never lie to him. But it was difficult to swallow the fact that he, too, thought Peter had been right in telling Aviara what he thought of her. Alexander lifted his eyebrows at Myles as if to silently convince him to reconsider his opinion before turning away and heading back toward the tower with the stairs leading down to the bailey. Myles was trying not to feel confused, or uncertain about an event he'd felt strongly about, when they heard Alexander as he shouted down the stairwell upon entering it. That took the knights to the other side of the wall, facing the inner ward, where they saw Christopher standing with Alexander's wife.

Myles lifted a hand in greeting at his sister.

"We were just discussing you," he called down to her. "Westley, in particular, was speaking of you."

Christin de Lohr de Sherrington lifted her hand to shield her eyes from the sun overhead. A beautiful woman with her mother's gray eyes and her grandmother's dark hair, she was the only person in the family who had been born a brunette. In her fourth decade, she'd given birth to seven children and could easily pass for a much younger woman. Her older boys had followed in their parents' footsteps by serving in the Executioner Knights, while their only daughter, at nine years of age, was a fiery lass who ruled the house and hold.

Not that anyone minded.

In the de Lohr family, it was the women who generally ruled the empire. Christopher liked to joke that he simply lived there, with his wife's permission. Christin was no different than her mother, only a younger version. When she heard Myles calling, she lifted her shielded eyes to the western wall.

"Oh?" she said casually. "And what did dear West have to say about me? Wait, do not tell me. Let me guess."

Myles grinned at her. "I could make you quite angry at him if I told you."

Christin shook her head in exasperation, lowering her hand when she caught sight of her husband coming out of the tower. "Never you mind," she told Myles. "Sherry will tell me."

"You will still be angry."

"Probably."

As Myles chuckled at his brother's expense, Westley had heard all of the shouting and decided that he wasn't ignoring his family any longer. He came to stand next to Myles, looking at his eldest sister as her husband greeted her down below.

"Whatever they tell you, they are lying," he called down to

her. "Do not believe a word of it."

Alexander, with a gleam in his dark eyes, leaned over and whispered in Christin's ear. She listened without reaction, nodding when he was finished.

"I see," she said calmly. "Was that all he said?"

Alexander nodded. "All of it."

Christin turned to look at her brothers on the wall, but particularly, she was looking at Westley.

"When you least expect it, West. I would be on my guard if I were you."

With that, she turned away, heading back the way she'd come with Alexander at her side. Westley made a good show of being unafraid of her threat, but it lasted just a few seconds before he was bolting off the wall, going in pursuit of his sister to ensure she didn't end his life prematurely at some point. As he ran, Myles and Douglas and Broden laughed, once again entertained by Westley and his posturing. Myles was about to turn his attention back toward the west when he heard his father's voice.

"Myles?" he shouted. "Attend me."

It was a command. Myles came off the wall and headed over to his father. Before he could reach the man, however, two of Christin and Alexander's boys came rushing out from the stable yard, converging on the man they called Grandpapa, or *Taid*, the Welsh name for "grandfather." Liam and Maxim de Sherrington were barely more than children, boys verging on manhood, and home from fostering with the Earl of Wolver-hampton for the time being. Christopher had brought them home because he wanted to send them to Thunderbey Castle in East Anglia to continue their training, as he felt it would behoove the boys to learn different skills from different masters.

But for now, they were at Lioncross Abbey, and as their Uncle Myles approached, they showed off the new practice swords, known as *rudis*, that their father had commissioned for them. They wanted Christopher to see them, as the smithy had only recently finished with them, so Christopher and Myles properly praised the weapons. As the boys ran off, convinced they could now ride to battle with their uncles and grandfather and father, Christopher watched them go with a wistful expression.

"It is good to have young lads at home again," he said. "They remind me of you and your brothers. I will admit that I was sorry to see you grow up. You were quite entertaining at that age."

Myles watched the boys disappear into the stable yard. "You have plenty of grandsons now to comfort you," he said. "Between Christin and Brielle and Peter and Curtis, you have a house full of children, growing larger by the year."

Christopher returned his attention to Myles, his sky-blue eyes glimmering. "Someday, you will understand what I mean about sons growing up, God willing," he said. "But that is a conversation for another day. I have a task for you, Myles."

Myles may be stone cold and dense when it came to women, but he wasn't when it came to men. Especially his father. He seemed to be intuitive when it came to the man, more than the rest of his siblings at times. He couldn't help but notice that his father hadn't looked him in the eye until this very moment, which made it seem to Myles as if the man was guarded somehow. As if, perhaps, there was something more than his need to send him on an errand.

Something told him to be cautious.

"By your command, as always," Myles said. "But I want to

ask you a question first."

"What is it?"

"If de Serreaux's missive wasn't for me, was it *about* me?"

Christopher maintained his expression, but the glimmer in his eyes seemed to fade. After a small eternity of gazing at his son, he forced a smile.

"If you ask me a direct question, you know I will not lie to you," he said quietly. "May I tell you of the task before we delve into the missive?"

"Then he did say something about me."

"He did. But I do not wish to speak of it first."

Myles sighed impatiently but nodded his head. "Proceed."

Christopher knew that Myles' patience wouldn't hold out forever, especially now that he knew the missive did indeed concern him. Therefore, he spoke quickly but firmly.

"I do not know if you ever met the man who prepared my maps, but his name was Edgar de Wolviston," he said. "The man produced the best maps I have ever seen, and I have several of them. He was a wealthy man, but he lived without protection over in Worcester. I suppose he liked to live simply. Whatever his reasons, he died recently, and I have received a request to provide an escort for his daughter so that she may be delivered safely to her betrothed in Manchester. I should like you to lead that escort, Myles. De Wolviston was a worthy man, and it would be the generous thing to do."

Myles clearly wasn't impressed by the request. He sighed heavily again, averting his gaze, making it clear with his body language that he didn't want anything to do with such an assignment.

"Why can't Douglas lead the escort?" he asked. "Or any number of knights we have here?"

"Because I want you."

Myles looked at him then. "Why?" he said. Then he eyed his father suspiciously. "Does it have something to do with the contents of de Serreaux's missive?"

"It does," Christopher said without hesitation. "Myles, I was going to wait to tell you what the missive contained. Your mother and I discussed it, and to spare your feelings, we thought it best to tell you once you'd taken the de Wolviston lass to Manchester, but you have asked me bluntly, and I cannot avoid giving you an answer."

"What did it say?"

"That Lady Aviara has married."

That brought a reaction. Myles frowned, but it was an expression of puzzlement more than anything. As if he simply couldn't believe what he was hearing.

"Married?" he repeated. Then he actually grinned. "It is a joke."

"It is no joke."

"Who in the world did she marry?"

"Oliver."

Myles' smile vanished unnaturally fast. "Ollie?" he said incredulously. "De Grey?"

"Do you know of any other Ollies competing for the lady's hand?"

Myles didn't, but he had to be clear. He felt as if he'd just been hit by a battering ram as the wind got sucked right out of him.

"You cannot be serious," he said.

Christopher could see that the news was finally starting to register. "I am afraid that I am," he said. "The missive was a wedding announcement. They were married last month."

Myles was dumbfounded. He had to take a few moments to process what his father was telling him before he could speak again.

"Do you mean to tell me that she chose Ollie over me?" he finally said. "Ollie? Who has half of my intelligence and possesses the appearance of a boar's arse?"

"Aye, *that* Ollie," Christopher said. "He has the Ilchester earldom, Myles. Surely that played a part in this."

Now, the rage was starting to come. Myles went from disbelief to anger in a split second. "Impossible," he said. "Ilchester or not, this is impossible. It is a mistake. I will go to Aldsworth Castle immediately and get to the bottom of this."

"Nay, you will not," Christopher said firmly, grasping Myles by the arm when the man tried to push past him. "Myles, listen to me. The contest for Lady Aviara's hand is over. Ollie is the victor. You will accept this because you have no choice."

Myles' jaw was twitching dangerously. "Ollie must have coerced her somehow," he said. "He must have forced her or… or threatened her. She would have never agreed to this otherwise."

Christopher could see the abject denial in his son's face. "Or it is possible she accepted of her own free will," he said quietly. "Myles, it is over. And I will not permit you to go to Aldsworth. You would only make a mess of the situation, and I will not let you shame yourself, or your family, in such a manner. It is finished."

Those three words hung in the air between them, but Myles was still in denial. He absolutely refused to accept it. But then something more sinister began to fill his thoughts. In the absence of the ability to accept the situation for what it was, he was looking for someone to blame.

He knew who had caused this.

"Peter did this," he growled through clenched teeth. "This is *his* fault."

Christopher was shaking his head before the man even finished speaking. "It is *not* his fault, and I forbid you to blame him," he said. "Do you understand me? You will not hold this against your brother."

"He did this!"

"He would not have had to do anything if you had done your duty as an Executioner Knight."

That brought Myles pause, because there was an accusation there. His manner cooled dramatically.

"What is that supposed to mean?" he asked.

Christopher dropped his hand from Myles' arm. "Do you think I am oblivious to the operations of the Executioner Knights?" he said. "Do you think I did not know about Tidworth and how Lady Aviara did her very best to keep you from carrying out your sword duty? Are you truly so blind, Myles? The woman is no good for you. She never was. Peter did what he had to do in order to force you to do your duty, and I cannot say I would not have done the same thing in his place. Let her be Ollie's burden from now on. You are destined for better things… and a better woman."

Myles was taken aback by his father's sharp words. Christopher wasn't usually so harsh with his children, but in this case, he evidently felt he had to be. He didn't hold back. Rather than understand that, quite possibly, his father might be correct, Myles was in a maelstrom of disappointment, disbelief, and anger.

It was a bad combination.

"I *was* doing my duty," he said, his voice gritty. "At no time did I shirk anything, and if Peter said so, he is a liar. I will tell him to his face. A true brother would not have said that about me."

Christopher frowned. "What do you mean by that?"

Myles was so angry that his restraint had vanished. He was saying things he'd never even thought of in his entire life, lashing out in his anger. "He is only my half-brother," he said. "We share a father. That is all. And if he told you that I somehow shirked my duty, then he has proved it. Any man who lies about me is *not* my brother."

Christopher was becoming quite displeased. "Is it not proof enough that Lady Aviara is not good for you if you would turn against your own brother because of her?" he said. "Can you not see what this woman has done to you, Myles? Would you truly want to marry a woman who would turn you against your own blood?"

"Peter is *not* my blood," Myles snapped. "Your blood may run through his veins, but so does the blood of a whore."

Christopher slapped Myles across the mouth before he even realized he did it. Suddenly, Myles' head was snapping back, and Christopher felt the sting of an impact on the back of his left hand. When he realized what he had done, he simply turned away and began marching back toward the keep. He was horrified. He'd never struck any of his children in anger. In fact, he'd never struck anyone in his family in anger. Ever.

But he'd struck Myles.

He was afraid of what more he would do if Myles said anything else.

He had to get away from him.

Myles could taste the blood on his lips as he watched his father walk away. Actually, the man was nearly running away. It had been a shocking and brutal moment, but suddenly, all of the anger was draining out of Myles' veins. He felt as if his entire world was crumbling as his father turned his back on him. But he'd done this... With his rage, he had done this. Rage caused by a woman who had taunted him over the course of a couple of years to the point of madness.

The madness had finally caught him.

*Is it not proof enough that Lady Aviara is not good for you?*

The proof had just been laid out before him with his father's hand to his mouth.

A woman who would cause his own beloved father to turn against him.

"Papa!" he called as he began to run after Christopher. "Papa, please stop. Please!"

Christopher didn't stop. He marched all the way to the steps leading into the keep as Myles quickly closed the gap. Christopher was up the stairs and nearly through the entry door when Myles grabbed him from behind.

"Papa, *please,*" he said with quiet urgency. "Forgive me. I did not mean any of it. Please... forgive me."

Christopher stopped. Taking a deep breath to compose himself, he turned around and put his arms around Myles and held the man so tightly that he nearly squeezed the life out of him. All the while, Myles held him and repeatedly begged for forgiveness as Christopher blinked away the tears and shushed him quietly.

"I need your forgiveness more than you need mine," Christopher muttered, finally releasing Myles and pinching his chin so he could get a look at his mouth. "I see that I drew blood. I... I do not know what to say, lad. I do not know what happened."

Myles wiped at his mouth. There was very little blood, certainly nothing to worry over. "You are without blame," he said. "It is my fault. Please… do not tell Peter what I said. I did not mean it."

"I know," Christopher said, his hand on Myles' cheek. He could see the genuine remorse, and it doused whatever anger he was feeling. "Sometimes passion makes men behave in a way they would not normally behave. This is an emotional situation, and for that, I am sorry. I am sorry for everything, lad. I should not have struck you."

Myles hugged his father again, kissing his cheek before releasing him. That was as much emotion as Myles was capable of displaying, but he was shaken. The entire situation had him shaken.

"When do you want me to leave for Manchester?" he asked.

Christopher looked at his weary, upset boy, seeing that he was trying to move past the incident by doing what his father wanted him to do. "By the end of the week, I suppose," he said. "Can you manage that?"

Myles nodded, hardly able to look him in the eye. "I can," he said. "Shall I pick my escort?"

"You may."

Myles simply nodded again, significantly calmer than he had been, but he needed to go off and collect himself. He needed to be alone. Those crumbling pieces of his world needed to be put back together again, somehow.

Everything, for him, had changed.

With a weary sign, Myles turned away, heading back across the bailey as Christopher watched him go. He was deeply saddened by their exchange but, in hindsight, not particularly surprised. Myles was known to have a temper, and Christopher, when roused, had one as well. Perhaps a clash like that, over a subject like this, had been inevitable.

And that greatly distressed him.

Something told him that it wouldn't be the last time they discussed Aviara de Serreaux.

God help them.

# CHAPTER THREE

*Cradley Heath*
*Worcester*

S HE WAS TRACKING a thief.

Thieves were rare in her world, but such was the case today. She had been in the rear yard of her father's manse, picking vegetables, when she caught sight of what she thought were vermin in the garden. Even though her home was in the city of Worcester, a sprawling estate on the edge of the River Severn, the truth was that they never really had any trouble with the locals because everyone knew them and her father was greatly respected. That meant that the usual thievery or shenanigans from the local populace had been limited.

Cradley Heath was something of a paradise.

In truth, it had been a wonderful place to grow up, nestled on the banks of a rambling river, a bucolic place Veronica de Wolviston had called home for all of her twenty years. When she had been younger, her family had consisted of her and her mother and her father, and they had had a wonderful world all to themselves. But her mother had passed away when she had seen thirteen years of age, and then it had only been Veronica and her father.

That was where the paradise had somewhat ended.

From that time, Veronica had been forced in many ways to carry on where her mother left off, but she didn't mind. She didn't mind managing the house or the finances, because it was something her father had no talent for. She had been rather young to have such responsibility thrust upon her, but she found that it was quite to her liking. In fact, she had always considered Cradley Heath *her* home, *her* domain. Her father, a very busy and very talented cartographer, was always wrapped up in his commissions and perfectly happy to leave everything else to a daughter who had a talent for management and for mathematics.

Veronica was quite intelligent that way.

Life had rambled on, as steadily and as strongly as the river that flowed by the great stone walls of Cradley Heath. But then came the passing of Veronica's father, and even though it was not an unexpected event, because he had not been in the best of health over the past year, it had still been a shock. That had been three months ago, and Veronica still felt the daily shock of waking up and realizing her father was gone. But that wasn't the worst of it. Her father's brother had come to town to settle his brother's estate… and that was where the problems began.

Veronica had no knowledge of the fact that upon the death of her mother, Edgar de Wolviston had asked his older brother to take care of his estate and of his family should anything happen to him. As far as Veronica could determine, that had happened years ago when her father was feeling particularly vulnerable and probably in great fear of what would happen to his daughter should he die. Clearly, he never imagined how Veronica would rise to the occasion and thrive, but over the years, he'd never rescinded his request. Edgar was forgetful, and simply forgot to tell his brother that no help was needed upon his passing.

Her Uncle Gregor showed up at Cradley Heath the week after Edgar passed.

Oddly enough, Veronica's father and his older brother had been estranged for the past several years of his life, or at the very least, they had hardly been in touch with one another. Edgar never spoke poorly of his brother, but he never spoke favorably of him, either. He was the only sibling he had. But the lack of communication meant that Gregor was walking into a situation he knew nothing about, and Veronica was not exactly receptive to a man she hardly knew taking over her father's estate. They didn't fight over it, but there had been some strong discussions regarding the situation, and Gregor was not at all convinced that Veronica could handle what needed to be done.

But Veronica sensed there was more to it than that.

*Greed.*

Veronica got the sense early on that Gregor was there for the money. Fortunately, she controlled the finances, and the money that her father had earned over the years was tucked away with Jewish bankers in Birmingham and in Hereford because they were very trustworthy. Given the fact that Edgar never really saw the need to employ armed men to protect his home and valuables, Veronica had sent almost all of the money to the bankers to protect it. She kept very little coin at Cradley Heath.

That was something Gregor did not appreciate.

Therefore, it was a power struggle between Veronica and her uncle for control of her father's estate, because Gregor wanted to know where the money was and Veronica would not tell him. What coinage there was at the manse, he'd already taken control of, so Veronica knew that if he got his hands on his father's fortune, she would never see a penny of it. She had tried to convince him that there wasn't much else by way of wealth because her father had been foolish with his money, but she wasn't entirely sure he believed it.

Therefore, he moved against her the only way he could.

*The betrothal.*

When Edgar had sent the request to Gregor for the management of his estate, he mentioned the betrothal and asked Gregor to ensure it happened when his daughter came of age. Well aware that removing Veronica would also remove the blockade from him being fully in charge of the estate, Gregor sent word to his brother's liege, the Earl of Hereford and Worcester, for an escort to take Veronica to her intended. It was time for her to finally marry the man who had been waiting for her until she came of age, which was actually next month, but Gregor was neglecting that little detail. He simply wanted his troublesome niece out of his hair.

Veronica didn't know about the request to Hereford, but she knew her uncle was tired of her. He was frustrated that she wouldn't tell him where her father's money was, or even if there was any money left, and he was frustrated with the fact that his brother had left a bullheaded daughter who impeded him at every turn. With the money that he could find, he had purchased a good deal of wine and food, and every night, he drowned himself in fine wine and ate until he could eat no more. While his plot to remove Veronica was already in motion, she was plotting to do the same thing—to remove her uncle.

But she had no idea that he'd already beaten her to it.

In fact, removal of her uncle was on her mind that morning when she discovered the thief. She had been out in the garden, pulling root vegetables for the evening's meal and lost in thought, as it so often was these days. But those thoughts had been dashed when she saw movement at the edge of the garden and realized that two children had managed to get in.

She began to follow.

Veronica wasn't quite sure how the children were going to get back over the wall, which was twelve feet or more in places, but they did have a postern gate that opened onto a field to the north of the manse. It was the gate where business was conducted with the kitchen and was usually locked, but it was possible they would make their way to the iron gate and try to escape with their stolen booty.

A plan began to form.

Off to Veronica's right was the daughter of the cook, a young woman that she had grown up with. Named Snowdrop after the flower, she was a little rough, capable of chores usually reserved for men. In great contrast to her delicate name, Snowy was the closest Cradley Heath had to a majordomo. Tall and pretty, with dark hair she kept cut above her shoulders because she hated having to deal with the feminine problem of hair dressing, she was ripping turnips out of the ground and tossing them into a basket.

Veronica hissed at the woman.

"There," she whispered, pointing toward the children hiding near the wall. "We have visitors. We must block the gate."

Snowy's head came up, and she strained to see what Veronica was pointing at. When she realized there were intruders in the garden, her eyes narrowed and she nodded quickly.

"Send them my way," she muttered.

Leaping up, she gathered her dusty skirts and rushed toward the postern gate as Veronica began to flank the thieves. She had to make it to the south side of the garden so she could sweep up and flush them away from the wall, toward the postern gate where Snowy was waiting.

But she had help.

Off to Veronica's left, she could see her dog resting under a sapling tree, looking at her curiously. The dog's name was Mud because he was the color of mud and tended to lie in it, making him not only a filthy creature, but virtually undetectable when he and the earth became one. But he was a big dog, a long-legged wolfhound, very ugly but very smart. Veronica loved Mud as if he were her very own child, and as she began to pick up speed to chase the thieves from her garden, Mud leapt up and ran after her.

Veronica was fast, but the thieves were faster. When they saw her coming, they began to run, tearing through the vegetable garden on their way to the postern gate. Mud was faster than they were, however, and the big dog caught up to them. He jumped on them, pushing them down as they screamed and tried to escape. Whatever vegetables they'd managed to steal fell away as the dog pounced. He didn't bite, but he did grab clothing and pull. All the while, the two young girls were crying and yelling. They somehow made it to the postern gate, where Snowy suddenly appeared and growled at them. Terrified, the girls nearly killed themselves trying to push past her and out of the gate with the dog in pursuit.

Without the vegetables they came for, they ran like the wind.

"Let them go," Veronica said as Mud continued to chase after them. "I do not think they will return anytime soon."

Snowy watched them go before whistling loudly for the dog, who came to a halt but continued to bark as if to tell the thieves not to come back. "He does not like trespassers in his garden," she said, then stepped back through the open gate. "Did they get anything?"

Veronica reached down to pick up the two cabbages and several carrots that they'd been carrying. "Nay," she said, inspecting the cabbage. "I wish I could let them keep it. They are probably only stealing because they are hungry. But if I let them keep it, there will be others, and this food is for us."

Snowy brought the dog back into the yard and pulled the heavy iron gate shut, throwing the bolt to lock it so no more trespassers could find their way in.

"We can do what we have done before," she said. "If they come back and work for it, we will let them keep it as payment."

Veronica handed her the vegetables. "Mayhap," she said. "But I do not like to do that, either, because we'll have every starving child from Brandsford to Droitwich begging for work. There are charities and churches that will feed them. We must worry about ourselves, since I cannot buy anything right now. Not without Gregor wondering where I got the money."

Snowy knew that. It was all they knew since Gregor had arrived. They'd been living on what they grew and what they could kill rather than buying anything, because Gregor had taken what money there was, and if Veronica tried to get more from the bankers, Gregor would know for certain that she was hiding it somewhere.

And she would do anything to keep him from knowing.

Even starve.

As if on cue, Gregor emerged from the manse. They were in the rear yard, which was on the river's side, while there was an entire enormous front yard, walled, that faced the street. The manse was in the middle of the complex, the crown jewel of southern Worcester. But the moment Veronica saw her uncle, her expression tightened.

"God's Bones," she muttered. "He must have known we were talking about money."

Snowy saw the man as he took a step through the door and simply stood there, beckoning his niece with an imperious flick of the hand. Even a brief glimpse of the man made her angry, so she quickly looked away.

"Speak of the devil and he will appear," she said quietly.

Veronica grunted in agreement. "I wonder what he wants now."

"Knowing him, it could be anything," Snowy said. "I am certain he has come to yet again make demands for your father's money."

"And he will be disappointed," Veronica said, holding up a hand to acknowledge his summons. "He has started selling things, you know. Your mother told me that he took several silver plates that were in the hall. I've not checked yet to see how many, but she said he took them yesterday."

Snowy grunted softly. "As long as he does not get his hands on the money your father left."

"And you sent the missive to the bankers not to release it to him if he somehow discovers where it is?"

"I did it weeks ago when your uncle started hunting for your father's wealth," Snowy said, assuring her of something she'd assured her of before, many times. "You have been doing business with Eli ben Shir for years, my lady. He knows you and he knows your father. He will not give your uncle anything."

Veronica sighed faintly. "I hope not," she murmured. "God,

I hope not."

With that, she left Snowy as the woman carried the stolen vegetables over to the basket that they'd been filling for supper. Veronica was focused on the short, red-haired man who looked a good deal like her father but had none of his kindness or character. She'd struggled to maintain a polite relationship with him in spite of his unwelcome presence, but the truth was that she disliked him intensely, and she knew the feeling was mutual.

It made for many awkward moments.

"Good day," she said evenly as she approached. "Did you require something, Uncle?"

Gregor was dressed for travel in fine leather and silk. "I am going to Cheltenham," he said, tightening up his leather gloves. "I have business there. I shall more than likely be gone a couple of days."

"I see," Veronica said. "Is there any reason for you to return here when you are finished?"

He stopped tugging at his gloves and looked at her with small, dark eyes. "Of course there is," he said, exasperation in his voice already. "Why wouldn't I?"

Veronica shrugged. "Why *would* you?" she said. "There is no reason for you to return to us. You should go home to Lincoln because Cradley is mine. Mine and my father's. Truly, Uncle, we do not need you here any longer. Surely you can see that."

He stared at her a moment before shaking his head in frustration. "Are we speaking of that again?" he said. "Aye, I will return, much to your disappointment."

"Are you going to sell the pewter plates you took from the hall?"

His expression tightened. "That is none of your affair, girl."

"It is my affair because it is my property," Veronica said, unwilling to surrender to the usurper. "In fact, I have sent word to the local magistrate about this. I think it is time we take this situation before someone who dispenses justice and see what he thinks about your attempts to steal my home and steal my money."

Gregor began to turn red in the face. "Is that so?" he said. "Then I welcome it. I have a missive from your father asking me to manage his estate."

"A missive I've never seen. Mayhap you will show it to the magistrate."

Gregor was trying hard to control his temper. Exploding at her had never done any good. "I will do so happily," he said. "And we can finish this once and for all."

"We can and we will."

He cocked his head. "I would not be so smug if I were you," he said. "You seem to forget that you will soon be leaving. Don't you have a betrothed waiting for you in the north?"

God, she hated to be reminded of that. Hearing it from his lips was like a slap to the face. A stupid contract her father had arranged when she was a child, a contract with a man she'd never even met before. Gregor knew about it because her father had told him when he asked him to manage the estate. The problem was that Veronica had no idea if he'd actually done something about it—perhaps he'd summoned her betrothed and demanded the man come to collect her.

She wouldn't have been surprised.

"I would not be so smug if I were *you*," she said. "When he marries me, he inherits Cradley. He will manage it, not you. Therefore, I would not be in such a hurry to marry me off, because you will lose your free source of coin."

She was right. As her father's heiress, she would inherit his estate, and when she married, it would become her husband's. Infuriated by the logic, Gregor turned for the house, disappearing into the dark innards as Veronica stood there and struggled with her rage.

The man was positively infuriating.

"What did he say?" Snowy asked, coming up behind her with the basket in her arms and the dog in tow. "Is he leaving?"

Veronica was still lingering over the annoying conversation. "Aye," she said. "He says he will be gone for two days."

"Where is he going?"

Veronica looked at her. "Probably to sell the plates he stole," she said. Then she cocked her head thoughtfully. "I told him not to return, but he said he would. If he is going to, I'll not make it easy for him."

"What do you mean?"

Veronica gestured at the manse. "I mean that we shall keep the gates locked," she said. "We'll lock everything, and I shall tell everyone that they are not to let him in. We shall lock him out."

Snowy liked that idea. "Good," she said, her dirt-smeared face aglow. "No one likes him as it is. They will not let him in if you command it. But... but he has men with him, my lady. What will we do about that?"

Veronica gathered her skirts and headed inside. "He brought four men with him," she said. "Four men who serve him, though they are not men at arms. They drink our wine and eat our food, and they chase the maids, but they serve no purpose."

Snowy was following, lugging the basket of vegetables with her. "You do not think they will fight for him or try to break in?" she asked.

Veronica was heading for the kitchens. "With what?" she said. "I think only two of them are armed. I only saw swords on them, and they did not seem to be very good swords at that. We have weapons here, more weapons than they have."

"But there are mostly women," Snowy reminded her. "You, me, my mother, seven female servants, and three male servants. No one knows how to use weapons."

"Then we can hire men to keep them out."

Snowy was very much agreeable to that idea. "Where will we find the men?"

Veronica shook her head. "I do not know," she said. "Mayhap I shall go to the nearest tavern. Mayhap the tavernkeep will know. If not him, then I will send word to the Earl of Hereford. He is our liege, after all. My father was a faithful servant. Mayhap if I tell him the situation, he will send men to protect us."

They had reached the kitchen by that time, and Snowy's mother, Iris, came to collect the basket. A big woman with a crown of white hair, she was as solid and tough as her daughter. The kitchen was steamy at this time of day, with boiling cauldrons of water for food and laundry and other things. Preparations for supper were underway, and Snowy was pulled into assisting her mother as Veronica headed to her chamber to wash off the dirt of the garden. But she was feeling more hopeful. She didn't know why she hadn't thought of sending word to Christopher de Lohr before, but it was of little matter. She'd send the man a missive in the morning.

Help would come.

She only hoped it was in time.

Little did she know that help—and chaos—was already on her doorstep.

# CHAPTER FOUR

"**I** THINK THAT is our destination," Douglas said, pointing. "That is the manse the priest indicated as being Cradley Heath."

Myles could see the big, gray-stoned manse a short distance away. It was on a lesser-traveled avenue on the south side of town, with trees and flowers all around, looking quite idyllic and verdant. Once he and his escort had arrived in Worcester, they'd gone straight to the cathedral to ask after Edgar de Wolviston's residence and been directed to this lush place on the banks of the River Severn. Now, they had it in sight on this sightly cool and blustery day, but they also had something else in sight.

A group of men departing through the gates.

"I wonder who they are?" Myles muttered.

Douglas shrugged. So did Westley and Broden, all of whom had come with Myles, along with thirty men at arms and a carriage loaned to the de Wolviston escort by Lady Hereford. She thought it would be more comfortable for de Wolviston's daughter to travel in. It would make the journey slower, but it would be better suited for the lady.

Myles had reluctantly brought it along.

As they drew closer, they could see the five men leaving through the open gate of the manse. In fact, their party literally ran into the departing group, and Myles called a halt as the five men came toward them. He called to the man in the lead riding a fine red steed.

"Is this Edgar de Wolviston's residence?" he asked.

The five men came to a halt, eyeing the heavily armed escort bearing the colors of Hereford. The royal-blue tunics with the yellow lion were on full display, and there was perhaps no better known standard in all of western England, but the five men didn't seem to recognize it. In fact, they seemed rather curious.

"Who are you?" the man in the lead asked.

"We have come on the command of the Earl of Hereford," Myles said. "He is my father. We have come to escort de Wolviston's daughter to her betrothed, by her uncle's request."

The man on the red steed stared at him. Myles couldn't have possibly known what the man was thinking. He couldn't have possibly known that the man thought, finally, his day of vengeance had arrived. That the woman he was desperate to be rid of had no idea what was in store for her, and, when she found out, he was positive she wouldn't go easily. Myles couldn't have known that the man was concocting a lie right in front of him, a lie that would put his brother's daughter into the hands of the Hereford knights and Cradley Heath into his possession. At least for a little while.

Myles couldn't have known how gleeful the man was to realize the moment had arrived.

The show was about to begin.

"This is Edgar's residence," he said, suddenly sounding

friendly. "I am his brother, Gregor. I sent the missive to Hereford."

Myles removed his helm so he could see the man better. Due to his long, thick hair, his helm was designed with extra room at the top because he would bind his considerable mane up at the top of his head so it would not escape the helm.

"I am Sir Myles de Lohr," he said, propping his helm on the front of his saddle. "These are my brothers, Douglas and Westley, and our cousin, Broden du Reims."

Gregor was clearly delighted. "I am honored, my lords," he said. "Truthfully, it was my brother's request that you escort her. I was simply carrying out his wishes. He passed away a few months ago, and I am now in charge of his estate."

Myles nodded. "Very well," he said. "Is the lady prepared to depart?"

All of the friendliness that Gregor had displayed began to morph into something akin to fear. There was hesitation in his manner as he glanced at the manse.

"I am afraid this will not be a simple thing," he said, lowering his voice as if what he was about to say was a brittle secret. "The lady you seek is inside, and she will kill you if you try to take her, so you must be swift and firm. You have my permission to enter the manse and take her by any means necessary. Tie her up and bind her mouth so she cannot speak, for she will try to curse you. Did you bring this carriage for her?"

Myles was slightly taken aback at what he was hearing. He glanced at Broden, at Douglas, before answering.

"Aye," he said. "My mother sent it for her comfort. What do you mean she will try to kill us? She does not want to go?"

Gregor shook his head. "She does not," he said. "But it is her father's wish, and the contract is binding, so she has no choice. You must make this carriage her cage. Put her in there and do not let her out, for she will escape if you let your guard down. Take her to Manchester and give her over to her betrothed. She can become his problem. I have feared for my life every moment of the day since my brother died because of the lady's violent tendencies. Help me, my lord. Get her out of here!"

That was a most unexpected bit of information. Myles looked to his brothers again, his cousin, exasperation on his face. Evidently, they were to corral a banshee, which wasn't what they had anticipated, but that seemed to be the situation. Not that this had been something he wanted to do to begin with, but here they were.

Ready or not.

"Is she armed?" he asked Gregor.

Gregor nodded. "She will use anything she can against you," he said, pointing to the manse. "Charge in there and take her. Do not falter in your bravery, for she will use your weakness against you. And whatever she says... they are lies. She lies and she deceives. Be cautious."

Myles was coming to hate this task more than he already had. He hadn't wanted to come to begin with, but he had agreed as a show of respect and as an apology to his father for the way he'd behaved regarding Aviara's marriage. He was here as penitence. But to hear that the very woman he was supposed to escort was dangerous only served to infuriate him.

"Are there weapons in the manse?" he asked, clearly annoyed.

Gregor gestured back toward the house. "Nothing obvious that I know of," he said. "There are fire pokers and pieces of wood that can be used as clubs, but I do not know if there are any swords or daggers."

"Then she intends to try to kill us with her bare hands?"

"With anything she can."

"What does she look like?"

"Dark hair and eyes so blue that they seem to burn from within."

"Where is she now?"

"The last I saw, she was in the garden, but I think she was finished with her task."

"Where is her chamber?"

"Second floor, north side."

Myles grunted at the information, which the uncle seemed more than willing to provide, and turned to the men behind him.

"Douglas," he said. "You and West and Broden will go inside with me. I want the men at arms to surround the manse. They are not to let anyone escape, and those who try will be captured and held until this situation is settled. We will treat this as if we are capturing a keep—we will go in, take prisoners, and subdue those who resist. But let us be sure we do not kill the lady we are looking for. You heard him—we are looking for a woman with burning blue eyes. Understood?"

As the knights nodded and began to spread the word to the escort, Gregor and his men swiftly vacated. Myles didn't even realize they were gone until he went to ask the man a question and saw that they were quite alone. Alone with an enormous manse and a woman inside who wanted to kill. That was all the information Myles had.

He proceeded carefully.

The gates to the enormous yard of the manse were open, and the knights advanced along with several of the escort. It was the escort's job to cover all of the doors and windows that might be used by someone trying to flee, so they fanned out in the yard and ran for the house while Myles, Douglas, Westley, and Broden headed for the door. Myles had left his helm back on his saddle, but he wasn't going to go back and get it. He could fight a mere woman without his helm. Reaching the entry door, he carefully put his hand on it and lifted the latch.

The door wasn't locked.

He wondered if that should worry him.

❧

AT FIRST, VERONICA couldn't believe her eyes.

She'd just finished stripping down and scrubbing off the dirt from the garden when she caught sight of heavily armed men entering through the open main gate of Cradley. Shocked, she watched as thirty or forty of them poured through the opening and then fanned out all over the compound.

But that wasn't all.

There were four enormous knights heading for the front door. They were wearing blue tunics with some kind of animal on it, though she couldn't make it out. She hadn't spent her time fostering in prestigious castles or even keeping abreast of the politics of England, so she didn't recognize standards on sight. She'd never had to, and had therefore paid no attention to them. But as she watched the big men approach the front door, she very much wished she had.

Something terrible was about to happen.

In a panic, she threw on the first garment she came to, a broadcloth dress to pull over her shift. She stuck her feet back into the dirty slippers she'd worn in from the garden and rushed to her chamber door. Opening it, she could see that it was still quiet in the hall. At this time of day, the maids would either be in the kitchens or possibly laundering at the river's edge, so the manse was relatively empty except for those in the kitchens.

"My lady!" Snowy was suddenly bolting to the top of the stairs, running for Veronica's open chamber door. "Men are here! We have seen them in the yard!"

"I know," Veronica said, reaching out to yank Snowy into her chamber. "I saw them. They are at the door!"

"What shall we do?"

Veronica thought quickly. "I… I do not know," she stammered, startled and terrified by a situation she'd never faced before. "I do not even know why they are here. The front gate is always locked, but…"

Snowy's eyes widened. "Lord Gregor left through the gate," she said. "He left it open!"

Veronica looked at her in horror. "My God," she gasped in realization. "He let them in. He said he would be gone for two days, but mayhap it was only an excuse to open the gate and let them in!"

"They are going to kill us!"

After another second of abject horror, realizing that Gregor had set her up, Veronica swung into action. "Is that his plan, then?" she said angrily, rushing over to the chamber's enormous hearth. "Summoning an army to remove me from my home? To kill me? I am sorry to disappoint him, but it will not happen."

"It won't?"

"Nay!" she barked, grabbing a heavy iron fire poker that was nearly as tall as she was. "It will not happen. We *will* fight back!"

"But what if they—"

"I will not lie down and let them kill me!"

It seemed that there was no other choice but to fight. Clearly, Gregor had summoned men to either throw them all from Cradley Heath or, worse, kill them outright. Veronica wasn't going to go quietly.

It wasn't in her nature.

Seeing her mistress's courage forced Snowy to summon her own. If Veronica could fight, then she could as well. She grabbed a heavy iron pot that was hanging over the coals, used to heat water, as Veronica rushed for the chamber door.

"You must run to the stairs the servants use and bolt that door so they cannot use those stairs," she said to Snowy. "That means they must use the main stairs and we can defeat them at the top. We will not let them pass. *Hurry!*"

Snowy was still holding the iron pot as she raced nearly the length of the house, to the narrow servants' stairs that led to the kitchen wing below, and threw the old iron bolt that hadn't been used in decades. It almost didn't move, but she worked it until it did. With the door secured, she ran back to Veronica, who was moving to the top of the main stairs.

Because the stairs were a half spiral, a low wall blocked the view of those coming up the steps. That meant anyone at the top of the stairs would have full view—and full access—to anyone coming up. They were designed with that purpose, in case the manse was ever invaded, so this was the very moment those stairs had waited for. Since Cradley Heath had never been breached in its eighty-year history, this would be a first.

Veronica would do the repelling, ready or not.

Truthfully, she wasn't sure she *was* ready. Other than hitting them with pokers and pots, she wasn't sure what else she could do. The weapons she spoke of, the ones collected by her grandfather and his father, were stored in the stables, not in the house. There was no way to get to them without being seen, so they had to settle for what they had. Veronica was so terrified that her entire body was twitching, but she fought it, knowing she had to be clearheaded and brave when Gregor's paid men came to call. She thought, with great irony, that Gregor had probably paid for their services with the silver plates he'd stolen.

She'd paid for her own destruction.

But she wasn't going down without a fight.

As Snowy settled down behind her, Veronica peered over the top of the half wall, watching the stairwell and listening. She thought she could hear footsteps, but there were no voices. Minutes passed. Terrible, tense minutes. Then she could hear voices in the distance, and perhaps even screaming, as the armed men found the kitchen and the servants there. She felt sick in the pit of her stomach, knowing she couldn't help the kitchen servants, but she couldn't even think of how Snowy must have felt. The woman's mother was the cook. Veronica could only pray that Iris hadn't fallen victim to Gregor's assassins.

And so, she waited.

And waited.

Then she heard it.

Someone was rattling the door to the servants' stairs. She gasped, startled, as the door banged loudly and someone struck it, but it wouldn't budge. The door was made of heavy oak and wouldn't move unless they took an ax to it or tried to burn it down. She prayed it wouldn't come to that, but now the invaders knew they had only one stairwell to use.

It didn't take a genius to know the lady of the house was

probably lying in wait for them.

But still, they came. In fact, Veronica heard footsteps again—many footsteps, in fact—but they stopped at the base of the stairwell. Snowy was poised to brain the first man up the stairs with her iron pot, and Veronica had the fire poker to use like a battering ram, when a deep voice drifted up the stairwell.

"My lady?" the voice said. "I know you are up there. I hope we can solve our differences amicably. I do not want to harm you."

Veronica scowled. "Go away!" she shouted. "Get out of my home!"

"I will not go away. May I come up without being assaulted? I only wish to talk."

"Nay! I told you go to away!"

"I swear that I will not hurt you. Now, may I come up?"

"I said go *away*!"

The man didn't reply. Veronica was more angry than frightened now, waiting for the next move.

It wasn't long in coming.

Men began coming up the stairs. There were two of them, grouped closely together, and they were in full armor. Helms, mail, swords… everything but shields, which would have served them well, considering what was about to happen to them. When they got within range, Snowy slammed the pot on the helm of the first man. It was a hard blow, enough to stagger him into the man behind him, and it was enough of a pause for Veronica to leap out of her hiding place and plant her foot on the shoulder. She kicked, and kicked hard, and he went falling back into the man behind him.

The two of them tumbled down the stairs.

That brought two more knights, but only one had a helm.

The other had a mass of blond hair tied up on the top of his head. As Snowy used the pot like a hammer, right into the top of the helmed head, Veronica used the poker like a battering ram. It went right into the helmed man's chest, and he fell back, into the man with the blond hair, who stood aside as the other man tumbled backward.

Realizing her blow hadn't sent the blond man to the bottom of the stairs, Veronica stared at him, and he stared back. Perhaps it was only momentary shock, but it was enough of a pause to convey that they were both a little startled by the situation. But then he was coming up the stairs toward her and she panicked, running into her chamber as Snowy scattered. The man with the blond hair stormed into the chamber, but Veronica was ready for him. She started throwing things like a madwoman, clipping him on the shoulder with a heavy candlestick.

But that was only the first.

A barrage of items came flying at him—more candlesticks, bowls, a hairbrush, a small stool, and a variety of other things. The knight had his arms up in front of him, arms covered with mail and pieces of plate, so he wasn't truly being hurt by anything. But he wanted to keep it away from his face.

Veronica had good aim.

"Lady, I would take it as a personal favor if you would stop trying to maim me," he said as a wooden bowl nearly hit him in the head. "I told you that no one is going to hurt you. I swear upon my oath."

"Your oath means nothing to me!" she said, hurling a chamber pot at him and watching it smack him in the hip. "I told you to go away!"

"I have been very plain that I mean you no harm," the

knight said. "Why do you fight?"

Veronica was too far gone with panic to answer him. She was on the other side of her bed at this point, grabbing the three small daggers that her father had given her. She held one up threateningly.

"Get out this minute or I will throw the dagger," she said. "Unless you want to come away missing an eye, I suggest you leave."

The knight didn't lower his arms from their protective stance. "I do not want to come away missing an eye," he said. "I rather like my eyes."

"I don't!"

"Why not? Have you even looked at them?"

Dagger in hand, she scowled at him. "I have no desire to look at your eyes," she said. "Or any part of you, for that matter."

"Is that so? I'm told I'm rather handsome."

Those scowling eyes widened. "I do not care if you are a god from Olympus," she said in outrage. "Handsome or ugly, I want you to leave. This is your last warning!"

He sighed. "God knows I *should* leave," he said. "Not only am I being attacked, but I'm being insulted as well."

"Good," she sneered. "Are you going to leave, or do I start throwing the daggers?"

"I have a duty to perform. I cannot leave."

"A *duty* to perform?" she repeated, aghast. "A duty to kill me, you mean. How much did he pay you? Whatever it is, I will double it if you will leave me alone."

The knight frowned. "Who paid me?" he said. "And who am I to kill?"

That only seemed to infuriate her. "Feigning ignorance will

not help you," she said. "Tell me how much he paid you."

"No one paid me anything," he said, clearly puzzled. "Who are you speaking of?"

"Gregor, of course!"

The knight's puzzlement grew. "The man I just met departing the manse? On the red steed?"

"You know exactly whom I am referring to. Do not insult my intelligence."

The knight simply looked at her. Something was going on behind those pale blue eyes. Veronica could tell. After a moment, he dropped his arms, unbuckled the belt around his waist that held his broadsword, and removed the entire assembly. He laid it on the ground and began pulling daggers out of the folds in his mail, in his belt, and even out of a sheath on his arm. There were eight daggers total that ended up on the ground next to the broadsword. Carefully, he stepped away from the weapons and held out his hands to show he was unarmed.

"Now," he said in a deep, quiet voice. "I think we have a misunderstanding here. I was told, by Gregor, that you were violently opposed to the betrothal your father has agreed upon. He told me that you did not wish to marry. Isn't that what this is about?"

Veronica had no idea what he was talking about. "Betrothal?" she repeated. "Gregor told you about... What on *earth* are you talking about?"

The knight lifted his blond eyebrows. "Mayhap I should start from the beginning," he said steadily. "My name is Sir Myles de Lohr. My father is the Earl of Hereford and Worcester. May I know your name, my lady?"

*De Lohr*. When Veronica realized she was looking at one of

the earl's sons, she immediately lowered the dagger. "I am Veronica de Wolviston," she said, her voice trembling with stress and fear. "Are... are you truly from Hereford?"

Myles nodded. "Truly," he said. "I have been summoned, by your uncle, to escort you to your betrothed, but I met your uncle as I arrived and he told me that I had to take you by force."

Veronica dropped the dagger when she realized he wasn't a paid assassin. "God's Bones," she muttered, nearly collapsing on the bed. Sitting heavily, she struggled to make sense out of what was happening. "He told you that?"

"He did."

"I thought you had come to kill me."

Myles shook his head. "Hardly," he said. "I've come to escort you to Manchester."

Veronica wiped a trembling hand over her brow, smoothing back hair that had become mussed during the fight. "At my uncle's request, did you say?" she said. Then she snorted ironically, as if suddenly realizing the truth of the situation. "So that is how he planned to remove me. He planned to have me taken north."

Myles had no idea what she meant, but he was certain of one thing—he'd never seen a more beautiful lady. She had perfect skin, lips like a rosebud, and dark, silky hair. But those eyes—Gregor hadn't been exaggerating when he said they looked as if they burned from within. Myles had never seen such brilliant blue eyes in his life.

"Who planned to have you taken north?" he said. "My lady, if you could clarify this situation, I would be grateful."

Veronica was still lost in her own thoughts, but she heard his soft plea. Perhaps the man did deserve an explanation.

"I do apologize for... for thinking ill of you, my lord," she said, standing up and facing him. "The truth is this—when my father died three months ago, his brother showed up on my doorstep with the declaration that my father had asked him to manage his estate in the event of his death. I've never seen the missive from my father giving Gregor such permission, but Gregor will not leave. He has taken what money I have and has spent it foolishly. Two days ago, he stole silver plates from our hall, and I thought he had used it to pay assassins—you—to remove me from this house. He wants what I have. That is why I fought you off, my lord. I thought you had come to harm me."

Quite a bit became clear in that softly uttered explanation. Myles shook his head. "Nay, lady," he said. "I am not here to harm you. Gregor sent a missive to my father saying that it was your father's wish that my father provide an escort to take you to your betrothed. Is there even a betrothal?"

Veronica nodded, but it was with remorse. "There *is* a betrothal," she said. "I'm surprised Gregor knows about it, but then again, he is my father's brother. My father surely must have told him at some point. But Gregor hasn't mentioned it since he arrived, and now I know why."

"Why?"

"He was plotting to use it to be rid of me."

That made sense to Myles. "And that was why he sent the request for the escort."

"It seems so."

Myles eyed her. "Would your intended even be expecting you?" he asked. "Or would you be surprising the man?"

Veronica sighed faintly, averting her gaze as she moved to pick up the broken pieces of a bowl near her feet. "I would not be a surprise," she said. "Not really. The terms of the contract stated that I would be delivered to my intended when I came of age, which will be next month. He will be expecting me next month, in any case. But I may as well go now, because the sooner I wed, the sooner my new husband shall be lord of Cradley Heath and the sooner he can chase Gregor away from the property."

Myles thought she sounded rather defeated. It was clear that he had walked into a family battle of sorts, something that was taking its toll on a young but fiery lady.

"It seems that this is a complex situation," he said quietly.

Veronica nodded with regret. "It is, indeed, my lord," she said. "I am sorry it has troubled you."

"It is no trouble," he said. "But if this situation is as you say, that seems wholly unfair to you."

Veronica set the broken pieces of the bowl on the nearest table. "Unfair is a word for it," she said. "I can think of others. But my main concern is my uncle. He wants all of this. The man bleeds greed and envy."

Because the situation had calmed considerably, Myles bent over to pick up his weapons. "Then mayhap I should have a talk with the man," he said. "I do not like being part of his games. Clearly, you did not know he sent for an escort."

"Nay, I did not."

"Then he is making me part of his plan to remove you from your home."

"I must go sometime. He knows that."

"Then mayhap you are right—the sooner you wed, the sooner your husband can chase your uncle from your home."

She nodded. "I suppose," she said. "But I feel stupid now. Stupid that I did not anticipate this. Gregor is more devious than I thought."

Myles, the stone-hearted knight, was feeling a strange twinge of... something. It was more than pity. He wasn't sure what it was, exactly, but he knew that it was strong. Uncomfortable, even. He didn't like the idea of the brave, radiant creature before him falling prey to a predatory uncle. A woman like that was something to be protected.

Nay, he didn't like the twinge in his chest in the least.

It made his stone heart feel something.

"Nothing is going to happen today," he said as he began tucking daggers back where they belonged. "Your uncle said he would be gone for the night, so you have a slight reprieve. With your permission, my men and I will stay the night, and then we can leave on the morrow if that is agreeable. Or mayhap you need tonight to decide if you truly want to go."

"I want to go," she said. "I will not change my mind. I cannot."

"Very well," he said. "But you will need time to pack your things, especially if you were not expecting to depart."

Veronica was looking at the mess on the floor. "You needn't worry," she said. "I suspect this has already been a great deal of trouble for you, and your father has been most generous in sending an escort, so I will be ready. But I do apologize for the fight. I hope your men are not terribly injured."

The corners of Myles' mouth twitch with a smile. "I was just going to see to them," he said. "Would you care to come with me? I believe everyone needs to see that we have not killed one another and that there is peace between us."

Veronica nodded. "I agree," she said. "There are probably a few of my servants who must be calmed. I thought I heard screaming."

"You did, but only out of fear. No one was harmed."

"Then there may be some frayed nerves to ease."

"And a head or two that needs tending."

He meant the knights that had been conked on the head with the iron pot. Veronica looked at him, grinning guiltily because she knew it was her fault that those knights were seeing stars.

"I hope they are not too angry with me," she said.

Myles shook his head. "I will explain the situation," he said. "They will not be."

They came to the doorway, and she stopped, gazing up at him. Then she looked him up and down as if truly seeing him for the first time.

"You are quite tall," she said. "And big. No wonder I was so frightened of you."

He was more than a foot taller than she was, because she came to about his sternum. "My father is very tall," he said. "So are my brothers."

"How many do you have?"

"Five."

"Are you the eldest?"

"I am in the middle."

"Middle Son Myles."

He cracked a grin. "Something like that."

"I hope you do not hold our introduction against me, Myles."

"I hope *you* do not hold our introduction against *me*."

Veronica shook her head. "I will not," she said. Then she peered closely at his face as if she'd spied something worth studying. "You were right about something."

"About what?"

"You do have nice eyes."

He couldn't help it. The cracked grin grew into a broad smile. "You noticed."

She nodded, her lips twitching with a smile as she continued to inspect his face. "And you *are* handsome enough," she said. "Is that something you go around telling women you have just met?"

"Not usually," he said. "Why? Should I?"

She shook her head as she turned for the door. "Probably not," she said. "It makes you sound conceited, and I am sure your wife would not appreciate it."

"I am not married."

She grunted. "Shocking," she said. "You should be."

"I should?"

They were on the landing now, heading for the infamous stairs. "Of course," she said. "You're old enough. And you said yourself that you're handsome, so it should be no trouble attracting women. But, most importantly, you're an earl's son. You should have a line of ladies from here to London vying for your hand."

"I do not."

"Then something must be wrong with you. What is it?"

Myles couldn't help it—he burst into soft laughter, refusing to answer her as they headed down the stairs. He was embarrassed to admit that a beautiful young woman had actually rendered him speechless with her praise and probing questions. She didn't hold back, and he thought it rather hilarious.

Maybe the escort to Manchester wasn't going to be so bad after all.

# CHAPTER FIVE

WESTLEY AND DOUGLAS were not exactly in the forgiving mood.

At least, not in the beginning.

They had been the first ones up the stairs in pursuit of the lady, following Myles' order, and they had been the first ones to encounter the woman with the iron pot and the second woman who kicked them back down the way they'd come. Westley had fallen into Douglas, so Douglas received the brunt of it when he fell all the way down the stairs with his brother's weight on top of him. He'd fallen on his left shoulder and arm, and even now he was nursing a sprained elbow. Westley was the one who had been smacked in the head, and it had briefly knocked him unconscious, so he was sporting one hell of a headache.

Myles could tell by the expressions on their faces that they were not open to any manner of apology. At least, not at the moment. They weren't finished being angry yet. Neither one of them had wanted to go up the stairs first, but Myles commanded it, so they had been forced to comply. Their anger was directed at him more than it was the lady, whom Myles had managed to subdue. Oddly enough, she wasn't bound in any way, but seemed to be accompanying their brother of her own free will.

A strange situation, indeed.

Once they got a good look at the lady, however, their mood changed a little. They both thought she was quite beautiful, and sometimes beauty was the great absolution when it came to hard feelings. It was difficult to be angry with someone so lovely. When Myles explained the situation and it all came clear, there was far more of a willingness to understand what had happened, and perhaps even some forgiveness, at least where the lady was concerned.

But Myles was another story.

They were still angry with him.

Veronica, for her part, was feeling a good deal of guilt for the beat-down she had put on the younger de Lohr brothers. Between Snowy's bashing and her kicking, the stairs had done the rest, and both knights were nursing bruises and sprains. But Myles, who professed to be their brother, simply stood there and shook his head at the pair, seemingly making no move to actually tend their injuries, so Veronica took over.

It was the least she could do.

While the de Lohr men at arms began to set up their encampment in the bailey of Cradley Heath and the situation was defused, Veronica left the wounded knights in the entryway and headed back to the kitchens to gather the things she needed to help them, but also make sure her servants were well. They had certainly suffered a scare at the hands of Gregor's misunderstanding, and when she entered the kitchen, everyone seemed well for the most part, except for the cook. Iris couldn't seem to get off the chair she was sitting in because she'd had such a fright. The woman sat there and panted while Snowy fanned her with a cloth, but when Veronica explained the situation, they were most understanding. Several of them even volunteered to assist the knights who had been injured in the scrap.

That included Snowy.

Armed for service, Veronica and her servant army returned to the entryway and went to work. Westley was the one in most obvious need, because he not only had a large bump sprouting out of the top of his head, but he also had a gash that was turning his blond hair pinkish with blood. Veronica had never sewn such a gash before because she'd never experienced a battle before. She dabbed the blood, cleansed the wound, but hesitated to stick a needle in the man. It was finally Myles who ended up putting three stitches in his brother's scalp as Veronica watched closely and tried not to become ill.

This was all quite new to her.

Once the knights were tended, that was where Veronica and Myles parted ways. He and his brothers went out to the bailey where Broden was supervising the encampment setup, but before they departed, Veronica invited Myles and his men to sup in the hall. Considering what had happened, she felt that it was the least she could do.

Myles agreed.

Maybe a little too quickly.

With the knights out in the yard and the door shut, Veronica stood there a moment, thinking on how the day had transpired. She'd awoken this morning with the same thoughts she always had—of Gregor and how to keep her father's money from him—but now, her life had changed in a matter of minutes. Gregor had found a way to remove her from Cradley Heath, and it was legal. He had summoned an escort to take her to a place south of Manchester, called Adlington Castle, where a man by the name of Abner de Correa would become her husband. A man her father had known, but a man she'd never even met before.

But that was of little matter.

She would soon be his wife.

And that marriage would take her away from Cradley Heath, leaving Gregor to do what he wished with it, at least until de Correa married her. Then it would be his, so anything Gregor had done—like sell possessions or animals and keep the money—would belong to de Correa. Veronica actually cracked a smile when she thought of Gregor having to pay back everything he'd taken.

Perhaps this betrothal was the best thing after all.

At least, she kept trying to tell herself that.

"My lady?"

Veronica heard a voice and looked up to see Snowy standing in the doorway that led into the hall. It was enough to break her from her train of thought.

"Are you well?" she asked the servant woman. "I did not have a chance to ask you personally. You were not hurt in the struggle, were you?"

Snowy shook her head. "Nay," she said. "But what happened in your chamber? I heard things being broken. Did that enormous knight try to fight you?"

Veronica shook her head, grasping Snowy by the arm as she headed into the hall. "He never made a move against me," she said. "What you heard was my throwing things at him. Trying to chase him away. But then we discovered something surprising."

"What was that?"

"That Gregor has summoned an escort to take me to Manchester," she said, looking at the woman. When Snowy looked confused, Veronica hastened to explain. "It is the misunderstanding I spoke of when I told everyone that Sir Myles and his men were not a threat. Gregor knows of my betrothal. My father must have told him. Gregor sent word to the Earl of Hereford requesting an escort to take me to my betrothed. That is why Sir Myles is here—to take me to be married—only Gregor evidently told him that I would not go without a fight, so that is why they came in armed. Gregor's lies have caused this, Snowy. Yet more lies in a situation that has been full of them."

Snowy looked at her with surprise, but also with some fear. "You are to be married?"

"Aye. We always knew it would happen."

"But… *now*?"

"Now."

"What will you do?"

That was a very good question. The more Veronica thought on the answer, the more she realized that it was her salvation. "I will go, of course," she said. "There is a betrothal, and come next month, I will be expected to fulfill it. Don't you see, Snowy? This is the beginning of Gregor's end. The man I marry will inherit Cradley Heath. He will claim his property and throw Gregor to the wolves. I wonder if Gregor realizes that with this latest subversion to remove me from my home, it will mean his own demise."

Snowy wasn't an educated woman. She couldn't read or write, but she had a good mind. She was sharp. As she watched Veronica head into the corridor that led to the kitchen, she spoke softly.

"What if your new husband does not help us?" she asked

softly. "What if he does not care about you or Cradley Heath?"

Veronica paused and looked at her. "Then I suppose Gregor will win," she said, something that was difficult to admit. "But something he shall not have is my father's money. I will take that secret to my grave. And so will you."

"They could not burn it out of me, my lady."

Snowy was serious, and Veronica knew she meant it. Other than Veronica, she was the only person who knew about the Jewish bankers. Veronica knew the secret was safe. But she very much hoped Snowy wouldn't have to suffer Gregor's wrath in her absence, because the man knew the two of them were close.

Perhaps some things needed to be said between them.

"You must stay here when I go north," she said, taking Snowy by the hand. "I leave you here to protect Cradley Heath and do all you can to keep it, and everyone who lives here, safe from Gregor. I do not know how long I will be gone, but I swear to you that I will return as soon as I can. Hopefully I will bring an army with me to purge Gregor from these walls, but until I do… you must be brave, Snowdrop. I know you will be."

Snowy nodded, but it was with some uncertainty. The entire future was uncertain, as far as she was concerned, but Veronica seemed to think otherwise. She seemed optimistic about her new husband, that the man would leap to her aid and charge back to Cradley Heath to reclaim his wife's property.

Snowy sincerely hoped she was right.

God help them if she was wrong.

☙

"A PITY SHE is to be married," Westley said. "I would say that she is a rare beauty. I've hardly seen finer. And you said that her uncle is trying to get rid of her?"

He was attempting to look at the stitches in his scalp with a hand mirror of polished bronze. They were sore, and they itched, and the hair around it was a faded-blood color. Westley was in Myles' tent, a big one pitched near the main gates to the yard, and he'd been complaining bitterly about the treatment they'd received since arriving at Cradley Health until Myles told him about the supper invitation.

After that, he wasn't so inclined to complain.

"It is a complicated family squabble," Myles said, carefully shaving his chin, which was difficult to do because of the big dimple in the middle of it. "It seems that we have become pawns in the battle for Cradley Heath."

"And we intend to remove the lady?"

Myles didn't answer right away because he was dragging the straight razor across the cleft of his chin. "We intend to escort the lady to her betrothed, and the lady's husband will punish her greedy uncle when he inherits this place," he said, rinsing the razor off in warm water. "I already told you all of this."

"I know," Westley said, still trying to look at his wound. "Don't you think we should send a missive to Papa about the situation?"

"I already have," Myles said, glancing at his youngest brother. "Truly, West, do you sleep through everything? Douglas sent a missive about an hour ago. Tomorrow, we are escorting the lady to Manchester. When we are finished, we will come home and that will be the end of it. The... end of everything."

He suddenly sounded pensive, and Westley looked over him, noticing that he had stopped shaving and was simply looking at himself in a small mirror by the light of a few tapers.

"What is it?" Westley asked. "What is wrong?"

Myles stared at himself a moment longer before continuing

because he had his entire left cheek to finish. "I was just thinking," he said.

"Of what?"

"Of what I shall do when I get home," Myles said, beginning his shave of the left cheek. "There is nothing left for me there. Or anywhere."

Westley frowned and put his mirror down. "What do you mean by that?"

"I mean no marriage," Myles said. "No wife. Aviara is marrying Ollie, of all people. God, I still can't swallow that. I cannot even say it without wanting to throw this razor through the wall."

Westley eyed him as he lay back on his brother's bed, which he'd been sitting on. "I heard Mama and Papa talking about it," he said. "They think you view her as a prize to be won. They do not think you are in love with her."

Myles frowned and turned to look at him. "When did you hear that?"

"The day Papa gave you the directive to come to Cradley," Westley said. "Before you think that I was deliberately eavesdropping, I was looking for Mama, and the cook told me that she had gone to Papa's solar. The door was shut, so I listened to what was being said, to see if I could interrupt her. But what I heard was them talking about you and how you were going to deal with the loss of Aviara."

Myles eyed him a moment before slowly returning to his shaving. "You *were* deliberately listening," he said. "I know you, West. You've got the curiosity of a woman. One of these days, you're going to hear something that you do not wish to hear."

"Do you want to know what they said or not?"

"Nay," Myles said flatly. "I am certain that I already know

what they said. They've told me."

"Did they tell you that sending you on this escort was to keep you away from Ollie and Aviara's marriage?"

Myles paused, looking at his brother in the reflection of the mirror. "I assumed as much," he said. "Papa told me to stay away from Aldsworth. I'm assuming that is where the marriage will take place, unless Ollie wants to marry at his seat of Ilchester."

Westley shook his head. "I would not know," he said. "But Papa said you are hard."

"I *am* hard."

"He means you are hardhearted. He fears you will never know happiness because of it."

Myles was staring at his reflection in the mirror, hearing his father's words coming from his brother's mouth. Somehow, that hurt him. He didn't mean to be hard or even dense, as Aviara had accused him. He simply was. That was his nature. He didn't know how to be anything other than what he was, so the fact that his father feared for him made him feel sad.

It also made him feel very alone.

But he couldn't admit it.

"Papa worries too much," he finally said, finishing with the last patch of hair on his jaw. "I am sure he says the same thing about all of us to varying degrees."

"Mayhap," Westley said. "But what will you do, knowing that Ollie is marrying Aviara?"

"Nothing."

"What will you do when you see Ollie again?" Westley pressed. "And you know you will. What will you say to him?"

Myles splashed water on his face, cleaning off the slimy soap he'd used to shave with. "Stop asking questions," he said.

"Why don't you go and clean yourself? At least change into a clean tunic. We have been invited to sup, and I should not like the House of de Lohr represented by filthy barbarians. Papa deserves better representation than that."

Westley sat up, rubbing his head because it throbbed a bit. "Do you want to know what else I heard Papa say?"

"Nay."

"He said he might send Peter to the wedding because he and Mama did not want to go."

Myles was drying off his face, but his movements slowed. "How ironic," he muttered. "Peter would go to witness Ollie marry the woman I should have married. It should be *my* wedding he's attending."

Westley stood up from the bed. "Myles, may I say something?"

Myles cast him a long look. "Haven't you said enough?"

Westley shook his head. "Not nearly enough," he said. "I know a little something about women. They just seem to like me, and I understand them. I think that is a fair assessment. Don't you?"

Myles shrugged. "For whatever reason, they do like you, and you do seem to enjoy them."

Myles put himself in front of Myles so he could look him in the face. "I want to tell you something," he said. "I tell you this because you are my brother and I love you. I only want the best for you. So I will tell you this—I have been watching Aviara flirt with you for two years. When you were not around, she flirted with any man she could. We have all seen her. With Ollie, she pitted you two against one another like two dominant roosters. She wanted you to fight for her so she could feel powerful."

Myles rolled his eyes and tried to turn away. "I know what

you think," he said. "I know what my entire family thinks. Does no one even stop to consider that I am not a complete fool when it comes to women?"

Westley wouldn't let him walk away. He grasped his brother by the arms. "Myles, listen," he said. "Just this once, please listen, and I will never speak of this again. You are not a fool. But sometimes, when we are caught up in our own feelings, we fail to see the truth that others see. Aviara is a pretty woman and witty, but she was never in love with you. To her, you seemed to be a prize. Something to be won. I may not be married, but I know enough to know that is not how marriage should be. She would have made you miserable for the rest of your life."

With that, he dropped his hands, but Myles didn't walk away. He stood there and looked at his brother with an unhappy expression on his face. Then that expression faded and he averted his gaze, as if thinking on what his brother had said.

"At least I had her attention," he said after a moment. "That does not often happen with me."

He stripped off the tunic he was wearing and tossed it aside, going to hunt for a clean one in his saddlebags as Westley watched him.

"Do you know why?" he said.

Myles pulled forth a dark blue woolen tunic. "You must if you are asking that question," he said with some sarcasm. "Impart your wisdom on me, little brother. Why?"

A hint of a smile crossed Westley's lips. "Because you are unapproachable," he said. "You do not smile, you do not laugh, and if you told a woman she was pretty, I might actually faint. There is nothing warm or charming that comes from you, Myles. You are the most beauteous brother—I can admit that.

We're all handsome enough, but you... you look like God carved you out of a piece of marble. And you're just as cold. Women do not respond to a man who is cold."

Myles pulled the tunic over his head. "That is not the first time I've heard it."

"And what do you do about it?"

Myles smoothed down the tunic and raked his hair back with his fingers to straighten it. "Nothing," he said. "I cannot be something I am not."

Westley shook his head with pity. "Can you not try to be a little nicer?" he said. "Tonight, for example. We will be supping with the lovely lady... What is her name, anyway?"

"Veronica de Wolviston."

"The lovely Lady Veronica," Westley said. "We will be supping with her tonight. Why not try to be kind? Practice being charming with her."

Myles scowled. "I will *not* practice being charming," he said. "The woman is going to marry another man. What is the point?"

Westley went to the table that held the razor and soap and water and began to wash his hands. "The point is that you can practice being nice to her," he said. "That does not mean you have to marry her. Simply be... nice."

Myles looked at him dubiously. "Nice?"

"Aye... *nice.*"

Myles wasn't so sure it was a good idea. He didn't want to give the woman the wrong impression. But, on the other hand, the fact that he wasn't very charming or sociable had always been his downfall. With Aviara now out of his reach, marrying a man who was, in fact, much more charming than Myles, he supposed Westley wasn't too far wrong. With a heavy sigh, he nodded his head in resignation.

"Very well," he muttered. "I'll try. *Nice.*"

Un-truer words were never spoken.

# CHAPTER SIX

"AND THEN *MY* cousin, a vile bastard if I've ever known one, swooped in and stole her away from me. We just received the wedding announcement!"

It was a scene out of a horror tale. Westley was sure of that. Two hours into a lovely supper that Lady Veronica had provided, including very strong cider made from their apple orchards, and the drink had gone straight to Myles' head. The man was usually quite tolerant of drink, but not hard cider. It went through him like a tempest, and even now, he was spilling the entire event with Aviara and Oliver for the benefit of their hostess.

Westley and Douglas and Broden couldn't have been more mortified.

"Myles, surely Lady Veronica does not want to hear about your misfortunes with Lady Aviara," Westley said. Truthfully, he was fairly drunk himself off that potent cider, but at least he had some of his wits about him. "It is over and done with. Tell the lady about the new horse you purchased in London last month. The big white beast with the long black mane."

Myles' head was swimming. Positively swimming. He

looked at his brother, his sodden mind slow to change subjects. "That beautiful animal," he said, nearly slurring his words. "He is the younger brother to the horse I ride now. Tempest is his name, and he is like a brother to me. But the new horse—his name is Lune—will be astonishing once I break him in. The horse has perfect conformation, including plump hindquarters that look like a woman's naked arse the way they flow and curve."

Douglas, who was also fairly drunk, wasn't so far gone that he wasn't dismayed by his brother comparing a horse's rump to a woman's naked arse. In front of a lady, no less. He slapped a disbelieving hand over his face as Westley looked as if he'd just heard something outrageously awful. He had, in truth, but Veronica, sitting next to Myles, didn't flinch.

"My father has three fine horses here," she said steadily. "To be perfectly honest, I am afraid to keep them here, afraid my uncle will try to sell them. They are worth a good deal of money."

Myles looked at her, frowning. "We must discuss your uncle," he said. "Where does he come from?"

"Lincolnshire, my lord."

"Why won't he go home?"

"Because he says my father has tasked him with managing his estate," she said. "I believe I mentioned that earlier."

Myles lifted his cup and downed the rest of the cider, motioning to a servant to pour him more. "And you have been fighting with him since he arrived?"

Veronica shrugged. "Not exactly fighting," she said. "But he wants all of this. I mean to keep it from him."

Myles was looking at her as she spoke, his half-lidded eyes drifting over her face, her neck, the necklace that she wore. "I must ask you a question, Lady Veronica."

"Please do."

"Do you *want* to marry?"

Veronica seemed to falter. "Every woman wishes to marry, at some point."

"But do you want to marry someone you love?"

She smiled thinly. "I have never met my betrothed," she said. "But I hope I would grow to love him, someday."

Myles wiped his mouth with the back of his hand, a mildly uncoordinated gesture. "You are very pretty," he said. "Beautiful, even. Did you know that? It is my opinion that your betrothed is a fortunate man."

Her smile turned modest. "That is very kind of you, my lord."

But Myles waved her off. "Kindness has nothing to do with it," he said. "It is the truth. You are beautiful. And you are brave. Not many women would fight back against men twice their size. That was impressive."

"I am glad I did not injure you, my lord. I was careless and frightened."

He frowned, leaning over and grasping both of her hands in his enormous mitts. It was a rather bold gesture.

"Do not say that," he said, shaking his head at her. "Never apologize for defending yourself. It is a sign of weakness, and you are not weak."

His face was close to hers, the smell of alcohol on his breath, but Veronica didn't back away. She was watching him like a hawk, noting every move he made because there was nothing about him that wasn't mesmerizing.

"Again, you are kind to say so," she said quietly. "And you are very understanding."

Myles gave her a saucy smile, drunk as he was, that came easily to him. He winked at her, kissed her hands, and then let her go.

"Did you hear that, West?" he said to his brother across the table. "She says I am *very* understanding."

Westley eyed his brother, wondering if he and Douglas should try to get the man out of there and into bed before he started talking about Aviara or arses, or both, again.

"I heard," he said. "Well done, Myles."

Myles smiled, a truly handsome gesture, as he looked at Veronica but pointed to his brother. "West told me that I should be nice to you tonight," he said. "I have been, haven't I?"

Veronica was confused, looking to Westley for clarification. "You have been," she said, answering Myles' question. "You have been nice since the start of our acquaintance."

Myles shook his head. "You misunderstand," he said. "My entire family thinks I have a heart of stone. I am not the friendly sort. I am not the *nice* sort. My talents lie elsewhere, my lady. I could not be charming if my life depended on it."

That clarified it a little for Veronica, but in truth, the entire supper conversation had been quite odd. It had been an event that she was strangely looking forward to throughout the afternoon, planning a plentiful and tasty meal, hoping to make up for the misunderstanding they'd had. She'd wanted to be kind to Myles in particular, since he was the one she'd sinned against the most. The first hour of the meal had been relatively quiet, without a good deal of conversation, but once the fermented apple cider took hold, Myles started chatting nonstop.

About somebody named Aviara.

"I do not agree, my lord," she said after a moment. "Whoever has told you this is mistaken. You've been kind and charming since we were able to work through our differences."

Myles picked up his newly full cup of cider and took a long drink. "No one has ever said that to me," he said. "Is it possible you say that to me because you know I will escort you to Manchester and you want to ply me with flattery, or do you say it because it is true?"

"I want to ensure we have as smooth a journey as possible, that is true," Veronica replied. "But I do not lie. If I say it, I believe it."

Myles' blue eyes were glimmering, something they didn't normally do. He was looking at Veronica with a gaze that sparkled with drunken warmth. He'd been drunk before, but not on cider. Not like this. It seemed to be invading cracks in the hard shell that he surrounded himself with, bringing forth traits and conversation that weren't usual with him.

Unfortunately, it was like watching a runaway beer wagon.

"But I've been told I am dense," he said before picking up his cup again and swigging a gulp. "She told me I was dense. Do you not see that in me?"

Veronica cocked her head. "Who told you?"

"Lady Aviara," Myles said deliberately, enunciating each syllable. "She called me dense because I did not know she wanted me to court her. After two years, she finally tells me she wants me to court her. How was I supposed to know that?"

"Myles," Douglas said from across the table. "The lady does not care about Lady Aviara. Can we not change the subject to something more—"

Myles cut him off by turning to Veronica and grasping one of her hands again. "My lady, you are a woman," he said with more animation than a sober Myles was capable of. "You are a lovely woman who seems to be reasonably intelligent. You are certainly courageous enough. If you wanted a man to court you, would you tell him? Or would you expect him to simply know it?"

Veronica should have been put off by a very big, very drunk man demanding all of her attention. Were it anyone but Myles, she might have been. But there was something comical, but also strangely endearing, about the man. Something she couldn't quite put her finger on, but it was something she didn't want to discount.

Oddly, it drew her in.

"I see no reason not to tell him," she said honestly. "Or I would have someone else tell him. It would be a bit forward for me to do it. Or mayhap I would not have to tell him at all if my actions were obvious to him."

Myles stared at her a moment before letting go of her hand and sinking back in his chair. It was a big wooden chair with a high back, the one her father had always used, and Myles closed his eyes and began banging his head against the chair back.

"She *was* obvious," he said as he continued to slowly bang away. "She flirted with me. Flattered me. Toyed with me. My entire family felt that she was using me, teasing me, and I suppose she was. I knew she was. She flirted with me and then she would flirt with my cousin, Ollie. Ollie is more charming and far more intuitive with women, but he looks like a horse's arse. I thought my appearance alone would be enough to win her hand. But it was not. Ollie's charm and wit were more appealing, and he was able to gain the upper hand. That is why she married him. He won her over where I could not."

The head banging continued as Veronica motioned to Snowy, who had been bringing food and drink to the table, and whispered to the woman to bring *very* watered-down cider. It was probably too late for Myles, but she had to try something. The man was becoming increasingly animated, which, she deduced, wasn't his normal state. As he banged, she leaned forward in her chair.

"Then she was not meant for you," Veronica said evenly. "You should not have to fight so hard for a woman's affection. Either she gives it freely or she doesn't. And if she is using you to make another man jealous, then she is not worth your attention."

"Hear, hear!" Douglas said, slamming his cup on the table. "That is what we have been trying to tell you, Myles. If you will not believe us, then believe the lady. She makes good sense."

Myles stopped his head banging and looked at his brother. "That is easy for you to say," he said. "You can communicate with women. All I do is make a mess of things."

As Douglas shook his head in disapproval at his brother's self-pity, Veronica spoke. "When you find the right woman, you will know how to communicate with her," she said. "It will be completely natural. Better still, she will understand you for who you are. She will not expect you to be someone you are not."

Myles looked at her, hearing her words through the alcohol that was clouding his mind. "And you?" he said. "When you meet your betrothed, do you think that you will understand him and he will understand you? Do you apply the same logic to your own marriage?"

Veronica shrugged. "I've not thought about it much, to be truthful," she said. "As I said, my father made this bargain when I was a child. Therefore, I must make the relationship work. I have no choice. But you do. You will find the right woman someday, Sir Myles. I am sure of it."

He made a face that suggested he was doubtful. "That makes one of us," he muttered. "But I appreciate your faith, my lady. I truly do."

He seemed depressed, but he stopped talking about it. And he'd stopped banging his head. Veronica took his stillness and silence as an opportunity to study him. He was a truly fine example of male beauty—she'd noticed that when she first laid eyes on him. The long, luxurious blond hair, messy as it had been when he arrived, was now combed and flowing past his shoulders. It was hair a woman would be proud to possess. He had a square jaw, perfect lips—a perfect face in general that was set off by eyes the color of the sky. Even when he smiled, his teeth were perfect. But beyond his face, he had an enormous body that was muscular and powerful. There wasn't anything about him, in her opinion, that was imperfect, but he seemed to think there was a good deal wrong with him. Other than the fact that he got drunk on apple cider, Veronica couldn't really find anything else amiss with the man.

She was coming to think that Aviara was a very fortunate woman.

Or, at least, she could have been.

"Myles," Douglas said from across the table. "Why not go to bed? It has been a long day, and the hard cider has not been kind to you."

Myles' response was to down the contents of the cup in his hand, which was at full strength. It was his sixth such cup. "I will go to bed when I am ready," he said, blinking rapidly because now, the room was starting to move around. "The lady has gone to the trouble of providing this fine meal, and I will not eat and depart so quickly. A meal like this deserves to be lingered over."

Douglas glanced at Westley, rolled his eyes, and downed his own cup of cider, but it was only his third. Westley, however, was apologetic to Veronica.

"He is not used to the cider, my lady," he said quietly. "He is not usually this talkative. Please make allowances."

Myles suddenly pounded the table near his brother with a ham-hock-sized fist. "I heard that," he said. "You will *not* make apologies for me, Westley. There is nothing wrong with me."

Westley cocked an eyebrow. "As you wish," he said, but he didn't mean it. "Let us talk about horses again. Wait… mayhap not horses. Mayhap we'll speak of—"

Myles cut him off. "When I breed that horse, I'll have the finest horses to sell in all of England," he said, jabbing a finger at his brothers. "Mayhap I'll use one of them to buy myself a wife. Surely a horse that fine will be an even exchange for a woman."

Veronica, who had been expecting more chatter about a big white arse, suddenly looked at him with a frown. "You intend to *buy* a wife?" she said. "What an appalling thought."

Myles looked at her seriously. "Is it?" he said. "Explain."

"Because a wife is not meant to be purchased. Certainly not with a horse."

"But women come with dowries," Myles pointed out. "Is that not meant to buy a husband?"

Veronica shrugged. "It is meant to make the bride more attractive to a prospective husband."

"And that is not buying him?"

"I suppose if you look at it pragmatically, it is."

"Then what is the difference if I exchange a beautiful horse for a beautiful woman?"

"Do you consider women no better than horses, then?"

"Myles," Westley said in a warning tone. "If I were you, I would be very careful with my answer."

As Westley and Douglas and Broden started to laugh, Myles looked at them as if he had no idea why. What was so funny? Veronica, too, was fighting off a smile, waiting for the little jewel of an answer to come forth from Myles' beautiful lips. But Myles let his gaze linger on his brother's cousin, now having a suspicion about what they meant, before he returned his attention to Veronica.

"I am certain I will enrage you with my reply, but let me see if I can explain what I mean," he said carefully, though his words were still slightly slurred and his movements exaggerated. "A man is a man. He is a creature of habit, of tradition. There is nothing special about a man. If he is lured into a marriage by a large dowry, it is because he is stupid and does not know that there are more important things in a marriage. But women and horses... A horse is a fine creature of muscle and bone and honor. Sometimes he is smarter than a man. Yet a woman is the most glorious creature God has created. She is an angel of wit and charm and beauty. She is far better than a mere man. If I exchange a horse for a wife, then I am exchanging one glorious creature for another. They are the most perfect things in God's kingdom and meant to be revered."

That was not the answer Veronica, or any of them, had expected. Westley rose to his feet and started to applaud his brother. Douglas and Broden followed. Having no idea why the knights at the dais were applauding, the de Lohr men in the hall, mostly senior men, stood up and began to applaud, too. Myles looked around, confused, until Veronica also stood up and applauded him. He gazed up into her smiling face, having no idea why she was praising him but liking the feeling that she was. That hadn't happened often to him where a woman was concerned.

"Well said, Myles," Westley said from across the table. "Well done, old man."

When Myles realized he'd said something good for a change, a weak smile broke through. Then he took another big drink of the cider, only to spray it out all over the table. As the applause abruptly stopped, Myles rose to his feet, scowling at the cup.

"Someone is trying to poison me," he declared. "What foul liquid was put into my cup?"

Veronica knew exactly what he meant. Trying not to laugh at his over-the-top reaction to the watered cider, she put a gentle hand on his arm.

"Forgive me, my lord," she said. "That was my fault. It is not poisoned, but watered cider. I feared the strong cider was going to make you ill, so I had the servants add water to it. If it was wrong, I apologize."

Myles felt the hand on his arm before he ever looked at her face. *That hand…* It was warm and soft. It wasn't trying to tease him or taunt him. It wasn't trying to pit him against another man or make him jealous. It was simply a hand, and simply a touch, but it was perhaps one of the most significant touches he'd ever experienced. When he finally looked into Veronica's face, into those glowing blue eyes, he felt all of the rage and indignation drain out of him like water through a sieve.

All he could see was her.

He'd never experienced anything like it.

"It was not wrong," he finally said. "But you could have told me. I'm afraid I have spit cider out all over my brothers and their food. They will be unhappy with me now."

Westley and Douglas were already calling for more food, pushing aside the half-eaten meal that had watered cider on it thanks to their brother. Veronica smiled at Myles, pleased he was the forgiving sort, and called for more of the strong cider for his cup. As that was being brought forth, she stood up from the table and toward the hearth. As the knights settled back down again, she reached for the small harp that was propped up against the stone. It had been mingled with some other implements used around a fire, so it was inconspicuous. Collecting it, she brought it back over to the dais.

"Mayhap this will cheer everyone," she said. "Your father has taken the trouble to send his very own sons as my escort, so I would like to sing for you, if you will allow."

Myles was greatly intrigued. He liked music, and oddly enough, he loved to dance. He was very good at it. Reclaiming his seat, he gestured at the harp.

"Please," he said. "I would very much like to hear you."

Veronica sat down, settling the harp on her thighs and against her left shoulder. She plucked all of the strings in succession, listening to any that might be out of tune, and tightened one of them. Playing the strings again, she was satisfied that they sounded well enough.

Softly, she began to play.

*O lovely one… my lovely one…*
*The years will come… the years will go…*
*But still you'll be… my own true love…*
*Until the day… we'll meet again…*

Her voice was sweet and pure. Her tone and pitch were

perfect, in delicate combination with the heavenly sound of the harp. The realization of her talent had shocked the de Lohr men into silence, along with the rest of the hall. Conversation ceased; men stopped gambling. Everything came to a halt as she continued with the second verse.

*O lovely one... my lovely one...*
*My love for you... will never die...*
*My heart is yours... till the end of time...*
*When you will be... my own true love...*

When she finished, she looked at Myles with a timid smile on her face, and he suddenly bolted to his feet, clapping and cheering loudly for her, so loudly that he nearly ruptured her eardrums. The entire hall did the same thing, clapping and demanding more song as Veronica sat there and blushed furiously. She wasn't used to such attention because the only person she had ever played for had been her father.

Not a room full of strangers.

"My lady, that was beautiful," Douglas said from across the table. "Please bless us with another song. We've rarely heard such lovely singing."

Hugely embarrassed by the praise, but also hugely flattered, Veronica began to strum the harp again, bringing forth chords as the room settled down. But they didn't settle down fast enough, and Myles bellowed at the men to shut their mouths, which they did immediately. As the hall quieted, Veronica lifted her voice in song.

*Come roam with me, my love,*
*Come roam far with me,*

*Away from this hard world,*
*And love only me.*

*They said that you loved me*
*They said that you cared.*
*They said that your strong heart*
*Wasn't mine to be shared.*

The words tapered off, but she continued humming the tune as she played the harp. She had Myles thoroughly mesmerized as he sat back and watched her through half-lidded eyes. There was something so sweet and warm about her singing, something that was hypnotizing. She continued to hum and play, glancing up to see that Myles was watching her like a cat watches a mouse. Embarrassed at the attention, she grinned at him and stopped playing.

"Is there something you would like to hear?" she asked.

Myles shook his head. "Nay," he said, his voice husky. "Sing what you will. I could listen to you all night."

Veronica chuckled softly. "I am afraid I must still pack what I plan to take with me tomorrow," she said. "Otherwise, I would be happy to play for you all night."

"We do not have to leave on the morrow if you do not want to."

Veronica's smile faded. "I do," she said. "We discussed why earlier today. But I have been thinking…"

"What about?"

She glanced over her shoulder to where the servants were congregating, preparing to bring more food and drink out into the hall. She could see Snowy directing the servants, instructing them where to replenish drink or perhaps put more wood on the fire.

"My servants," Veronica finally said, turning to look at Myles. "I worry what will happen to them when I have gone. I intend to return, of course, but there is no knowing how long that will take. I worry what will happen when Gregor returns. He... he will not be kind to them. Some of the older servants were here when my grandfather was alive, and if Gregor turns them out, they have nowhere to go."

Myles turned to look at the servants moving in and out from behind a painted wooden screen near the wall. "I suppose we can station some men here," he said. "I will send word to my father and tell him what has happened with your uncle. I will tell him there is some dispute about your uncle's role in your father's estate. Since your father was a loyal vassal, I am certain my father should like to take the property under his protection until you marry and can return with your husband."

Veronica's eyes widened. "You can do that?" she said incredulously. "Only today I was speaking of locking the gates and preventing him from entering when he returned, but it would be difficult to keep him out because we have no men at arms."

"I do," Myles said. "Does your uncle have an army?"

Veronica shook her head. "Nay," she said. "He brought four men with him when he came, four men who eat our food and chase my servants."

"Then I shall leave twenty men here," he said. "That will reduce our escort by nearly half, but I do not like traveling with too many men as it is. We will still have ample protection and make good time with thirty men. In fact, I will even leave Broden here. Your uncle will think twice before challenging a du Reims knight. But I will send word to my father to send more men to bolster what I've left here. Believe me when I tell you that your uncle will not be able to gain access, or anything else, until you and your husband return."

Veronica stared at him in disbelief for a moment before breaking down into quiet tears. "Thank you," she whispered, trying not to make it obvious that she was weeping with joy. "You cannot know what this means to me. My father's home—our home—will be preserved from someone who is trying to pick our bones clean."

"Not to worry, my lady."

She tried to smile, but the tears kept getting in the way. But quickly, she wiped what she could and struggled to compose herself by propping her harp up again.

"What would you like for me to sing?" she said with more joy than she'd felt in months. "Tell me what you would like to hear, and I will sing all night if you wish."

Myles had already downed half of the cup of strong cider, making it nearly seven cups of the stuff. With the latest jolt, he was slipping further and further in the direction of a drunken stupor.

"Sing anything," he said. "I will listen to whatever you play."

With renewed vigor, Veronica began to play and sing. She made it through four songs before Myles, unable to handle the overload of strong cider, passed out in the chair he was sitting in. His head was back against the chair, his mouth open as he snored loudly. Westley and Douglas and Broden tried to decide what to do with him—either leave him there or take him back to his tent—but they ultimately decided to leave him where he sat.

He was sleeping like the dead.

The night deepened and men began to filter out of the hall,

back to the encampment to prepare for the morning departure. Little by little, they left, until it was only Myles and Douglas and Westley left. Even Broden had followed the men out to ensure preparations were made for the morning.

True to her word, Veronica continued to strum her harp, singing softly as Myles snored to the rafters, until Westley finally called her off. There were, perhaps, two hours until sunrise, and Veronica still had packing to do, so they banked the fire in the hearth and left Myles to sleep off the drink in darkened silence.

He remained in that chair, head back and mouth open, until dawn.

# CHAPTER SEVEN

*Somewhere near Stoke-on-Trent*

"**M**UD!"
Veronica was peering from one of the barred windows in the fortified carriage that she'd been riding in for the past three days. She'd been trying to locate her dog, who had come with her because he wouldn't remain behind. Not even in the care of Snowy. Mud, the enormous wolfhound who spent his day running up and down the length of the escort, rolling in the mud puddles on the side of the road, and then getting everyone filthy when he jumped on them, wanted to be with his mistress.

That had been the most excitement the journey to Manchester had seen so far.

The weather for the journey had been surprisingly mild. Even at this time of year, rainstorms could be expected, but they'd had clear sailing for three days. The roads were in decent shape and the carriage that Myles had brought was wonderfully comfortable, all of it adding up to a pleasant journey.

But it was a journey that was causing increasing anxiety to Veronica.

She had been surprisingly calm the first day she found out about her uncle's intentions to send her north to join her betrothed. She had accepted it and, perhaps, even been mildly pleased by it. She'd rationalized it as being a good thing overall. But that had only been the first day, because after that, reality had set in. The reality that she was going to have to marry a man she'd never even met before.

That was when the anxiety set in.

Meeting unexpected men in her life, as of late, had not produced pleasant results for the most part. Gregory was the prime suspect in that opinion, because he had caused nothing but misery since the day they met. Myles was perhaps the exception to the rule, but even that hadn't gone entirely smoothly. Their introduction had been rough, no doubt, but she thought they had managed to smooth things over. At least, that had been her impression, but ever since they'd departed Cradley Heath on a cold, misty morning, Myles had been withdrawn and distant.

Somehow, that had been greatly disappointing to her.

His brothers, however, had been friendly enough. While their cousin, Broden, had been left behind to manage Cradley until her return, Myles' two younger brothers were part of the escort. Douglas was a few years younger than Myles and a seemingly mature individual who wasn't very talkative, but Westley was a typical younger brother. He was animated and loud at times, and he wasn't afraid to give his opinion. He had been the one who was most thoughtful to Veronica's needs along their journey, and he wasn't beyond carrying on a lively conversation when they stopped for the night.

No matter how exhausted they all were.

Veronica had found herself sitting by the cooking fires of

the encampment they would set up nightly, listening to Westley tell stories. The stories were mostly about others, and it was clear early on that he liked to make fun of people. He told stories about his sisters, his sister's children, his older brothers—including Myles, until he threatened Westley the second evening and told him that any more talk would see an unfortunate accident with a knife to his tongue.

After that, Westley veered away from telling stories about Myles.

But he was still entertaining and friendly, and Veronica came to appreciate his positively annoying nature. She'd never had any siblings, and she certainly had not spent any time around young men, so this dynamic was something quite new for her. She wasn't hard-pressed to admit that she liked it. If nothing else, the de Lohr brothers made her feel accepted.

At least, Westley and Douglas did. Myles hardly spoke to her except to ask her if she was comfortable or hungry. He seemed to leave everything else to his brothers while he dealt with the men or simply went to his tent and shut the flap. He didn't seem to want to socialize, and as the third day of their journey dragged on, Veronica was wondering if it was something she had done.

Or perhaps he'd realized that he simply didn't like her.

The problem was that, being far removed from any male companionship as she was, she had perhaps put too much stock in the supper at Cradley Heath. She was well aware that Myles had been drunk throughout the entire meal, but he had been sweet to her and shockingly affectionate, which was something she had never before experienced. The man had held her hands, even *kissed* her hand, and once or twice he had winked at her. When she sang for him, he couldn't praise her strongly enough.

It was male attention on a glorious scale, but now those scales had evidently broken, because Myles seemingly wanted nothing to do with her. The more time passed, the more disheartened she became about it.

Adding to her burdens, of course, was the fact that she was soon to marry a man she didn't know. Since there was no one to really talk to as the hours of the day rolled by and the road seemed endless, her imagination had a chance to flourish. She was increasingly concerned that her husband would be more beastly than Gregor ever was, concerned she was going to end up in a far worse situation in Manchester. Her imagination began to run wild.

By the third day, her fears had her in their terrifying grip.

"*Mud!*"

She was calling for the dog again, trying to keep her thoughts away from the terrors that awaited her at the end of her journey. She could see the dog running in the meadow alongside the escort, chasing the birds who would fly up from the grass, and generally having a marvelous time. He was ignoring her and, frustrated and needing to stretch her legs, Veronica opened the door of the carriage, which was at the rear, and leapt out onto the road. As the men at arms following the carriage watched, she ran off into the meadow to chase down her errant dog.

Mud, however, would not be contained. He saw her coming, ran at her, jumped up and put his muddy paws on her, and then darted back toward the escort. The soldier knew enough about the dog to know he was sweet but incorrigible, so they tried to protect themselves when the big beast began running through the ranks. He jumped on backs, shook the mud off his fur and sprayed it on anyone within five feet of him, and then tripped one man as he ran in front of him. The soldier went down, the dog jumped on him as if playing, and Veronica grabbed for him.

But Mud was too fast.

It was a naughty dog that ran to the front of the escort after leaving a trail of destruction at the rear. The warhorses weren't disturbed by dogs, so none reacted to the overly playful mutt as he ran among the knights. When Veronica appeared, however, the horses were suspicious. That brought a word of warning from Douglas.

"Nay, lady," he said, holding out his hand. "Do not come any closer. The horses might react badly. They are bred for battle, you know. They might see you as a threat."

That left Veronica walking by the side of the road, watching her dog settle down amongst the warhorses and walk with them like a well-behaved beast. Douglas and Westley, riding side by side, grinned at the dog between them.

"He is a happy dog," Douglas said.

Veronica was watching Mud, waiting for him to break out and run again. "Happy is one word for him," she said. "Annoying is another. He usually minds better than this, but he thinks he has found many new playmates, so he is ignoring me."

Westley snorted. "I saw many of the men more than happy to feed him scraps last night around the cooking fires," he said. "That dog is going to fatten up like a holiday goose."

About twenty feet ahead of the escort, Myles came to a halt and turned his horse around. He'd been riding alone, mounted on his big white steed and isolating himself as he usually did. When leading an escort, he always ran point, and he always stayed away from the men so talk would not distract him. But it was difficult not to be distracted by what he was hearing.

He spied Veronica.

"Why are you walking?" he said, pointing at her. "You and that filthy dog should be back in the carriage."

He sounded unhappy, and Veronica shrugged in an exaggerated gesture.

"I would like nothing better," she said. "But he will not come. He escaped about an hour ago, and I cannot gain control of him."

"Then you should not have brought him."

"As I said, he is not usually so disobedient. Many new friends excite him."

Myles didn't reply. He turned his horse around and began to move forward again. The rest of the escort hadn't stopped, so they simply caught up to him and followed. That included Veronica, who was still walking on the edge of the road, watching her dog and again wondering why Myles was being so cold.

Perhaps she just needed to accept his behavior and move on.

The village up ahead possessed the unlikely name of Stone, and Veronica heard Myles tell his brothers that they were going to stop there for the night. It was Westley who dismounted his warhorse while it was still walking, collaring the dog and leading both Mud and Veronica back to the carriage, where he loaded them inside and shut the door. After making his way back to his steed, who was still plodding along, he remounted the beast just as they were coming to the edge of the village.

Night was beginning to fall, the mild temperatures of the day becoming cool and damp as the moisture from the surrounding fields rose and created a mist that lay against the ground. The village itself had a wall around it, with gates that were beginning to close and torches that were being lit. Douglas rode on ahead to make sure the watchmen kept the gate open so their party could pass through, and once it did, the iron gate was shut for the night.

And that struck Veronica as strange.

They'd camped out for the past two nights, meaning that Myles, for some reason, was seeking shelter inside the village on this night. As she was pondering that very question and wondering if she could find a trough to bathe her dog in, the carriage came to a halt about the time the door opened.

Veronica found herself looking at Myles.

"Come, my lady," he said, stepping back and motioning to her. "Out."

Veronica grabbed her satchel and stood up. "Where are we going?"

Myles gestured off to his right, into the darkening town center. "There is an inn over there," he said. "It is called The Nag and the Stallion. We will spend the night there."

Veronica came to the door, and Myles held out a hand, helping her down from the carriage. The dog tried to bolt past him, but he grabbed it by the back of the neck, and the animal settled right down. He looked down at the canine, his expression severe.

"You will behave yourself," he said sternly. "Any further running about and I will tie you up for good."

Veronica almost laughed at the man, expecting Mud to obey him, but a funny thing happened. Mud actually remained right by Myles' side as he took Veronica's satchel and started walking in the direction he'd indicated. Veronica quickly followed as Douglas and Westley settled the escort for the night, sending everyone over to a large barn that was just off the main road. She could see the roof in the setting sun. As the men and the carriage began to move, Myles led Veronica and the dog to a tavern with a painted sign over the door. It was just a horse's head, or something that resembled a horse's head, but it was enough to indicate a place of rest and food.

In they went.

The tavern was deceptively small on the exterior, as it was actually quite large inside. It was a long building with a common room that held dozens of people. There was a big firepit in the center of the common room giving off a good deal of heat and smoke, which wafted up to the ceiling and escaped through holes in the roof. As Veronica stood at the door and took hold of Mud so he wouldn't go charging into the room and frighten people, Myles sent a serving wench for the proprietor.

Quickly, a man with a round, red face and a balding head emerged from the kitchens and, with the exchange of a few sentences, Myles procured two rented chambers. Veronica was ushered to one, about midway down the long common room. The proprietor opened the door for her, and she went inside along with her big, dirty dog, but when the door shut behind her, she quickly threw the bolt because she'd never stayed in a tavern before. Suddenly, she was in a strange tavern in a strange town with strangers all around.

She'd never felt more alone in her life.

Slowly, Veronica turned away from the door and looked at her rented chamber. It was not very large, but there was a bed, a table with two chairs, and a small hearth that, upon inspection, was a pass-through to the chamber on the other side. One fire in the hearth heated two chambers. That didn't do anything to ease her nerves, because a bold fool could crawl through the hearth opening and end up in her room.

But not if there was a fire in it.

The room was nearly dark because of the encroaching night outside, but Veronica set her satchel down and quickly went to work building a fire. There was a bucket next to the hearth full of kindling and wood, and she managed to locate a flint and stone on the table next to the unlit oil lamp. Piling the wood into the hearth, she managed to light a piece of kindling after several tries and, with careful coaxing, saw it catch one of the larger wood pieces on fire. More coaxing from her, which simply meant blowing on the infant blaze, and a larger blaze sprang up.

Large enough to burn a drunken fool crawling through the hearth to molest her.

Rather proud of herself, and feeling marginally better about the rented space, Veronica stood up and brushed off her hands, then went back to the table and lit the oil lamp. A soft glow filled the chamber, making it seem a little more comfortable. A little more inviting. But then she heard snoring, only to see that Mud had jumped up on her bed and was now lying on his back, sleeping like the dead. Nothing much bothered him, and a day like today, with wild running and men at arms to pet him, was just like heaven to old Mud.

Veronica had to shake her head at her silly dog.

As Mud snored his head off, she tried to get a closer look at the bed, to see if the mattress was at least somewhat clean and free of vermin. She held the oil lamp up to the corners of the bed only to see the little creatures scooting away in the light. Realizing the bed had bugs, she was forced to awaken the dog and move him over to the hearth, which he would like better because of the warmth, while she was resigned to sleeping on the floor, on her cloak, for the night. As she petted the dog to settle him down, there was a knock at the door. Veronica opened the panel to find Westley standing there.

"My lady," he greeted her. "Is everything to your satisfaction?"

Veronica glanced at her chamber, thinking of the infested bed, before answering. "I would not mention it otherwise, but I am assuming Sir Myles is paying well for this chamber," she said. "I am afraid the bed is covered with vermin. He should not have to pay at all because of it. I will sleep on the floor."

Westley looked past her, into the chamber that was lit by an oil lamp and an inviting fire, before holding up a finger to her as if to beg patience.

"A moment, lady," he said. "Stay there. Do not move."

With that, he headed toward the entry to the tavern, and Veronica craned her neck to see that Myles was standing there, speaking to a couple of the de Lohr men at arms. When Westley muttered to him, it was only a matter of seconds before Myles was looking over at Veronica standing in the doorway. Just a few more words from Westley, and Myles sent the men at arms on their way before charging all the way across the common room with Westley in tow, back to the kitchens, from where Veronica heard a loud, stern voice.

It was Myles.

Things began to happen.

The first thing that transpired was that Westley emerged from the kitchen and approached Veronica, holding out his hand to her.

"My lady," he said. "Come with me. Please."

Hesitantly, Veronica complied. Westley led her over a pitted, well-used table near the hearth that he had secured. Douglas was already there, talking to the serving wenches, seeing about sending food over to the barn where the escort was settling in for the night. Westley had Veronica sit down while chaos seemed to be happening all around her. Men were moving, doors were opening and closing, and back in the kitchens, Myles sounded as if he was tearing the place apart.

An angry Myles was a formidable thing.

While the shouting and chaos was going on, people began to rush out from the kitchens and dart into her rented room. Veronica leaned sideways in her chair to gain a better view, peering into her room and noticing that they were doing something with the bed. Mud, who had been nesting by the hearth, must have decided that new playmates had joined him, because Veronica could see him milling around the servants and wagging his tail. But the servants didn't notice the dog. They seemed entirely focused on the bed, pulling off all of the bedding, including the mattress, and then rushing out of the room and back toward the kitchen with all of it.

Once that had happened, someone else came out from the kitchens with a bucket and rags, and as Veronica continued to watch, they began washing the floors. Mud had no respect for the newly washed floors and walked all over them, annoying a woman who was trying very hard to clean the wood. In most taverns and public houses, the floors tended to be hard-packed earth, but this place was different in that it had wooden floors. Veronica could see that the dog was completely getting in the way of the woman, so she rose from her chair and headed over to the door, calling to Mud, who reluctantly wandered in her direction.

The silly mutt was living up to his name that night, still filthy from all the mud he had rolled in during the day. He had a layer of it all over his body, something he was tracking on the floor as he walked. Veronica very much wanted to rinse him of the mud, and when she mentioned the fact to Westley, he abruptly picked the dog up and carried it back toward the kitchen. As Veronica watched with some concern, Westley disappeared into the yard behind the inn. When he next appeared a few minutes later, it was with a soaking wet but clean dog.

He placed Mud at her feet.

"What did you do?" Veronica asked, inspecting the dripping dog. "He's completely sodden!"

Westley pulled Mud over toward the hearth, and the animal began steaming from the heat. "You were concerned that he was filthy, and he was," he said. "There is an animal trough back there, so I threw him in. Is this usual with him?"

Veronica looked up from the dog. "Is what usual with him?"

"The dirt."

"His name *is* Mud."

Westley conceded the point. Veronica grinned at the knight, who was dirty himself after handling the dog. He seemed rather disgusted by it all. Mud picked that moment to shake himself off and spray everyone within five feet of him with cold water. But the big, ugly wolfhound was clean, or at least clean*er* than he had been, so Veronica didn't mind too much. Mud didn't seem to mind too much, either, because the truth was that he loved to be wet. Westley, however, did not. He moved away from the spray zone, looking for something to clean himself off with.

As Veronica ran her fingers through the dog's heavy fur to help dry him in the heat, the food began to come. Piles of bread, bowls of butter and stewed fruit, bowls of beans that had been baked in honey and spices, and hunks of boiled beef. Having last eaten that morning, Veronica plowed into the food with gusto. For every bite she took, she gave the dog one, and they were well into their meal when Myles emerged from the kitchen carrying an enormous beef bone that was stringy with pieces of meat and fat. He handed it off to Mud, who took it eagerly. As the dog lay in front of the fire with his bone, Myles sat opposite Veronica at the table.

He didn't say a word as he began piling food onto a small wooden trough that had been brought out with the food. Instead of trenchers, there were wooden cribs for holding the food. They were well scrubbed and clean, fortunately, and as Veronica watched, he filled his up and delved into the meal.

But the silence was uncomfortable.

And he knew it.

Truthfully, Myles wasn't quite sure why he was so angry about the dirty bed, but it had something to do with providing Veronica with something inferior. What he couldn't decide was if his rage was the result of having been made to look bad by unknowingly renting a filthy chamber or if it was because that dirty chamber was meant for Veronica *personally*.

Therein was the dilemma.

He wanted her to have the best.

God help him, something was happening to him. It had started the morning they departed Cradley Heath. With as much as he'd had to drink the night before, and from the sheer fact that he'd passed out from it, he shouldn't have remembered anything about the evening. But he did. He'd awoken at dawn, still slightly drunk and with a throbbing head, but he'd remembered everything that had happened. The conversation, the singing...

Everything.

That memory had only worked against him. He'd awoken with a pasty mouth, his head aching, his mind muddled, and all but charged out into the dawn as his men began to break down the encampment as if he wasn't feeling poorly at all. Douglas was up but Westley wasn't, so it was Myles and Douglas who set about forming the escort and selecting those who would remain behind with Broden, who wasn't particularly thrilled at being left at Cradley Heath. But Myles explained the situation and why he felt strongly that the property had to be protected from what was evidently a greedy uncle until his father could make a decision about it, so, begrudgingly, Broden agreed to remain.

For a time, focusing on the escort distracted Myles from thoughts of Lady Veronica and the night before. He was dealing with the men, planning their route with the help of one of the senior men at arms who also acted as the quartermaster, and engaging in other duties that kept the bright-eyed beauty out of his mind. Quite honestly, he couldn't imagine why she was occupying his thoughts when he was pining for Aviara, who was already someone else's wife. Aviara was the woman he wanted, the woman he cared for. Perhaps *cared* for was too strong a word, but certainly, she was the woman he wanted. He thought he'd loved her, but only in the sense that she was the woman he'd hoped to marry.

The prize, as his mother had said.

Aye, Aviara was the prize.

*Was.*

Certainly, it wasn't healthy of him for his thoughts to linger on Lady Veronica. It was even disloyal to Aviara for him to do so, but he couldn't help it. Perhaps it was only because Veronica had been brave and kind and attentive. She clearly had talent when it came to singing, but lots of women were. She wasn't unique. Once he was finished with the quartermaster and his focus inevitably returned to Veronica, he couldn't quite put his finger on *why* he found her so intriguing. The woman hadn't flirted with him or thrown herself at him like Aviara had, nor had Veronica tried to capture his attention only to flirt with another man when he was looking. When he thought of it that way, somehow, that sort of behavior seemed so beneath her. She didn't seem like that kind of woman.

The kind of woman that Aviara was.

Then it began to dawn on him.

Veronica was the type of woman that didn't *need* that kind of attention.

The kind of woman who had to make others suffer so she could feel good about herself. So she could feel powerful. Although he didn't know Veronica well, he suspected she hadn't fostered in big houses or fine castles where, often, women were taught the finer arts of flirtation and selfishness. That was true, because he'd seen it for himself. At Lioncross Abbey, his mother was very selective about the young ladies she allowed to live there, to learn from her, because Dustin was, and always had been, a no-nonsense woman. She didn't tolerate things like jealousy or pettiness or bullying, which could happen among highborn young women. He knew that was why his mother hadn't liked Aviara. What Myles called spirited, Dustin called stupid maliciousness.

Perhaps it was.

Myles had four sisters—Christin, Brielle, Rebecca, and Olivia Charlotte. All four of them were fine women—kind and compassionate and just. But they were spirited, too—especially Christin and Brielle—so he was well aware of what a decent woman behaved like. With Aviara, however, he'd overlooked those qualities because she was pretty and vivacious and made him feel special with her attention.

But she gave that same attention to others.

Perhaps he hadn't wanted to acknowledge that until now.

It had taken spending an evening with a woman of character for him to realize that, but that woman of character was off to marry another man. That was the very reason why he was there. Since he wasn't the type of man to steal a woman who belonged to someone else, he couldn't think of any other way to deal with his interest in Veronica other than ignore her. Perhaps if he did, he'd forget about those foolish thoughts he was entertaining. He'd only just met her, after all.

It shouldn't be difficult to forget about her.

At least, that was what he thought. He'd spent three days on the road essentially ignoring her while Douglas and Westley saw to her needs. Now, they'd ended up at this shabby tavern with a horse head painted above the door and bugs crawling on the bed. He'd become irate about something that was fairly normal in any place he'd traveled. But not for Veronica.

She'd already had a difficult enough time of it.

And perhaps that was why he'd become angry most of all. Between her father's death, Gregor's intrusion, and a betrothal she had to face, Myles didn't want her to deal with one more thing that was uncomfortable or difficult.

So, he'd lost his temper.

Even now, coming out of the kitchen after he'd whipped the tavernkeeper and his servants into a frenzy, he had seen Veronica sitting over by the hearth with a pile of food in her face and a wet dog.

Mud.

A stupid name for a dog, but he could easily see why the dog had the name. He'd seen it for the past three days, a giant dog who loved to roll in the mud. It was ridiculous. But it was also strangely endearing.

Taking a deep breath, he made his way over to the table.

Grabbing one of the wooden troughs that had been brought with the food, he piled food into it before he began to shove it in his mouth. All the while, he didn't look at Veronica or even acknowledge her. He knew it was uncomfortable, but the truth was that he had no idea what to say to her. He was afraid that any conversation, however benign, might stir up that interest he was trying so hard to forget.

But Veronica didn't have any such restraint.

"It was very kind of you to secure a room for me," she said. "I'm very sorry you had to go to some much trouble. I could have just as easily slept on the floor. I do not mind."

He stopped chewing and looked at her. "But *I* mind," he said. "I mind quite a bit. I paid good money for a bed, and if you are unable to use it, then I have wasted my money."

Veronica nodded quickly, lowering her gaze. "Of course," she said. "I completely understand."

"They sold me a bed that was covered in vermin."

"Aye, I know. I saw it."

"You could not use it."

"Nay, I could not."

She went back to eating, but Myles didn't. He tried. He tried very hard. But he kept looking at her because it seemed to him that his answer had displeased her. Was she expecting something more from him? He may not have wanted to speak with her, but he also didn't want to upset her, and she did seem... hurt. He had no idea why.

Myles sighed slowly.

He was terrible when it came to communicating with women. So awful it defied explanation. But he also knew that women liked to feel as if a man felt concern for her, even if it was only polite concern, and he could see he had conveyed that. He'd only spoken of the money he'd spent for something unusable. He hadn't spoken about how it affected her other than she couldn't use it.

That didn't show much concern for her in the literal sense.

"I suspect I've not said the right thing," he finally muttered.

She looked up from her food. "What do you mean?" Before he could reply, she continued. "Nay, my lord, you are not to blame at all. Surely I must have done something, and if I have, then I apologize. I never meant to annoy you."

He frowned, puzzled. "Annoy?" he said. "What are you talking about?"

It was her turn to look puzzled. "This… this journey," she said. "I thought I might have said something to upset you, because we've hardly spoken this entire journey. If I have offended you somehow, I beg your forgiveness. I did not mean to."

Now, Myles was starting to understand. All of that ignoring he'd been doing had not gone unnoticed by her. The very person he was trying to ignore. God help him, he didn't want his interest in her to grow, but as he looked into her anxious face with those glowing blue eyes, he could feel himself relenting.

He was starting to feel foolish.

"You have not done anything," he said quietly. "It is I who should apologize for you. I did not mean to cause you distress."

Her features washed with relief. "Praise the saints," she said.

"I thought I had said something awful to you. For a man who is going out of his way to do my father a great service, I should have felt terrible if that had been the case."

He shook his head then turned back to his food but realized he didn't feel much like eating. Sitting back in his chair, he drained the cup of ale at his right hand. Unlike the night of the supper at Cradley Heath, he didn't pour himself another.

He didn't want to be drunk again in front of her.

But he did want to be honest with her.

"You have been charming and gracious since our little misunderstanding was cleared up," Myles said. "All I've done is get drunk and rent a chamber for you that was crawling with bugs. I should be the one apologizing, lady. You deserve better than what I've shown you."

Veronica shook her head. "There is no need," she said. "Sometimes two people meet and things do not go smoothly. That's all this was. But I do want to thank you for taking time away from your busy life to escort me to Manchester. You must surely have a thousand duties more important than this, yet you are here. I do not know if I will ever have the chance to thank your father personally, so I hope you will relay my gratitude when next you see him."

Myles drew in a long breath, thinking on what she'd said. "Duties?" he said. Then he snorted softly. "When you are the son of Christopher de Lohr, there are more duties than you can imagine. Not only important ones, but duties like this. An escort for the daughter of my father's cartographer."

Veronica looked at him, her eyebrows lifting at what was clearly an insult, and it took Myles a few seconds to catch on to what he'd said.

"I did not mean to imply that you are not important," he

said quickly. "I simply meant that some duties are life and death, but this one is not in the least. Oh, damnation… I do not know what I mean. The more I say, the worse it gets."

Veronica was struggling not to smile. "Do you know what your problem is?"

He looked at her, mildly startled. "Then I *do* have a problem?"

"You do."

He appeared concerned. "What is it?"

Veronica appeared thoughtful as she picked up the pitcher, pouring him more ale before refilling her own cup. "You speak to every person as if they are men," she said. "You speak to them honestly, without reserve, as if they know you and you know them. You have a level of comfort even with strangers where you feel you can be completely open with them. You did it with me the night of our supper at Cradley Heath. Your only problem is honesty, Sir Myles. You say what is on your mind."

He thought on that, hard. "No one has ever said that to me," he said. "But you are correct—I suppose I do say what is on my mind. I do not have the time or tolerance for anything else."

"I can see that," Veronica said. "But the difference between you and a man who can communicate well with women is something called tact. You do not have it."

"What do you mean?"

Veronica caught sight of Westley as he grasped one of the serving wenches, gently, to talk to her about more food for the men. She gestured at Myles' younger brother.

"You told Sir Westley on our last night at Cradley Heath that he knows how to communicate with women," she said. "I heard you tell him that."

Myles nodded. "It is true."

"But it is only because he has employed something you have yet to employ," Veronica said, looking at him. "For example, if I stood in front of you with a big streak of mud all over my face that I could not see, something my dog put there, how would you tell me? Would you simply walk up to me in front of everyone and announce I had mud on my face? Or would you do it discreetly so I would not be embarrassed by the obvious?"

Myles had to honestly think on that. "I would simply tell you."

"Would Westley?"

Myles grunted. "He would put his arm around you and pull you into a corner, kissing your lips before telling you about the mud," he said. Then he cocked his head. "But that is what you prefer? Is that what I should do?"

Veronica let her smile break through. "That is what women would have you do, aye," she said. "Mayhap not the kissing part, but putting a protective arm around a woman and whispering such news in her ear would be much more appreciated. Clearly, you would tell a man to his face. But sometimes, women need something gentler. Most have fragile feelings that are easily hurt."

"Like you?"

Veronica pondered the question. "I never thought so," she said. "But the truth is that my father was a very tactful man. I never had to worry. But I realize all men are not like my father. There are men like Gregor, who are rough and unkind. They do not care what a woman thinks. But I believe you do."

Myles did, but he wasn't quite sure what to say about it. He ended up shrugging. "Women are a mystery to me."

"They are a mystery to most men."

He chuckled. "I have tried to be like my brothers," he said.

"They are all good with women."

"All of them?"

Myles nodded. "I have five," he said. "Peter is the eldest, and he married a Jewess. A more beautiful creature you will never meet. Curtis married a Welsh princess, and a more fiery creature you will never meet, but he managed to tame her and keep all of his fingers while doing so. Roi married a docile lady who dotes on him, and while Douglas and Westley are not married, they are both quite adept when it comes to reading women's minds. And me..."

He trailed off, unsure how to continue, so Veronica leaned forward and looked him in the eye. "You have something all women want," she said. "Do you not even understand that? Sir Myles, I think this Lady Aviara has somehow damaged your confidence. She made you think less of yourself, and that is not right."

He was listening, but there was doubt in his expression. "I do not know how she would cause me to doubt myself," he said. "I realize I have spoken of her, and since I told you the situation, I will not repeat it. But if you must know, Aviara made me feel... wanted. Worthy."

"Did she?" Veronica said dubiously. "Because if what you told me is true, she did not make you feel worthy. She made you feel worthless. If she thought you were worthy, she would not have tried to make you jealous by flirting with Oliver."

"You remembered that, did you?"

Veronica chuckled. "I did," she said. "You told me the tale. Sir Myles, the one thing you have that all women want is honesty. I do not think you could tell a lie if you tried. There are so many men out there who would tell a lie to get what they wanted. With you, a woman will know where she stands from the start. Lady Aviara was not for you, don't you see? You will find a worthy woman, I promise."

His gaze was lingering on her because, somehow, she was managing to flatter him. But it wasn't the kind of flattering Aviara had done. This was something sincere. Myles knew that simply by looking at her.

That touched him.

"Nay," he muttered. "I've not been honest with you, not entirely. But there are some things better left unsaid. We should reach your betrothed's home by tomorrow evening, and that will be the last we see of each other, so I will tell you that it has been a privilege coming to know you, Lady Veronica de Wolviston. Lord de Correa, whoever he is, will be a very fortunate man when he marries you. But will you do something for me?"

"What is your wish?"

Myles cocked an eyebrow and jabbed a finger at her. "If this man is terrible to you or gives you any trouble, will you send word to me?"

Veronica's brow furrowed. "Why would I do that?

"So my father and I can have a talk with him and tell him how he should treat Edgar de Wolviston's daughter," he said, lowering his hand. "You have already had to endure hardship with your uncle. I should not like it if I left you off with a man who treated you as badly, or worse. You will send word to me if he shows you anything less than kindness."

Veronica smiled broadly at him, a gesture that lit up her face. If Myles thought she was beautiful before, now he saw the woman had a smile as bright as the sun.

"Myles de Lohr, I think you are far more wonderful than you give yourself credit for," she said. "If I was not already betrothed, I might ride straight to Lioncross and ask your father for your hand."

Myles had never blushed in his life. He didn't even know how. Or, at least, consciously he didn't know, because once she said that, his face started feeling hot in a way it had never felt hot before. That hardhearted man who didn't have a charming bone in his body was feeling... giddy. Impossible as it was. He found himself grinning, embarrassed.

"Do you think I would make an easy catch, then?" he said.

Veronica laughed softly. "Probably not," she said. "I suspect that I would have to woo you. If your story of Lady Aviara is to be believed, then you like to be chased."

His smile faded. "Not necessarily," he said. "I am not sure what I like anymore."

Veronica's smile faded, also, as she realized she'd brought up a tender subject. "It was cruel of me to say that," she said. "My apologies, my lord. I did not mean to make light of something that clearly meant a good deal to you. I was unkind."

But Myles shook his head. "You were truthful," he said. "I told you of the situation when I should not have. But I did, and made a fool of myself, something I should not like to do again, so mayhap having a woman flatter and chase me is not something I should do again."

"Mayhap you should do the chasing next time," Veronica said helpfully. "Women do like to be pursued."

He looked at her as if a thought had occurred to him. "Then that must be what I did wrong," he said. "I let a woman chase after me when I should have done the chasing. Mayhap that was wrong all along."

Veronica lifted her shoulders. "It is possible," she said. "Personally, I have never been chased, so I would not know, but it seems to me that a woman likes to feel as if she is wanted."

Myles' gaze lingered on her. "That is the most ridiculous thing I have ever heard."

"That a woman likes to feel wanted?"

"Nay. That you have never been chased."

"It's true."

"Did your father keep you locked up?"

"Of course not."

"Then why have you not had any suitors?"

"Because I have been betrothed to de Correa since I was a child."

That reminded Myles of what she'd already told him. He picked up his cup, full of ale that Veronica had put there, and took a long, steady swallow.

"And what about de Correa?" he said, smacking his lips. "What do you know about him?"

"Very little," Veronica said, shaking her head. "I know that he and my father were friends and that he was married before, but his wife died in childbirth."

Myles' eyebrows lifted. "Then he is an old man."

"Possibly," Veronica said. "I do not know how old he is, but he is older than I am by quite a bit. I also know that he is a vassal of the Earl of Lincoln."

"De Lacy?"

"Aye," she said. "My father said this his family is quite rich, as they have made their money quarrying sandstone that rich lords use to build their castles with."

Myles considered the rich old man that Veronica would soon be marrying. "Interesting," he said. "Is he titled?"

"Baron Adlington and the third Lord Bucklow."

"Bucklow," Myles repeated thoughtfully. "I have heard that

name. Does he have a son who fights under that name?"

Veronica shook her head. "I do not know," she said. "Though I know he does have a son."

"If he has a son, then why should he want to marry again? It is not as if the man needs more sons to carry on his name."

Veronica sighed. "I do not know," she said, reaching for her own cup. "All I know is that my father made the bargain with him when I was about ten years of age. He wanted me to be taken care of, and de Correa was looking for a wife. I think it gave him peace, knowing I would have a husband, and a rich one, when I married."

Talk of her father seemed to bring on some melancholy. Myles, not usually intuitive, could see it in her eyes. When she took a gulp of the ale, it was as if she was trying to drown her sorrows with it. He'd seen it before.

He suspected why.

"How did your father die?" he asked quietly.

"Heart," Veronica said, forcing a smile that was more like a grimace. "We thought he was fine and healthy, because he never complained, but it seemed that he had been having pains in chest his for weeks until one night, they became worse and he confessed that he'd not been feeling well. I summoned the physic, who gave him a potion, and he went to sleep as usual. He never woke up."

Myles grunted softly. "I am sorry," he said. "And your mother?"

"She died when I was very young."

"No siblings?"

"None." She paused, seemingly wanting to say something but perhaps unable to articulate it. After a moment, she lifted her eyes to him. "My lord, may… may I tell you something?"

Myles nodded. "Of course."

"I must swear you to secrecy and a promise."

"You have my word."

Veronica believed him. "Mayhap I should not tell you this, but I feel compelled to because I am the only one who knows the secret," she said. "That is to say, Snowy, my maid, knows of it, but not the extent of it, and, not knowing what I will be facing when I marry de Correa, I feel that I must confide in you. I may not have the chance to confide in anyone else."

His brow furrowed. "You sound as if you are going to your execution," he said. "It is only a marriage, my lady."

She nodded quickly. "I know, but not knowing the character of my new husband, this may be something I keep to myself."

"What will you keep to yourself?"

"My father's wealth."

He understood, sort of. "I see," he said. "What did you wish to tell me?"

She took a deep breath. "This is something Gregor has been trying to get out of me since his arrival," he said. "I would not tell him. He would only steal the money, and I do not want him to have it. Not under any circumstances. I would rather see it go to your father, as my father's liege, than to my uncle."

"I am listening."

"My father was very wealthy," she said, lowering her voice so no one would hear her. "It is true that he entered into the priesthood, long ago, but his mother, my grandmother, did not want him to. That was my grandfather's doing. My grandmother deliberately gave my father the money she had inherited from her own father so that my father broke his vow of poverty. He did so willingly because, as he put it, the priesthood is for deviants and fools. My father was a talented artist, as you know, with a love of maps and history, and that is how he became a cartographer. Word of his talent spread, and very soon, he made up to six hundred pounds a year in his profession. His maps went for a high price."

Myles had heard from his own father that Edgar de Wolviston was wealthy, so it wasn't a surprise. But he was impressed. "That is a tidy sum," he said. "Your father did well for himself."

Veronica nodded. "He did," she said. "But that is not what I wanted to tell you. My father hardly spent any of his money. We lived very frugally. He kept his money with two Jewish bankers, one in Birmingham and one in Hereford. The name of the man in Hereford is Eli ben Shir. His cousin is the other banker in Birmingham. If anything happens to me... I do not want this secret to die with me. I want you to know where the money is."

Myles nodded seriously, but he was concerned that she sounded as if she was going to her death with this new marriage. "I will tell my father if you wish," he said. "But I am sure there is no need. Your new husband will be worthy of this secret."

Veronica shrugged, averting her gaze. "New men in my life, other than you, have made me wary of trusting anyone," she said. "My father's money is mine, and the truth is that it makes me an extremely wealthy woman. Between the bankers in Hereford and Birmingham, my father has saved over twenty-four thousand pounds."

Myles' eyes widened. "Twenty four *thousand* pounds?"

"Gold."

That caused Myles' mouth to pop open in surprise. "*Gold?*" he said. "God's Bones, lady. You were not jesting when you said that you are wealthy. That is a shocking amount of money."

"I know," Veronica said. "And that is why Gregor can never have it. And unless I trust my new husband, I do not want him to have it, either. But your father… I would rather see it go to him. I know he would do good with it. I will send you word within the year as to whether or not I've decided to tell my husband."

Myles simply nodded, shocked that this beautiful woman should live, and travel, so simply. A woman with that kind of money could live like a queen. Knowing how much she was worth didn't change his opinion of her, but it certainly made him look at her a little differently, because she had trusted him with perhaps her most precious secret. The keys to the kingdom, as it were. Her kingdom, at least. Myles had had a lot of people trust him over the years, and, as an Executioner Knight, trust was paramount.

But he'd never had trust that meant so much to him.

This was different.

He was precluded from replying when loud voices caught his attention as Westley and Douglas entered the tavern, complaining about something or cursing something. Myles couldn't tell what had them speaking so loudly and with some harshness, but they were obviously agitated about something. They approached the table, still half-full of food, removing gloves as they went.

"Christ, I'm famished," Douglas said. "You did not eat everything, did you, Myles?"

He sat down next to Myles while Westley sat next to Veronica. Myles frowned as his brothers grabbed at food and drink, finally slapping Westley on the hand when the man buffeted Veronica as he reached for the pitcher of ale.

"You two dolts," he growled. "I've just finished telling Lady Veronica how mannerly you both were and you come in here like bulls on the rampage. What is the matter with you?"

He meant one or both of them, anyone that could answer. Veronica picked up the pitcher Westley had been grabbing for and handed it to the man as Westley took it with gratitude, lest Myles berate him again.

"The man who owns the barn," Douglas said, tearing at his bread. "He wants a pence a head to let the men sleep in the barn tonight, and we told him we'd burn the barn down before we paid such a high price."

"He was driving a hard bargain," Westley said, spooning beans into his trough. "The man thinks we are made of gold."

Myles understood their agitation now. "Did you pay him?" he asked.

"We gave him half what he was asking for," Douglas said, shoving food in his mouth. "Rain is approaching from the west. You can smell it in the air, so the men need a roof over their heads."

Myles didn't argue with them. It was a small price to pay to keep the soldiers dry. As Douglas and Westley delved into their meal and kept up a steady stream of conversation with Myles, Veronica suspected her private time with Myles was over. She was sorry that it was finished, but also very grateful for it. Not only had she been able to tell him about her father's money, but they had cleared the air as well. Myles hadn't been angry with her, which was a relief, but he also hadn't told her why, exactly, he'd remained so silent and distant. She was coming to think she had simply imagined the entire thing. Myles was the head of the escort, and he'd only been doing his duty, which didn't include keeping up a running conversation with her throughout the day.

Even if she wished otherwise.

She was imagining problems where there were none.

Finished with her meal and feeling the alcohol as it made her sleepy, Veronica looked over at her rented chamber to see what the progress was. There were still servants in the chamber because the door was open and she could see them moving around, so she turned for the hearth where Mud lay on his side, snoring away. He was still a little wet, and she climbed off her chair and crouched on the floor next to him, running her fingers through his still-damp coat. But the heat was stronger here, and it was drawing her. She ended up sitting on the floor next to the dog, raking her fingers through his hair and listening to the conversation around her.

Mostly, she was listening to Myles' voice as he spoke to his brothers about a place called Croft Castle. Evidently, their father had just acquired the property through a treaty with a Welsh lord, and there was speculation that one of the brothers might be the garrison commander. There seemed to be some excitement at the prospect of managing a Welsh castle, and a big one, but from what Veronica had been told of the Welsh, the last thing they wanted was an English knight in command of one of their castles.

But it didn't seem to matter to the de Lohr brothers.

They were excited for a new challenge.

As Veronica listened, she began to regret having no siblings, no close family. It had only, and always, been her and her father. She'd lived a relatively sheltered life, tutored by the local priest so that she could read and write and do sums to manage her father's house, but her only friends had been local children, and now, as an adult, Snowy was her one true friend. She hadn't even realized that it had been a lonely life until the past few days when she saw Myles with his brothers. There was such camaraderie there.

A feeling of belonging.

It made her unknown future weigh even more heavily upon her, not knowing what she was facing once she reached Adlington Castle. The more time she spent around the de Lohr brothers, the more she wanted to be part of what they had. If she were completely honest with herself, the more she wanted to be part of Myles. That awkward, blunt, gorgeous man had her interest, and she deeply regretted that.

She regretted what could never be.

Perhaps, for her sake, it would be better if he continued ignoring her.

Veronica sat for a few more minutes, listening to the de Lohr brothers, grinning when Myles and Douglas ganged up on Westley for knocking Douglas' cup of ale onto the floor. Douglas took Westley's cup, and before Westley could take *his* cup, lying on the ground, Myles booted it across the common room. It had been both cruel and hilarious, but when Westley got up, miffed, to find the cup, one of the serving wenches informed Myles that Veronica's chamber was ready.

Veronica heard her.

Rising to her feet, she awoke the slumbering dog and dragged the animal back to the room that was now relatively warm and smelling of vinegar. Someone had even brought her a basin of hot water so she was able to wash her arms and legs and face, cleaning off the dust of the road. As Mud settled back down in front of the warmth of the hearth, Veronica took advantage of the hot water.

Using a small piece of lavender-scented soap from her

satchel, she quickly scrubbed the parts of her body that she could get to, including her face and hair. She simply dunked her entire head in the basin, upside down, and washed. She had a bit of an obsession for washing and always had, so it was something that was important to her. Clean and dried, she donned her sleeping shift and sat in front of the hearth to dry her hair out before going to bed. It was nearly dry when the door in the chamber through the pass-through hearth opened and she could see booted feet enter. Three pairs.

The de Lohr brothers had arrived.

Veronica put more wood on the fire to create more warmth, but also a barrier between her and the brothers. She figured they would want their privacy, and probably didn't realize that the hearth didn't have a fire back, so she built up the blaze to the low hum of their conversation until one of them must have realized that the fire in the hearth was growing bigger.

Suddenly, Veronica found herself looking at Myles.

She smiled weakly.

"The hearth is open between the chambers," she said, pointing out the obvious. "I thought to build up the fire to give you and your brothers some privacy. I will go to sleep quickly, so I will not hear whatever you wish to speak of."

He grinned at her through the flame. "I do not mind if you hear us, but we will be quiet so you can sleep."

Westley crouched next to his brother, looking at her through the fire. "What is this madness?" he said, looking at the open hearth before focusing on Veronica. "'Tis good that you warned us. Now we will not speak about things that only men should speak of and women should not hear."

She couldn't tell if he was jesting or not, but she started to laugh. "God's Bones," she muttered. "What on earth would that be?"

Myles looked at his brother to see just what Westley would concoct. He wasn't surprised with what his clever little brother came up with.

"Farting," Westley said. "We speak of farting constantly. Do you ever wonder what men talk about when they are alone? We speak of who farts the loudest and the longest."

Myles rolled his eyes. "Good Christ," he muttered. "We do *not*."

"We do!" Westley was trying not to laugh. "But do not worry, my lady. We will keep talk of farting to a minimum. Mayhap we will speak of how far we can vomit when we've had too much to drink. Would that be a better subject?"

Veronica burst out laughing, but she was also groaning. "Go to sleep, Westley de Lohr," she said, standing up. "I've had enough of your man talk."

"Wait!" Westley called to her, trying to see where she was going. "Come back! I'm not finished!"

"You are," she said, though her voice was faint because she was across the room. "Good sleep to you."

Westley's response was to make farting noises—loud ones—with his mouth. "Come back or you will have to listen to this gassy symphony all night."

Veronica sat down on her bed, silently laughing at him, as she braided her nearly dry hair. She was about to reply when she heard Westley grunt in pain. Someone was forcing him away from the hearth, and she suspected it was Myles. Westley wasn't moving from the hearth voluntarily, or easily, but she heard him complain as one of his older brothers dragged him away. Just as she lay back on the clean linens, she could hear Westley's distant voice.

"Good sleep to you, Lady Veronica," he said. There was a pause. "Ooch! I only wished her a good sleep. You've no reason to strike me, sir."

More low conversation that Veronica couldn't hear. Low and threatening. Still chuckling, Veronica rolled onto her side, away from the fire, hearing Westley continue to complain that he'd done nothing wrong. She heard Myles tell him, clearly this time, that he was going to gag him if he didn't shut his mouth.

That seemed to settle him down.

Veronica fell asleep with a smile on her lips in one of the most entertaining moments she'd ever had.

# CHAPTER EIGHT

*Cradley Heath*

"I DEMAND YOU open this gate immediately!"

Broden was on the other side of the gatehouse of Cradley Heath, listening to a man with bushy gray hair and a pockmarked face make demands. He'd seen the man before, the day that he arrived at Cradley Heath with Myles and the escort, so he knew the man to be Lady Veronica's uncle.

This was the moment he'd been waiting for.

Broden was surprised it had taken this long. He'd been at Cradley Heath for four days without any sign of the uncle in question. It had been his understanding that the man was going to return shortly after they'd witnessed his departure on the day the de Lohr escort arrived at the manse, so four days later, the man who seemed to have caused all of the trouble made an appearance.

And he wasn't happy.

But Broden knew what he had to do. He wasn't sure the uncle would understand, but that wasn't his problem.

He had orders to carry out.

"I will again repeat what I have just told you," he said

steadily. "Since there is a dispute about who manages Edgar de Wolviston's estate, I have been ordered to lock it up and admit no one until Lord Hereford has all of the facts. The order to admit you will come from him, not me."

The man had been standing several feet back from the gate. He had four men with him, all of them looking quite insulted as well as quite confused. They'd returned to Cradley Heath to find a stranger in command. Worse still, he was denying them entrance.

It was all quite puzzling.

"Where is my niece?" the man demanded. "She will tell you to let me in."

Broden cocked an eyebrow. "Did you forget that you sent for the de Lohr escort to take her to her betrothed?" he said. "She is not here."

The man chewed on his lip, agitated, before approaching the iron gate. "I did not forget," he said, trying to sound reasonable because rage wasn't getting him anywhere. "Mayhap you are unclear on who, exactly, I am. My name is Gregor de Wolviston, and Edgar was my brother. Veronica is my niece. Edgar requested that I manage his estate after his death, so you have no right to keep me out."

Broden held his ground. "It is Lady Veronica who asked that you not be admitted," she said. "Word has been sent to Lord Hereford about this matter. He will decide what is to be done."

So much for keeping his temper. Gregor slapped his thigh with an angry hand. "This is not his concern," he said. "I have instructions from my brother!"

"If you have written instructions, then you must present them to Lord Hereford," Broden said. "If you do not, then it is your word against Lady Veronica's. Moreover, once she marries, Cradley Heath becomes the property of her husband. It does not belong to you."

Gregor was becoming more enraged by the moment. "I *am* Edgar's brother," he nearly shouted at Broden. "I have always been welcome in his home. You do not have the right to keep me out."

"I do have the right, given to me by Lady Veronica."

Gregor couldn't fight the circular logic. It all kept coming back to Veronica's wishes. Weeks of contention with her had now turned against him because somehow she had convinced the de Lohr knight to side with her.

That was something Gregor hadn't anticipated.

Now, he was at a crossroads. He wasn't sure he could convince the knight to let him in, and unless he wanted to go back to Lincolnshire, back to the small, dingy cottage where his hag of a wife lived, he was going to have to figure something out.

That was going to be a problem.

He had just spent four days in Birmingham, where he had sold his brother's pewter plates and lived like a king off the money. Those plates were very valuable, more valuable than he had anticipated, and he had found a metal smith who gave him a good deal of money for them. It was more money than Gregor had seen at any one time in his entire life, to be truthful, so he went to the nearest tavern, where he had purchased food and drink for him and his men for four solid days. Every meal was a banquet, and, at one point, he had even bought food for the entire common room. Everyone cheered him and thanked him, and he had felt the respect that he had deserved. Finally, he knew what it felt like to be rich and powerful.

That was a feeling he would not easily surrender.

He could have spent weeks in Birmingham spending that money, but he didn't want to. There were more plates at Cradley Heath, and if he could sell them, then he could pocket the money and do as he pleased. When he had first come to his brother's home, it was with the intention of taking what he could. The truth was that he *did* have a missive from his brother that he had received several years ago, right after his brother recovered from an illness, and in the letter, his brother asked him to watch over Veronica should something happen to him.

But that had been a long time ago.

The problem was that Veronica was nearly of age now, and given that she did have a future husband, there was really no reason for her to have a guardian. Her husband would do that, and any legal system would acknowledge this. Cradley Heath would belong to her husband, meaning a wayward uncle would have no place there. It was true that Gregor had sent the Earl of Hereford and Worcester a missive so he could get his niece out of his hair, but he had been anticipating weeks, perhaps even months, before her husband was able to come to Cradley Heath and survey what he had inherited by marriage. During that time, Gregor had hoped to ransack the manse and take everything of value that he could.

But now, that wasn't going to happen.

It seemed that Lady Veronica had yet again thwarted him.

That didn't sit well with Gregor. He and his brother had never been close, and while Edgar had gone on to make an excellent living as a cartographer, the truth was that Gregor had run their family estate into the ground. Their father, and his father, had made their money from a small fleet of fishing vessels, selling their catch at market. They had a comfortable home in Butterwick, near Boston in Lincolnshire, where the family had a large and popular fish stall.

Selling fish wasn't something Gregor had ever wanted to do.

Victor de Wolviston tried very hard to teach Gregor the business of what he would inherit as the eldest son, and Gregor pretended to care, but the truth was that he didn't. He'd remained in Butterwick, marrying the prettiest local girl he could find and drinking away his father's money. After his father's death, Gregor let the family business die, sold off the fishing fleet, and ended up losing Butterwick because of gambling debts. His wife, that pretty lass, had proven barren, so he had no children.

He had nothing.

But his brother did.

*Damnation...* He wasn't going to let it go so easily.

"It seems to me that you have listened to only one side of this situation," he said after taking a few moments to rethink his strategy. "Every circumstance has two sides, and no one has asked me what my truth is."

"That is not my decision, my lord," Broden said. "I am doing as I am ordered."

Gregor sighed sharply. "Then when is Lord Hereford expected?" he said. "I have proof that my brother has asked me to manage his estate."

"If you do, I suggest you go to Lioncross Abbey Castle and present it to Lord Hereford, because I do not expect him here anytime soon," Broden said. "If you want action, then go to Lioncross."

Gregor didn't exactly want to do that because he knew the only proof he had was somewhat ambiguous. Still, he would use it, and he would argue that he was interpreting his brother's wishes.

But he didn't want to leave Cradley Heath.

Not yet.

Another idea came to mind.

"If I promise to behave and do as you instruct, may I at least stay here until Lord Hereford decides what's to be done?" he said. "I will not be any trouble at all, I swear it."

"Nay, my lord."

"Please?"

Broden simply shook his head.

Once again foiled, Gregor knew he had to think of something else or he would be stymied for good. His options were limited, but he still had some of the money left from the sale of the plates. He could go back to Birmingham and see if he could hire some men to help him regain the manse, which was probably his only option at that point. He didn't know how many men the de Lohr knight had with him, but from what he could see through the gate, it didn't look like many. Perhaps if he could hire ten or fifteen men to breach the walls and kill the de Lohr men at arms, he could strip the manse for anything of value and get out before de Lohr found out what had happened.

It was one idea of many.

Without another word, Gregor turned away from the gate and headed toward the southern end of Worcester, where the businesses were gathered, but it was not so crowded. In this section, there was one main road, lined with a few businesses and anchored on each end by taverns. The one to the north was called The White Hart, and it was more of a lodge than a tavern, but the one on the south end was called The Bull and the Buck. He'd been there a few times, and the patrons were rougher than most.

Perhaps he would find what he needed there.

He had plans to make.

# CHAPTER NINE

*South of Macclesfield*
*Six miles from Adlington Castle*

THEY WERE DRAWING closer.

Closer to something Myles didn't want to draw closer to, which was odd. His thinking was odd. It had been ever since last night, when he had a long and surprisingly comfortable conversation with Veronica. He'd never had a comfortable conversation with a woman in his life, Aviara included. Her conversations had always been about people or clothing or politics, which she didn't readily understand but was very curious about. Myles always felt as if he was teaching Aviara something every time he talked to her, because she wasn't particularly bright. She was shallow, but he knew that. He'd always known that.

It had been a shock speaking with a woman who wasn't shallow.

He'd had three distinct conversations with her—the conversation the first day they met, the conversation when he'd had too much of that hard cider, and then the conversation last night. He was coming to deeply regret having ignored her for the first three days of their journey, because he realized that he liked talking to her. He didn't feel like he was desperately trying to keep her attention because he was fearful that she was going to go off with someone else. Aviara had always made him feel desperate, like he'd had to go above and beyond in order to keep her interest. As if what he was, as a man, simply wasn't enough. He had to do *more*.

But Veronica didn't make him feel that way.

It was so strange, truly. He was the god of the de Lohr brothers, but he was also the odd man out. He knew his parents worried about him. He knew he wasn't like everyone else when it came to showing warmth or joy or compassion. He'd known many women in his life, all of them fawning over him because of his appearance. He wasn't so stupid that he didn't know that. But, gradually, most of the women had fallen away, and he knew why. He'd never shown the same interest in return, or even an ounce of charm. But Aviara had been different.

He knew why.

God's Bones, he did.

His own parents thought he'd viewed Aviara as a prize to be won. He'd wanted her not because he was in love with her, because he wasn't. The deep, dark secret of Myles de Lohr was that he didn't know *how* to fall in love. In concept, he wanted to, but he'd never met anyone to show him how. Aviara had paid him attention long after other women fell away, even if that attention had been to pit him against his cousin, whom she was now married to.

And then it occurred to him.

He'd not lost her because of Peter.

He'd lost her because he'd never shown her enough interest to *keep* her.

Oliver had been the one to show Aviara attention and kindness and understanding and warmth, things that Myles didn't really possess. Yet he'd just spent the previous night with an astonishingly impressive woman who made him feel something he was unfamiliar with. She'd made him giddy at one point, which was perhaps one of the better feelings he'd ever had. He thought about having such a woman by his side on a daily basis, speaking to her, listening to her, having conversations that delved beyond fashion and politics. A woman like that could give advice he would listen to. She hadn't been tainted by fostering in great houses like Aviara had been.

She was special.

And she was going to marry someone else.

A phenomenally depressing thought as he plodded along the road, heading toward Adlington Castle, where a man named de Correa was waiting. It occurred to him that he didn't want to take her there, not tonight. He wanted one more night of talking to her, of listening to her, feeling as if, somehow, there was some normalcy deep inside of him and he was like everyone else. He could feel something and show warmth and compassion, but in this case, it was only to someone very specific.

It was to Veronica.

God... he was in trouble.

"What's amiss, brother?"

He heard someone speaking to him off to his left, and he turned to see Douglas as the man reined his steed next to his. Douglas, perhaps one of his only true friends. There was a sister born between him and Douglas, and there were six years between them, but they had always been close. Douglas looked like him, and they essentially had the same hair in length, color, and texture, so much so that Christopher had always called them Odin's twins. He joked that they looked as if their father had been a Norse god, clearly in denial that he, too, looked as if he'd been fathered by a Norse god because of his blond, fair looks. Westley had the same look to a certain extent, with shoulder-length blond hair, but he also looked as if he and a comb were mortal enemies.

The flowing blond mane of the younger de Lohr lads were legendary.

Douglas was the brother who perhaps understood Myles the best. Myles never felt judged by Douglas. The truth was that none of his family really judged him, but Douglas was more in alignment with Myles' thoughts and hopes and fears. Douglas was the one who initially told him that Aviara was no good for him, and he knew his brother would not lie to him, but still, he didn't want to believe it.

Maybe he should have listened.

"Nothing is amiss," he said after a moment. "Why do you ask?"

Douglas glanced at the escort behind them before speaking. "Because you could not be moving more slowly," he said. "You were moving at a regular pace when we departed Stone, but you have become slower and slower, and we are all setting pace with you. Poor West is struggling not to fall asleep. Why are you moving so slowly?"

Myles looked at him a moment before turning away, sighing long and heavy. "I did not realize I have slowed so much," he said. "I suppose I have been thinking."

"About what?"

"You do not want to know."

"Aviara?"

"Nay," Myles said, shaking his head. "Someone else."

That had Douglas' interest. "Truly?" he said. "Who else is there? Someone I do not know about?"

"You know her."

"Christ, Myles, *who*?"

Myles hesitated. Then he tipped his head back in the direction of the carriage. When Douglas didn't understand him, he pointed. Several times. Then Douglas started to catch on.

"Who?" he said. "The lady? De Wolviston's daughter?"

Myles kept his eyes on the road ahead. "She has made me realize something."

"What?"

"That you were right."

"About what?"

Myles wanted to answer, but he couldn't quite bring himself to do it. "I have a question for you," he said. "What happens when a man believes he missed the opportunity with a woman who may, or may not, be the right one for him? I feel as if… as if something is about to slip away."

Douglas wasn't much clearer on the subject. "Aviara, you mean?" he said. "She is gone, Myles. The sooner you accept that, the better."

But Myles shook his head. "Nay, not her," he said. "I am speaking of Lady Veronica. I seem to have a level of comfort with her that I've never had with anyone. It is the first time in my life that I feel as if a woman hasn't wanted something from me, and she is kind to me all the same. Does that make sense?"

It did, sort of. The corner of Douglas' mouth tugged up in a smile. "The way women throw themselves at you, aye, it makes sense," he said. "I agree with you. Lady Veronica is much different from the highbred, spoiled women that we are used to."

Myles looked at him then. "Mama was highbred, but her father kept her education in great houses to a minimum," he said. "I think she only fostered for a couple of years at Warwick Castle, but that was all. She received her education at home, from her parents. Hell, our sister, Rebecca, is even named after her best friend who died many years ago, a peasant girl she has never forgotten. Our mother is much more grounded than other noblewomen. But those highborn, spoiled lasses are the women we happen to be exposed to and introduced to. I thought all women were like that. But it seems they are not."

Douglas shook his head. "Nay, they are not," he said. "They are not all like Aviara."

Myles kept shaking his head. "That is what I have been thinking about," he said. "I wish we did not have to take Lady Veronica to her betrothed, because I like speaking with her. She is good conversation."

Douglas nodded. "She is," he said. "She is bright and articulate and very beautiful. But I do not suppose you have noticed that."

Myles glanced at him, looking down his nose at the man. "Have *you*?"

"I asked you first."

"She is betrothed to another man. It does not matter what I think."

"Doesn't it?" Douglas said. Then he heard barking behind him and turned to see Mud rushing out of the carriage and off into a sparsely wooded area next to a stream. "You just told me you had been thinking about her."

"I should not be."

"But you *are*," Douglas said. "Look at it this way, Myles—

her betrothed has been waiting a long time for her. Years, even. That is enough to take the edge of excitement off any betrothal. He might even have another woman in mind after all this time and fears he cannot break this betrothal."

Myles shrugged. "Possibly," he said. "If I had to wait ten or more years for my bride, I might forget about her altogether. But what are you trying to tell me?"

"I'm trying to tell you this," Douglas said. "Because he has waited so long for her, he might consider it if someone offered to buy him out of his contract. Forty pounds should do it. That's a princely sum for a bride, but he might consider it worth it."

It took Myles a moment to realize what his brother had said, and when he did, he began shaking his head vigorously.

"Nay," he said flatly. "That is ridiculous, Douglas. I have only just lost the woman I wanted to marry, and now you suggest I *buy* a bride? So soon? That would make me look like a fool. A fickle fool."

"Or it would make you look like a man who realized he'd been pining for the wrong woman," Douglas pointed out. "Myles, love is not about timing. It is about opportunity. And we cannot predict opportunity."

Myles geared up to argue with him but abruptly stopped, hissing with annoyance, but that was all. He didn't become angry or tell his brother how wrong he was, but it was clear that he wanted to.

"It would not work," he said, growing animated, which was something he didn't normally do. "I cannot simply go to a man and say, 'Here, take all that I have because I want to purchase the woman you have been waiting for'!"

"Why not?"

"That is ridiculous!"

"You still have not told me why."

Myles turned to him, exasperated, only to catch movement by the carriage. He turned to see Veronica emerging, pursuing her dog the same way she had since they'd departed Cradley Heath.

Myles pursed his lips irritably.

"It seems all she ever does is chase after that dog," he said. "And last night—that stupid dog managed to make it through the pass-through hearth and end up in my bed. When I awoke this morning, he was sleeping right next to me."

Douglas started to laugh. "And you never even felt him?"

"Nothing."

"You sleep *too* soundly, Myles. What if that had been an assassin?"

"Then I would now be dead."

Off to their left, they could hear Veronica as she called to the dog, who was barking and seemingly having a marvelous time running from his mistress. Veronica called, and Mud refused to come—in fact, he seemed to be running further away. Veronica's calls became more annoyed as she threatened her dog if he did not come to her. Mud barked, and seemed to be barking more than usual, until he abruptly sounded as if he was in a fight. That wasn't a sound that had ever come out of the dog, and immediately, Myles and Douglas and Westley, further back in line, began to turn their horses for the wooded area.

Then Veronica screamed.

Spurs dug into the sides of the warhorses as the knights sprinted in her direction. She was screaming, Mud was in a fight, and as the knights reached the trees, they suddenly came alive. Arrows and projectiles began to fly.

In an instant, they were in a battle.

The men at arms began to fly off the road, rushing into the wooded area as men literally dropped out of the trees on them. Myles, who could still hear Veronica screaming but couldn't see her, gestured wildly to Douglas.

"Clean out these woods," he shouted. "No mercy, Douglas. Leave no one alive. West! With me!"

As Douglas turned to manage the fight that had just begun, Myles and Westley plowed through the foliage, following the sounds of Veronica's screaming and Mud's barking. There was a stream bisecting the forested area, and they forged through it, onto the bank on the other side, and there they caught sight of Veronica as several men were dragging her away. Mud was in a fight with two other dogs, and it was a nasty struggle. As much as Myles wanted to help the dog, he had Veronica to focus on, but he called to a couple of men at arms to help Mud while he and Westley and about four more men at arms went to help Veronica.

The closer they drew to her, the more they could see that she wasn't making a willing victim. They had her by both arms and by her hair, but as Myles watched, she kicked one man in the crotch and kicked another in the stomach. She was twisting and kicking, trying to break at least one of her arms free, as Myles thundered up to the group holding her with his broadsword arcing. Half of them dropped her and fled in terror when they saw the enormous English knight, but two of them still held on. Myles made short work of them as Westley went after the group that fled. Reaching down, Myles pulled Veronica onto Tempest, who was gnashing his big teeth, and rushed off to help Mud.

The de Lohr men at arms were armed with crossbows, and one of the dogs fighting Mud had already been put down with an arrow through the chest. As Myles charged up, preparing to dispatch the other dog, an arrow came sailing out of the trees and hit him in the shoulder, in the joint where his left arm met his torso. The force of the blow caused him to grunt, and he staggered a little, but Veronica was behind him, holding him tightly and trying to prevent him from falling off the horse.

"I have you," she told him steadily. "You will not fall, Myles. I have you."

The sight of an arrow sticking out of his shoulder wasn't particularly shocking, but it did frustrate him. He couldn't tell how bad it was, but he tried to move his left arm and couldn't manage it very well. That meant that he was vulnerable.

*She* was vulnerable.

And that enraged him.

With a roar, he ripped the arrow out of his shoulder. It had gone deep, so it took him two full tugs to rip it free. Blood began to pour as he tossed it away, so bloody furious that all he could think of was killing every bastard out there who wasn't a de Lohr soldier or knight. The men at arms had managed to dispatch the other dog, but Mud was bloody and torn up.

Myles shouted to the nearest soldier.

"Give me the dog," he boomed. "Hand him to me!"

One of the men at arms grabbed the beaten dog and handed him up to Myles, who slung the pooch across his saddle. Driving his spurs into the sides of his horse, he charged off the way he had come.

He was trying to hold the dog with his left hand while directing the horse with his right. Behind him, he could feel Veronica pressed up tightly against him, one arm around his waist and the other clutching the dog she couldn't see very well. Her hand was on the bloodied gray fur, and when Myles glanced down to see that, something happened to him.

Something pulled at him.

His chest tightened.

Sorrow swept him.

But he couldn't focus on that. He had to get Veronica and the dog to safety, so he raced back through the trees where his men seemed to be winning the battle, and off toward the road where the carriage was.

Unfortunately, there was a bit of a battle going on at the carriage, too, as two men at arms tried to prevent about six men from stealing what was inside. They weren't losing the battle, but they were nearly overwhelmed until Myles charged up. Once the enemy saw the English knight bearing down on them, they scattered.

But so did Veronica's belongings.

They'd managed to get inside the carriage, so her satchel was on the road and some of her things were scattered. As soon as Myles came to a halt, he carefully handed the dog down to the nearest soldier as Veronica slid off behind him. But she held on to Myles' leg even as she directed the soldier to put Mud inside the carriage. Myles tried to ride off, but she yanked on his leg, and it nearly pulled her to the ground when he didn't stop fast enough.

"Nay!" she insisted. "Myles, you are injured. You must let me tend your wound."

Myles gazed down at her flushed face and could see the genuine concern. For him. He'd never had anyone so concerned for him, at least not like that. It touched him. *She* touched him. He would have loved to linger over the new sensation because it seemed to heighten his senses, and his emotions, but there wasn't time. Reaching down with his right hand, he gently touched her face and winked at her.

"Later," he said hoarsely.

With that, he spun his horse around and headed back into the battle, leaving Veronica standing there, watching him go and feeling sick inside. *That beautiful, brave, stupid man.*

But God... he was magnificent.

Tearing her gaze away from him, she quickly darted into the carriage as the two men at arms picked up her scattered belongings. When everything was collected, they tossed the satchel back into the carriage, and Veronica slammed the door and threw the bolt.

A rather final note on a most eventful morning.

# CHAPTER TEN

**M**UD HAD RECEIVED a thrashing.

Discovering that the damage to her dog had been extensive, Veronica spent the next hour or two cleansing the wounds and stitching what she could, bandaging the rest. All she had to clean them with was the ale that they'd brought with them from the tavern the night before, but it was enough. She had a sewing kit because all women—peasant or noble—had a sewing kit, and she had very fine silk thread, which she used to sew up a big gash on Mud's ear where the other dog had nearly ripped it from his head. She didn't do a very good job, given that she was squeamish and Mud was in pain, but it would have to do.

The rest of the wounds were bound with what she could find in her satchel and in the cap cases she had packed. She ended up tearing up a fine shift to make bandages, half of those going on the dog and the other half waiting for Myles or anyone else who had been wounded in the fight.

And she waited.

Mud passed out from sheer exhaustion on one of two cushioned benches in the carriage. Veronica covered the dog up with a blanket she'd found under the bench while she sat on the opposite bench, watching Mus sleep and wondering what was happening outside. She didn't dare look out the windows for fear she might somehow put herself in danger again. She hadn't meant to the first time, following her wandering dog, but she'd gotten more than she bargained for. Truth be told, she was still shaken.

She was certain that Myles was going to give her an earful.

A knock on the door roused her from her thoughts.

Quickly, she went to the panel, demanding to know who it was, and Douglas announced himself. Throwing the bolt, Veronica was confronted by a weary knight and an escort that was trying to put itself back together again. Some of the men were wounded, but she didn't see anything serious except for one man who was bleeding through the wrapping on an arm he seemed to no longer be able to use.

"God's Bones," she muttered, looking around. "Was it terrible, then?"

Douglas shook his head. "It could have been worse," he said. "We did not lose anyone."

She looked at him. "How many outlaws were there?"

Douglas glanced off to the west, where the skirmish had taken place. "We have thirty-two bodies," he said. "But that wasn't the problem. A few escaped, and we chased them over the hill, where there was an encampment of many more. Men, women, children… An outlaw camp."

Veronica looked at him in surprise. "What did you do?"

Douglas shrugged. "Cleaned out the camp," he said. "Killed anyone we could. We let the women and children escape, of course, but the men fell. That's what took so long—we were cleaning out the encampment."

Veronica noted one man walking past her with a gashed thigh and a limp. "Can I help?" she said. "Some of the men look quite injured."

Douglas shook his head. "They can wait," he said. "I need your help with Myles."

Veronica nodded. "He was hit with an arrow, but he pulled it right out," she said, gesturing. "He seemed well enough."

Douglas sighed. "He's not," he said. "He is very pale, and cleaning out the outlaw encampment has taxed him greatly. He refused to let any of us look at his shoulder, but I think if you ask him nicely, he would let you. I fear the damage is worse than he lets on."

That had Veronica coming out of the carriage, looking around for Myles. "Where is he?"

Douglas pointed toward the trees. "Come with me, please."

Veronica did. She followed Douglas off the road and toward the stream, where she finally saw Myles talking to Westley. He was holding the reins of his horse as Tempest hungrily ripped up some of the foliage, but he paused when he saw Douglas approaching with Veronica.

The conversation with Westley was forgotten.

"My lady," Myles said. "How fares the dog?"

In just those few words, Veronica could see what Douglas meant. Myles looked oddly pale and his lips were pasty. The man looked as if he was about to keel over. Suspecting he would refuse her should she start making demands that she be allowed to tend his wound, she opted for a different approach. She had only known Myles a few days, but from what she knew, he was a proud man. And he was always, irrefutably, in control of himself. She suspected a man like that wouldn't take it well if a lady saw him in a weakened state, so she approached him carefully.

"He has taken quite a beating," she said. "They nearly ripped his ear off."

Myles nodded grimly. "He was very brave," he said. "He kept those dogs away from you."

Veronica held out a hand to him. "Come with me and see him," she said. "I think he has become very fond of you, so it would do him well if you were to visit him. Please?"

Myles shook his head. "I cannot at the moment," he said. "But I will come when I have finished here."

Veronica looked to Westley and Douglas. "That is why you have your brothers," she said. "They are your generals, are they not? A commander is supposed to comfort his wounded, and right now, Mud is wounded. He requires your comfort."

Myles eyed his brothers, but he was succumbing to her logic. "That ridiculous dog was in my bed last night," he said. "Did you know that?"

Veronica struggled not to laugh at his displeasure. "I did when I awoke and he was not with me," she said. "I assumed he made his way into your chamber, but he had to walk through the hearth to do it. Will you not come see the animal who walked through fire for you?"

After that, Myles didn't argue. He couldn't. He handed the reins of his horse over to Westley and reached out to take her hand. Veronica took up a place alongside him, slipping her other hand around his enormous arm. It happened to be his left arm, where he'd been hit, and she suddenly stopped.

"I'd forgotten you'd been hit, too," she said, peering at the mail and tunic, which had a big patch of crusted-over blood. "Mayhap you'll let me clean you up while you and Mud are bonding over your mutual wounds."

Myles hesitated. "You should not be troubled by me," he said. "It is nothing."

"Mud allowed me to tend him without complaint."

"I am not complaining. I am simply saying that it is not necessary."

"Are you telling me that a dog has behaved better than you when it comes to his wound?"

She cocked an eyebrow at him, and Myles could see that he had little choice. Heavily, he sighed.

"Very well," he said. "Look at the wound if it pleases you. But I seem to recall that I tended my brother's wounds better than you did back at Cradley Heath."

"I hardly knew you. Of course I let you tend your brother's knotty head."

Myles burst out laughing, even if it was at Westley's expense. "My lady, I think you and I are going to be very good friends," he said, resuming his walk. "Anyone who calls my brother a knot-head is, indeed, my friend."

Veronica grinned. "I seem to recall that he did not complain, either, when you wanted to tend his wound," she reminded him. "I expect you to behave similarly."

"I will, I promise."

"You'd better."

She held his arm all the way back to the carriage, and Myles simply let her. He let her pull him into the cab and he let her sit him down next to the dog, who immediately woke up and began wagging his tail. He even let her help him remove his tunic, his mail, and the padded undertunic that was soaked with sweat and stained with blood. Unfortunately, the blood had mostly coagulated and some of the torn fabric was in his wound. When she pulled the tunic off, part of the scab came off too, and he grimaced.

"Did I hurt you?" she said anxiously. "I am very sorry. I did not mean to."

He shook his head, trying to get a look at the wound, but with the location, it was difficult to see. Sighing with frustration, he leaned his head back against the side of the cab.

"I am afraid that the arrow took some of my tunic when it went into my shoulder," he said. "If it does not come out, it will fester."

Veronica was listening to him closely. "I can remove it," she said confidently. "I will do it right now."

Myles looked at her, seeing that she truly had the best of intentions but probably no idea the extent of what he meant. Then he looked at his tunic, picking it up with his good arm and seeing just how much he had bled. No wonder he felt weak. With two hands, he pieced together the tunic where the arrow had hit him and could see that a small piece of material was missing.

He held it up to show it to her.

"See how there is a small piece missing?" he said. "Right in the center. See it? That is what is in my shoulder."

Veronica didn't say anything. She simply nodded her head and peered at the shoulder wound, which was clean as far as wounds went but crusty. Timidly, she touched it, seeing that it was scabbing over already.

"The wound looks as if it is already healing," she said. "Are you certain the fabric is in there?"

"Certain enough," he said. "You'll have to remove the scab and use something to probe the wound to find the fabric. If you ask Westley, he should have something you can remove it with. Or you can simply have Westley remove it. He's an excellent healer."

Veronica was looking at him with a good deal of trepidation. She also happened to be standing very close to him as he sat naked from the waist up. He had a big, beautiful chest, muscular neck and arms, and a trim waist, something that surely must not have escaped her notice. At least, he *hoped* it hadn't escaped her notice. He felt very much as if he was trying to seduce the woman as she attempted to tend his wound. If he felt any better, he might very well try it. In fact, he reached down, picked up her left hand, and brought it to his lips for a gentle kiss.

"May I make a suggestion?" he asked softly. "It seems to me that you've not tended a wound like this before. Am I wrong?"

Veronica's breathing was quickening. Quite honestly, she'd not considered that she was leaning over a half-naked man until that very moment. Now, she found herself looking at Myles in all of his fleshy glory, and it was a sight that took her breath away. Literally. When he shifted and his long hair tumbled over one shoulder, she could smell it. She could smell *him*. Musky and heated, like leather and steel. She'd never been this close to a nearly naked man in her life, and when he took her hand and kissed it, the carriage around her began to swim a little.

God, she could hardly breathe.

"N-nay," she said, swallowing hard. "You are not wrong. But I will try very hard, I promise."

He smiled faintly and kissed her hand again. "I know you will," he said. "But it might be better if you assisted Westley. Even someone as talented as you must learn the techniques of battle wounds, so this will be your chance to learn something new. Will you do it?"

Veronica was being mesmerized by the man's eyes. They

were incredibly blue, like the color of a warm summer sky. She found herself staring at the shape of his face and wondering what it would be like to kiss his full, smooth lips.

*It would be so easy to...*

"Aye," she said, suddenly stumbling away. "I... I will fetch Westley. Stay there—do not go away. I will return."

Veronica opened the carriage door and nearly fell out. She managed to catch herself, however, embarrassed and over-whelmed by that big, glorious knight in the carriage. She had to take a deep breath to steady herself as she caught sight of Westley, who was bandaging up a soldier's arm. He saw her nearly tumble out of the carriage and looked to her with concern.

"My lady?" he said. "Is something wrong?"

Veronica shook her head. "Nay," she said. "But he has managed to remove his tunic so the wound can be tended. He asked me to fetch you to do it. He says that the arrow took some of his tunic with it when it entered his shoulder, and it must come out or it will fester."

Westley sighed. "It will," he said, quickly finishing with the bandage. Then he paused to collect a leather satchel he had with him. "Come along, my lady. Let us see to my stubborn brother."

Veronica followed him back to the carriage, and the two of them entered to find Myles leaning back against the side of the carriage and snoring steadily. Even the dog was snoring. Westley turned to Veronica.

"How much ale do you have in here?" he asked quietly.

Veronica quickly picked up a pitcher that had a stopper, opening it up and peering inside. "This is nearly half-full," she said. "Should I find more?"

Westley took the pitcher and peered inside. "We need wine,

not ale," he said, setting it aside. "Go to the quartermaster and ask him for a bottle of wine. I'll take whatever he has. And I need bandages."

Veronica pointed to the neat pile of bandages she'd made from her shift. "There are some," she said. "Do you need more?"

Westley inspected the bandages. By this time, Myles had heard the voices and opened his eyes, noting that his brother was now in the carriage with him.

"How are the men?" he asked Westley.

Westley put the bandages back in the pile. "Well enough," he said. "We did not lose anyone. My lady, where did these bandages come from?"

"I made them out of one of my shifts," she said. "I used them for the dog, too."

Westley glanced at the big mutt who had been wrapped up tightly. "I see," he said. "When you go to the quartermaster, ask him for boiled linen."

Veronica looked at him curiously. "*Boiled* linen?"

"If you please."

She nodded quickly and was gone. As soon as the carriage door shut, Westley went to work.

"This is not going to be pleasant," he said. "I wanted her out of here so I could probe your wound without upsetting her. She has had enough excitement for the day. Are you sure there is material in your shoulder?"

Myles nodded. "Aye," he said. "Give me that ale."

Westley did. As he dug around in his leather satchel for a long pair of tweezers and a probe, Myles downed three big gulps of the ale. He used some of the remaining ale to pour over the wound. It stung like the blazes, but he didn't react. He didn't even react when Westley peeled off the scab and began to dig through coagulated blood.

As Veronica had noted, Myles had already started to heal, so he had to turn his head away and clench his jaw as Westley did what he had to do. He was about two inches into Myles' shoulder when he found the piece of fabric. By then, the bleeding had started again, and he doused his brother's wound with the rest of the ale, making sure to get it into the wound, before packing the linen from Veronica's shift on it. By the time she returned, breathing heavily because she had run the entire way, Westley was nearly finished.

She climbed into the carriage and stood there with her mouth open.

"I brought everything you asked for," she said, watching Westley bind up Myles' shoulder. "But… you finished without me?"

Myles looked over, smiling weakly as he held out his good hand to her. Confused, Veronica came over to him and put the bandages in his hand. He set them down and extended his hand again. She handed him the earthenware wine bottle. Chuckling softly, he put that aside and put out his hand to her yet again. She came closer but didn't put her hand in his, highly aware that Westley was there.

He would know if she allowed Myles to hold her hand.

"There," Westley said, finished with the bandage. "I would suggest you rest for an hour or two before we continue on. How far away are we from our destination?"

When Myles realized that Veronica wasn't going to give him her hand, his smile faded and he lowered his hand. "Less than an hour," he said, sounding dull. "We will be there by nightfall even if I rest an hour or two, but I do not need to. I can ride."

"Nay," Veronica said. "Please rest. It will not matter if we arrive in an hour or by dusk. Either way, we will be there... today."

Westley heard the same thing in her tone that he heard in Myles'. Something between regret and interest. Suspecting there was something more going on than met the eye, which was surprising when it came to Myles, he picked up his leather bag and left the carriage, closing the door behind him. That left Veronica and Myles in awkward silence.

For a moment, no one spoke. Veronica saw the empty ale pitcher and picked it up, setting it back where she'd found it.

"Why did he ask for those things if he did not need them?" she finally said.

Myles was resting back against the carriage wall again. "Because he did not want you to see what he needed to do," he said quietly. "You are very brave, my lady, and very helpful, but this was something that did not need an audience."

Feeling foolish, Veronica went to pick up the bandages and the wine bottle, but Myles' hand shot out and he grasped her wrist before she could get away.

"Where are you going?" he murmured.

She looked at him, her expression guarded. "To take these things back," she said. "Please lie down and rest. I will make sure you are not disturbed."

"Will you stay with me?" he asked.

"Why?"

"Because I wish it."

Veronica sighed faintly. He could see her entire body seeming to deflate. Averting her gaze, she turned toward the door.

"I cannot," she said. "It would be better if I go outside."

"Veronica," he said, his voice low and seductive. "May I tell you something?"

She looked at him sharply. "Nay," she said. "Please do not tell me anything. Myles, I have been grateful to know you and I have enjoyed our conversations, but please do not tell me anything I should not hear."

"What makes you think I would tell you something unsuitable for your ears?"

Her manner was growing more agitated. "Because... because I can tell," she said. "The way your voice sounds... the way you are looking at me... You are my escort, Myles. That is all you will ever be. Please do not make me regret knowing you."

That brought him out of what was inarguably a romantic state. He was tired from blood loss and the ale had warmed his veins a little, so perhaps he was a little soft and his judgment was weak, but he didn't like what she said.

"What do you mean by that?" he said, sitting up. "*Do* you regret knowing me? Have I done something that would cause you to say this to me?"

She dared to look at him then. "Nay, not really," she said softly. "Not yet. But... but you are to deliver me to my betrothed tonight, and... and I will not let you hold my hand, or kiss my hand, or anything else. It would not be fair to de Correa, and I would be a weak woman, indeed, if I let you continue. I should not have let you do it in the first place. Therefore, please... please do not tell me anything that I should not hear. If I were your betrothed, I am certain you would not like another man who was not a family member showing me such affection."

He understood. She could see it in his face. His gaze lingered on her as the impact of her words settled before he looked away.

"If you were my betrothed and another man kissed your hand, I would kill him," he muttered. "You are a rare woman, my lady. If you were my betrothed, I would be the proudest man in England. And the most fortunate."

Veronica stared at him. She didn't move and she didn't speak. When Myles finally dared to look up at her, he could see that her eyes were full of tears. As he watched, she blinked and they poured down her cheeks. In a flash, she bolted from the carriage and slammed the door in her wake.

Myles sat there in stunned silence. He had no idea what to make of it, but he could only come to the conclusion that the idea of being betrothed to him was so horrifying that it brought her to tears. And why shouldn't she be horrified? He'd behaved abominably since nearly the moment they met. He'd become drunk, spoken of another woman, and generally made an arse out of himself. Then he'd kissed her hands as if it was so easy for him to jump from one woman to another. What was it he'd told Douglas? He looked like a fool. He'd made a fool of himself in front of Veronica, a woman he genuinely respected and admired. But he hadn't shown her that.

Instead, he'd tried to seduce her.

Christ, he hated himself.

He just wanted to go home.

Before the hour was out, the de Lohr escort with Lady Veronica in the carriage was on its way to their destination of Adlington Castle.

# CHAPTER ELEVEN

*Adlington Castle*

S ET IN A lush, verdant valley with rolling hills to the east and the dark mountains of Wales to the west, Adlington Castle commanded a fertile plain. One could see the structure for miles all around, and the de Lohr escort had spotted it almost as soon as they left the area where they'd been attacked.

A cool breeze blew in from the west and the smell of rain was in the air as they moved toward the sandstone castle with a fairly short curtain wall around it. They didn't need a wall, however, because the castle was surrounded by a lake. It had fish and lilies and waterfowl in it, all of them swimming about quite happily. It was a bucolic scene. In order to get to the castle, an attacker would have had to swim the lake, which would be quite difficult for an army. There was a wooden bridge that spanned the lake on two ends of the castle, a larger wooden bridge leading to what was presumably the gatehouse, and then a secondary bridge that possibly led to a postern gate. In any case, Myles took the escort to the larger bridge that led to the gatehouse, but he had the escort pause,

He wasn't going to let them cross the bridge until de Correa gave permission.

Truth be told, he wasn't feeling very well. He was tired from blood loss, and after his exchange with Veronica, he was eager to leave her and head home, although the reality was that he didn't want to leave her at all. He kept hearing Douglas' words about buying a bride, but considering how Veronica had flamed about exchanging a horse for a bride once, he wasn't at all certain that was a good idea. She might not be flattered by such an offer. Moreover, the last words he had with her convinced him that she wasn't as attracted to him as he was to her.

*Do not make me regret knowing you.*

He couldn't shake those words.

"Keep the escort here," he said, dismounting his horse as Douglas and Westley followed suit. "West, you remain here with the lady. Douglas, you will come with me."

After handing off the reins of their horses to a couple of men at arms, Myles and Douglas began their walk along the wooden bridge spanning the lake. The wind was picking up, creating waves and ripples across the water as their heavy boots slammed against the bridge with every step. The closer they drew, the more they could see men in the gatehouse and on the wall gathering to watch them. By the time they reached the gatehouse itself, which was three stories tall and built heavy and squat, there were dozens of faces looking down on them.

They came to a halt in front of an iron gate that God himself probably would not have been able to breach.

"I come on behalf of the Earl of Hereford and Worcester," Myles boomed to the men of the gatehouse. "I come on business with Abner de Correa. You will announce my arrival."

There was a good deal of hissing. They could hear men conversing and feet running. That wasn't unusual when the de

Lohr army showed up, and more specifically with de Lohr knights as big and fearsome as Myles and Douglas were, but the delay seemed excessive. No one had replied.

"Who is in command of the gatehouse?" Myles said. "I wish to speak with him."

More hissing and conversation. Men were moving around. Behind the enormous iron gate was an equally enormous pair of gates, with dragons carved into them, and they could hear someone tampering with the gates. Bolts were being thrown. After a few moments, the gate on the right began to creak open.

An older man appeared, his tunic and mail clean and his graying hair neatly combed. He came to the iron gate, his expression curious as he gazed upon the enormous knights.

"My name is Damon St. Bernardine," he said. "I have served the House of de Correa for almost thirty years. May I ask your business, my lords?"

He was calm and polite, so Myles didn't have a problem answering the man. "I am Sir Myles de Lohr," he said. Then he indicated Douglas. "This is my brother, Sir Douglas de Lohr. Our father is the Earl of Hereford and Worcester."

"Christopher de Lohr," St. Bernardine said with some awe in his tone. "Of course I know of the House of de Lohr. We are honored, my lords."

Myles nodded his thanks. "I do not mean to be disrespect-ful, St. Bernardine, but our business is with Abner de Correa," he said. "We have come with something he has been expecting, so I would be grateful if we could address him personally."

St. Bernardine could see the big escort on the shores of the lake, including the fortified carriage. "You have brought someone?" he asked.

"We have," Myles answered.

Realizing he wasn't going to get any more of an answer out of the big knight, St. Bernardine turned for the men behind him and gave them the order to unlock the iron gate. It wasn't a portcullis, but a gate that swung inward, secured by the most enormous lock Myles had ever seen. Someone brought two keys, because it evidently took two to secure it, and when the tumblers were turned and the bolts thrown, St. Bernardine opened the gates and stepped through. He came to within a foot or so of Myles and Douglas, fairly close for a man who was not armed.

He looked at Myles seriously.

"My lord, I see that you do not wish to tell me what your business is, and I respect your authority to do so," he said quietly. "But I must tell you that Abner de Correa is dead. His son is now Baron Adlington and the fourth Lord Bucklow. You must conduct your business with him."

Myles couldn't help it; a wave of shock rolled through him, and he turned to look at Douglas, but they were wearing their helms, so there was no way to see the man's expression. He could only imagine that Douglas was as shocked as he was.

*Dead.*

Abner de Correa was dead.

"When did the father pass away?" Myles asked.

"Almost seven years ago," St. Bernardine said. "It has been many years."

Myles couldn't help it then—he tipped his head, pulling off his helm so he could address the de Correa soldier more clearly. He hated speaking through a lowered faceplate. His long hair was bound up on top of his head as it usually was, but it was all a blond mess as the helm came off.

Myles looked at St. Bernardine in disbelief.

"And no one bothered to send word to Edgar de Wolviston about this?" he said incredulously.

St. Bernardine wasn't quite sure why the knight was growing annoyed. "De Wolviston?" he repeated. "Who is that?"

"A man that your lord had a contract with," Myles said pointedly. "De Wolviston of Cradley Heath. In Worcestershire."

That seemed to bring some recognition. "Ah," St. Bernardine said. "I remember him now. The cartographer."

"That is the man."

"He and Lord Abner were friends for many years."

Myles frowned. "Lord Adlington had a contract with him," he repeated. "A *betrothal* contract. I brought de Wolviston's daughter."

That brought St. Bernardine pause. He looked at the fortified carriage again, realizing that it was transportation for a woman. *A betrothal contract.* Knowing what he did about the de Correa family—and he knew everything because of his position of trust—his memory was jarred by the de Lohr knight's explanation. He seemed to remember something about this, vaguely. Lord Abner had mentioned a future wife years ago. St. Bernardine remembered because it seemed odd coming from a man who had been widowed for many years and never shown any interest in remarrying.

Trepidation swept him.

"I think you'd better speak with Lord Adlington," he said quietly. "The son, I mean."

"I think I'd better, too."

Throwing wide the gates of Adlington Castle, St. Bernardine led the way.

CB

"MY FATHER HAS been dead for seven years. There has been no communication from Edgar de Wolviston in all that time."

The hall of Adlington was like walking into a great hall of old, or a longhouse left from the days when Danes walked these lands. There was an enormous firepit in the center of the hall and a hole in the roof for the smoke to escape. The beams of the hall had been painted, long ago, but faded remnants of yellow and red paint still remained, of flowers and vines and mythical creatures. But the ceiling was the only thing heavenly about the hall, because if one looked at the floor, it was covered with dogs and dog shite, and it reeked to high heaven of human habitation.

The smell was enough to knock a man off his feet.

Myles and Douglas had entered this paradox of a hall only to be greeted by a rather slovenly, middle-aged man with a skin condition that had turned his entire face red. It was early for the evening meal, but the man was eating anyway, with a large spread of food before him. But he stopped when Myles and Douglas entered and, when they revealed that they had come on behalf of Edgar de Wolviston, was quick to answer.

Enos was his name.

Enos de Correa.

Myles didn't like him already.

"We are simply the escort, my lord," he said, watching de Correa stuff his face with something that leaked juice out all over his chin. "Edgar de Wolviston was a vassal of my father, the Earl of Hereford and Worcester. When de Wolviston passed away, his brother sent a missive to my father requesting an escort. There is a little matter of a betrothal, my lord. Surely you are aware."

Enos slowed his eating. He frowned, looking between Myles and Douglas as if puzzled by the message they bore.

"A betrothal?" he said. Then he swallowed the bite in his mouth and sat back in his chair. "De Wolviston... *De Wolviston*... Oh... *that* betrothal."

Myles watched the man's reaction. "Aye, that betrothal," he said. "Then you are aware of it."

Enos eyed Myles before returning to his food. "I am aware," he said. "I am rather surprised you have come, because, as I said, we've not heard from Edgar in many years, but in answer to your statement—I am aware of the betrothal. I remember when my father made it."

He didn't seem at all concerned with something as important as a betrothal, and that annoyed Myles greatly. "Then you know that the terms of the betrothal demanded that the lady be delivered to your father when she came of age," he said. "We have brought her. It is what her father wanted."

Enos was still stuffing something juicy into his mouth. There was liquid dripping all down his face. "He is dead, is he not?"

"He is, my lord."

"And my father is dead. Both men are dead, so there is no more contract."

That was true, in a sense, but not entirely. Myles glanced at Douglas, who simply lifted his eyebrows at what had become a rather unexpected situation.

"Then we will take direction from you, my lord," Myles said. Legally, any contract had to be honored by the heirs of whoever instigated it, so, like it or not, the betrothal contract was to be managed by the glutton stuffing his face in front of them. "Shall we return her home?"

Enos nodded as he swallowed the bite in his mouth and took a big swallow of the wine from the cup at his elbow. "Since both my father and de Wolviston are dead, I can tell you something about that contract," he said as he took another bite. "I remember it well because, at the time, I was quite opposed to it. I assume you thought the marriage was to be between the lady and my father?"

Myles nodded. "That is what we were told, my lord."

Enos shook his head. "Nay," he said. "It was to be between *me* and the lady, but I found my wife several years ago and married her without my father's permission. That means that if my father was alive right now, he would have to marry de Wolviston's daughter. He made the contract, so let him marry the girl."

More chewing and swallowing and flecks of food flying off the man's lips. He ate like a pig. After his initial surprise and confusion was over, Myles realized that he was elated. Actually elated. This meant that Veronica didn't have to marry a man she'd never met. That meant she was free.

*Free!*

Riding the wave of elation and wanting to get the hell out of that hall, Myles felt a distinct pull toward the door.

He wanted to run before de Correa changed his mind.

"Then we will return her home, my lord," he said. "I apologize that we have interrupted your meal."

As he and Douglas turned to leave, Enos stopped him. "Wait," he said, wagging a finger. "Wait just a moment. To be perfectly honest, I'd completely forgotten about this contract, but I seem to remember it is a valuable one. The lady is an heiress, is she not?"

Myles immediately thought of the twenty-four thousand pounds tucked away with Jewish bankers, something Veronica had sworn him to secrecy on. He certainly didn't want to tell this slovenly man the truth, even if it *was* his right. Therefore, he proceeded carefully.

"She is the heiress to Cradley Heath, a manse at the southern end of Worcester," he said. "I do not know if there is any money at the house, but I can tell you that the people of Cradley Heath live very simply. If there is any money, it is not obvious."

That was true for the most part. Since Douglas didn't know differently, he couldn't have known that his brother was withholding information from the man who had a legal right to retain the contract. A wealthy heiress would mean a valuable contract. Even if Enos couldn't marry her, he could sell the contract to the highest bidder. Myles kept hearing Douglas' words floating about in his head.

*He might consider selling the bride if someone offered to buy him out of his contract.*

Was it possible that Douglas might be right?

Did Myles find himself in that very situation at this moment?

"Then the heiress is only an heiress to the house and the land," Enos muttered, breaking into Myles' startled thoughts. "Still, that might bring some money. Is she pretty? If she's pretty enough, I may take her for a mistress."

Myles couldn't tell if he was serious or not, but the mere thought that this beast would lay a hand on Veronica nearly drove him to kill at that very moment. What was it he'd told Veronica if she had been his betrothed? That he would have killed any man who tried to seduce her? Well, she wasn't his betrothed, but he suddenly saw a future he never thought he'd have. With a woman who was more of a woman than any female he'd ever met, more than any of the hundreds of women who had thrown themselves at him, and certainly more of a woman than a thousand Aviaras.

She was a woman among women.

And the bastard in front of him either wanted to sell her or keep her as a mistress. Myles would kill him before he let that happen, so he knew he had to do something. Perhaps he'd only known Veronica a few days, but in those few days, he felt as if he'd lived a lifetime. He'd grown a lifetime. He wanted to keep growing and keep learning from a woman who had made him feel like no one else ever had. Perhaps these feelings were a whim, but it was a whim he was going to act upon. What was it Douglas had said?

*Love is not about timing. It is about opportunity.*

This *was* his opportunity.

"Then let us talk business, my lord," Myles said, approaching the table. "You have no need for her because you already have a wife, but I have spent the past several days with the de Wolviston daughter, and trust me when I tell you that this is not someone you would want to keep as a concubine."

Enos frowned. "Truly?" he said. "Why?"

Myles snorted. "Consider yourself fortunate," he said. "She is pretty, but she has the manners of a pig. And she smells. From what I've seen, any man would be well rid of her."

"Is that so?"

"It is," Myles continued in perhaps the most convincing speech he'd ever given. "You could not even sell her contract because she would shame you so badly that whomever you sold her to would want their money back."

Enos' eyebrows rose in shock. "Is this true?" he said. "God's

Teeth, I suspected as much. No word from de Wolviston in so many years, not even a note to mention his daughter or the upcoming betrothal. And why would he keep silent? Because he knew what he'd done. He knew his daughter was unworthy. Why would my father make a marriage betrothal sight unseen?"

Myles pointed a finger at him. "Because Edgar de Wolviston was smart," he said. "He knew he would have difficulty marrying his daughter off, so he swindled your father."

That brought instant anger from Enos. "He did!" he said. "And my father let him because he was an old friend."

"Exactly," Myles said. "Take my word for it, my lord. The angels have prevented you from making a grave mistake, so take this opportunity to refuse what we are delivering. Let me return the lady home, and you can forget about this… this unpleasant incident."

Enos scratched his head, brow furrowed, still thinking about his father's old friend, who had evidently tried to foist a banshee on him. But then he looked at Myles curiously.

"Why should you tell me this?" he said. "Are you not her escort? Sworn to protect her?"

Myles snorted. "I am the son of the Earl of Hereford and Worcester," he said. "I am only acting as the lady's escort because I was forced into it. I have no stake in this situation. But I do feel some pity for you, my lord. Had she been a suitable bride, you could have sold the contract."

Enos shrugged, but he was still unhappy. "Unfortunate," he said. "Mayhap I should see the lady. If she is pretty, as you've said, then I may be able to get something out of the contract. I'll simply sell it to a foreign lord, someone I do not know so they cannot hate me for it when she turns out to be a shrew."

But Myles shook his head. "That is not necessary," he said.

"My father thought this might be the case with her and has given me instructions to compensate you for the loss of the contract. He was ashamed his vassal would act so dishonorably."

The mention of compensation interested Enos. "What compensation did he have in mind?"

Myles shrugged. "It is negotiable," he said. "But since this could have been a lucrative contract for you should you choose to sell it, would you accept eighty pounds gold and a yearling colt, bred in Brussels, who was purchased at auction for almost two hundred pounds gold? You could sell the horse for far more than the marriage contract."

Enos' eyes widened. "Eighty pounds gold and... and a prize colt?" he repeated. "Are you serious?"

"Absolutely."

"And you swear to this?"

Myles nodded. "If you agree, I can leave the eighty pounds of gold with you this night and have the colt sent to you as soon as I return home," he said, his eyes glittering at the man as he tried to close the deal. "Do we have a bargain?"

"Sold!" Enos shouted, slapping his hand on the table and spraying food everywhere. "Take de Wolviston's daughter and do what you will with her."

"May I have that in writing, my lord?"

Enos nodded, hunting for his majordomo and shouting at the man when he spied him several feet away. "You heard the man," he said. "Put our bargain to vellum immediately, and I will sign it!"

As the majordomo rushed off, Myles was feeling such relief that he could hardly describe it. Jubilation, too. Incredible jubilation. He'd just bought Veronica's betrothal contract and was having difficulty believing it, but he knew one thing—he had to get Veronica away from Adlington because he didn't want to chance that Enos might see her. If he did before their bargain was signed, it might throw the entire thing in jeopardy.

He didn't want to risk it.

"Sit," Enos said, indicating his table. "Sit and feast with me. We will celebrate this night, and you will tell me more about this colt. I suspect I am getting the better end of the bargain."

He was essentially celebrating getting rich off Myles' hard-earned money—and a horse that Myles had spent a good deal of money on. But Myles didn't care in the least. He had what he wanted, and for the first time in his life, it wasn't prestige or money or possessions. He had something that was quickly becoming nearer and dearer to him than even that. But along with de Correa's agreement, he was feeling a good deal of anxiety. He very much wanted to leave Adlington, but he couldn't before their bargain was executed.

There was still a chance that Enos could change his mind.

"You are generous, my lord, but I am afraid we cannot stay," he said. "As soon as your majordomo has drawn up our agreement, we will depart. In the meantime, I will show you the brother of the colt that you are receiving from this bargain. I believe you will be pleased."

Enos' face lit up. "Truly?" he said. "Where is this animal?"

Myles was gesturing to Douglas to head for the door. "He is out with the escort," he said. "Remain here, my lord. I will bring him into the courtyard for you to inspect."

Enos nodded as he went back to his messy food. "I look forward to it."

As he began to shove meat into his mouth, Myles and Douglas headed from the hall. They passed through the relatively small bailey, past St. Bernardine and through the iron gates. They were walking at a clipped pace, set by Myles because he wanted to leave as quickly as possible. The sun was nearly set by the time they reached the bridge that spanned the lake. They could see the escort on the distant shore.

That was when Douglas let loose.

"You did it," he said. "You actually did it."

Myles was looking straight ahead at the escort. Some of the soldiers were lighting torches, which were being placed on the fortified carriage in iron sconces for just that purpose.

"You suggested it," he said. "I was simply taking your advice."

"Aye, I suggested it," Douglas said. "But eighty pounds gold? Myles, that's almost everything we brought with us, and it's Papa's money. And the colt on top of it?"

"Aye, the colt on top of it. And I'll pay Papa back."

"But you're mad for that colt."

Myles stopped abruptly, looking at his brother in the fading sunlight. "There is a woman in that carriage that I suspect is the one woman in this world made for me," he said. "I do not know how I know that, but I feel it. Something is telling me that Veronica is the woman I should risk everything for, and I hope that I am always willing *to* risk everything for her. My gold, my colt, my very life… Douglas, I have spent my life in the shallow pursuit of shallow women. Aviara was the shallowest of all. Veronica has made me realize that. Do you think I would be willing to give everything I owned for Veronica if I had one shred of feeling for Aviara?"

Douglas was listening to him quite seriously. "Nay," he said. "But it is not like you to do something on the spur of the moment. You usually think things through more deeply."

Myles took a deep, long breath, gazing up into the sky that was turning shades of purple and dark blue. "Mayhap that is my problem," he muttered. "I listen to my head in all things and not my heart. This time, I am listening to my heart, and it tells me that this is right."

Douglas nodded faintly, a smile playing on his lips. "I have something terrible to tell you, Myles."

Myles sighed sharply and looked at him. "Do your worst."

Douglas jabbed a finger in the direction of Adlington Castle. "You just paid for a bride with a horse," he said. "How are you going to tell Veronica?"

Myles burst out into soft laughter. "By telling her what I told her before," he said. "I am exchanging a glorious creature for the most glorious creature God has ever created. It worked the last time I told her that."

Douglas was chuckling because Myles was. "I wish you well, brother," he said. "Giving her a pretty speech, hypothetically speaking, is one thing. But putting it into practice is another."

Myles couldn't disagree. "It will be the truth," he said. Then he paused. "But… Douglas, would it be too much to ask you to tell her for me?"

Douglas looked at him, his brow furrowed. "Why would you ask me to?"

Myles shrugged, his gaze moving to the carriage lit with torches. "Because I am not an eloquent man," he said. "I will simply make a mess of things."

"That is not true."

"She insinuated earlier that she regretted knowing me."

Douglas scowled. "That is the most ridiculous thing I have ever heard."

"But that is what she said."

"Myles, there is something you should know about women," Douglas said, his gestures becoming animated. "Sometimes they do not always say what they mean. In Lady Veronica's case, I saw the way she looked at you when you were wounded. I have seen the way she looks at you the entire time we have known her. Trust me when I tell you that she does *not* regret knowing you. I do not know what she said to you, but you take things too literally."

Myles was still looking at the carriage. "Then you think I should simply come out with it and tell her what I've done?"

"I think you should go to her, tell her your shoulder is hurting, and when she looks at it and fusses over you, tell her what you've done," Douglas said. "But tell her *gently*."

Myles was listening intently. "Then I am to create a ruse before I tell her so that she will pity me? And that will lessen her anger when I tell her the truth?"

Douglas snorted, slapping a hand over his face in exasperation. "Come along," he said, grasping his brother by the arm. "Go and tell her now."

"But I told de Correa that I would show him my horse," Myles said. "He is also expecting payment."

"*I* will show him the horse," Douglas said. "When he is ready with the agreement, he'll receive his payment. Meanwhile, you tell Veronica that she will be Lady de Lohr someday, because if you do not tell her now, you may as well wait until your wedding day and surprise her. You *are* going to marry her... aren't you?"

Myles had the strangest look on his face. It was as if the realization of what he'd done suddenly occurred to him. *A marriage.*

"God's Bones," he murmured. "I have a bride."

Douglas snorted, leading him off the bridge and toward the carriage. "You certainly do," he said. "Congratulations, old man. I like this one much better than the one you thought you wanted. Veronica will be a fine match for you, Myles. I'm very happy for you."

"Providing she agrees."

They had come to the door of the carriage. Douglas lifted his hand to knock, but paused as he looked at his brother.

"She'll agree," he said softly. "Now... *tell* her."

With that, he rapped loudly on the door. A soft voice responded.

"Who comes?"

Douglas silently gestured to Myles' shoulder and made a sad face, as if he were in pain. Myles took the hint.

"'Tis Myles, my lady," he answered loudly. "My... my shoulder is troubling me. I was hoping you might be able to help."

The door swung open immediately and Veronica stood there, looking at Myles with concern. "Come in," she said, reaching down to pull him inside as if he actually needed help. "Did you speak with de Correa?"

Myles let her pull him up into the carriage. "Aye, I spoke with him."

"What happened?"

"Help me with my shoulder and I will tell you about it."

With that, he shut the door behind him, leaving Douglas to show Enos the example of the colt he would soon be receiving and delivering the eighty pounds that Myles had in his saddlebags. Because it was an escort mission and unknown expenses had a tendency to pop up, Christopher had sent his sons with enough money to cover any unexpected expenses, and this was certainly one of them.

A most unexpected expense.

Douglas hoped Christopher de Lohr would understand.

# CHAPTER TWELVE

*Aldsworth Castle*
*Gloucestershire*

BERTRAND HAD WALKED into a horror.

Summoned by a panicked servant, he'd run all the way from his solar to the gatehouse of Aldsworth, which was the size of most keeps. It was an enormous structure that had a tunnel running through it, from one end to the other, with gates on both ends. The problem with the gatehouse, in particular, was that the tunnel was sloping. Most men couldn't ride through it or they'd hit their heads. And that was evidently what happened here.

Oliver, his daughter's husband, had tried to ride through it on a skittish stallion.

It hadn't ended well.

Aviara was standing at the entrance to the tunnel, hands over her mouth and eyes wide with shock. By the time Bertrand reached her, others were standing around in shock, gazing down at the body of Oliver de Grey. Bertrand, too, suffered his share of momentary shock, but he hissed at a gatehouse guard to find a blanket to cover the man up. Meanwhile, he knelt beside the still-warm body to feel for a pulse.

There was none.

The blanket came from the guardhouse, kicking up a cloud of dust as the soldiers laid it over the body. Bertrand may not have liked Oliver, but he wanted the man to have some dignity. Even in death. And with that, he turned to his horror-struck daughter and grabbed her by the arm.

"*What* happened?" he said.

Tears were swimming in Aviara's eyes. "He said he was leaving," she half wept. "He said... terrible things, Papa. We quarreled. He said he was leaving, but the horse slipped and reared up, smashing him into the top of the tunnel."

She was gesturing to the ceiling of the tunnel, now with a big, bloodied mark on it where Oliver's helmless head had struck it. His hair was stuck to the stone. In light of the explanation, Bertrand motioned to the guards to carry Oliver away, but he didn't release his grip on his daughter. He began to drag her away, through the nearest door he could find, which happened to be for the family apartments. Once inside, he slammed the door behind him and faced her in the dim light.

"Tell me everything," he demanded. "You said you quarreled. What about this time?"

*This time.*

That had been the story of the marriage between Aviara and Oliver. Since the day they wed, they'd done nothing but quarrel. Aviara broke down in tears.

"It was nothing new," she said, sniffling. "The same thing we always quarrel about. He is not happy; I am not happy. He knows I am longing for Myles, and he is furious about it. He was leaving to speak to a priest and have the marriage annulled."

Oliver's eyes widened. "Annulled?" he repeated in shock. "How could he do that?"

"Adultery," she whispered. "He was going to tell the courts that I had committed adultery with Myles."

Bertrand frowned. "But that is not true."

"He was going to tell them the babe I carry is Myles' child."

It was shocking at the very least. Unfortunately for Aviara, the courts would rule against her because she had, since the day of her marriage to Oliver, spoken of Myles and how the marriage to Oliver was a mistake. She let Oliver know, clearly, that he had failed as a husband and a lover, and she'd told him many times that she wished they had never married.

And Bertrand had stood by and let her.

"My God," he breathed, finally letting her go and hanging his head. "Avi... *is* it Myles' child?"

Aviara's tears grew more hysterical. "Of course not," she said. "How could it be? I've not seen the man in months!"

Bertrand sighed heavily. "You could have met him without my knowledge," he said. Then he eyed her. "It would not be the first time."

Aviara sucked in her breath sharply, aghast at her father's insinuation. "Papa, that is a terrible thing to say!"

Bertrand shrugged. "You did not go to the marital bed a virgin," he said. "Oliver was greatly disappointed over that."

"Oliver was a terrible lover."

"He felt as if you had tricked him."

"My body is mine to give. It was a waste to give it to Oliver de Grey!"

"That is not the point," Bertrand said. "God's Bones... We have a problem, lass."

Aviara was still angry over the subject matter, upset over

having seen a man killed in front of her. She wiped her nose with her kerchief. "There *is* no problem," she said, sniffing. "Oliver is dead, and good riddance."

Bertrand hissed at her. "Still your tongue," he said. "You will not curse the dead. It will bring bad fortune. The problem I speak of is your being pregnant. No man wants a widow with a child, and especially not a widow who does not bring a fortune with her. Mayhap you tricked Oliver into marrying a woman who'd known men before him, but Oliver was not forthcoming with the fact that he was a virtual pauper. You may have the Ilchester title, but not the fortune, because there isn't one."

Aviara frowned. "So there is no fortune," she said. "What does that matter? I have Aldsworth. That will be attractive to any new husband as the Countess of Ilchester, whether or not I am a widow with a child."

Bertrand shrugged. "Aldsworth does not have the fortune it used to," he said. "We were hoping that Oliver would provide that, but alas, he did not."

"Nay, he did not."

"And you harassed him for it."

Aviara averted her gaze. "He vexed me," she said. "We married for the wrong reasons. He did it because he wanted a pretty wife. I did it to teach Myles a lesson."

"What about?"

"To make him jealous, of course."

Bertrand shook his head at his daughter, who'd used marriage to punish a man she was in love with. She'd been punishing Myles since nearly the day they met because he wasn't attentive enough or affectionate enough. Nothing was ever to Aviara's liking. He'd known that from the start, but as always, he simply let her do as she pleased. He didn't intervene.

But that was going to stop now.

"Do you think he was sufficiently jealous?" he asked.

Aviara looked at him. "Possibly," she said. "I do not know, as I have not spoken to him since the last time I saw him at Tidworth."

Bertrand stared at her for a moment in disgust before, slowly, his expression began to change. After a few moments, he looked as if he'd been hit with an epiphany.

"The man was mad for you, Avi," he said. "Surely he has not overcome his adoration of you in so short a time. If you were to go to him and beg his forgiveness for not marrying him instead of Oliver, he would be forgiving. He *must* be forgiving."

Aviara's tears began to dry up. "Of course," she said as if she, too, had her father's vision. "The man was mad for me and I was mad for him. Oh, *why* did I not marry him first? I could have convinced him to do it. The night of the feast at Tidworth, I told him that I wanted him to court me. He knew how I felt about him."

Bertrand could see a way to the future now that he hadn't seen before. "Then that is what we will do," he said. "I will send Oliver back to his parents, and you and I will go to Lioncross Abbey immediately. I wish to speak with Christopher, and you... you can speak with Myles. Seduce him if you have to. But you will not be able to find a more suitable husband than Myles de Lohr, so you *must* make him forgive you. Is that clear?"

"Aye," she said, but there was doubt in her expression. "But... should we not accompany Oliver back to Ilchester, to his parents? You simply want to send him home alone? Although I have no love for the man, that seems cruel, even to me."

Bertrand waved her off. "We must get to de Lohr before

208

Oliver's parents inform him of the state of your marriage," he said, watching her frown. "Do you think Oliver had not already told his parents what a mistake the marriage was? I know he sent missives home to his mother, so surely he has told her what kind of wife you have been. Do you want that information to get back to Hereford? Worse still, to Myles?"

Solemnly, Aviara shook her head. "But I would not be a terrible wife to Myles," she said. "It would be completely different with him."

Bertrand grunted. "Mayhap," he said. "But in any case, we must get to Myles and his father before Oliver's mother does. I must tell the story first, from our perspective. If she manages to convince Christopher that you are a pariah, then your chances for a good marriage are gone. I do not think you want that."

Again, Aviara shook her head. She knew her father was only looking out for her and the child she carried. It was true that her marriage to Oliver had been a battle from the start, in large part due to the fact that she couldn't forget about Myles. She knew marriage was permanent, in theory, but marrying Oliver to punish Myles and then not being able to walk away from said marriage had been a rude awakening for her. So was the realization that she was carrying the child of a man she didn't even like.

Her father was right.

She had to get to Myles before the truth of her marriage to Oliver did.

# CHAPTER THIRTEEN

"**Y**OUR SHOULDER *IS* a little red," Veronica said, holding up a taper so she could get a good look at the wound she had just exposed to the air. Then she put gentle fingers on the flesh around it. "It does not feel hot. Do you feel as if you have a fever?"

Myles was watching her closely in the dim light of the carriage. The sun had set upon Adlington Castle and the surrounding area, and a bank of tallow candles lit the inside of the fortified carriage as Veronica inspected his arrow wound.

He only had eyes for Veronica.

"No fever," he said after a moment. "The wound is simply sore and the bandages were uncomfortable. Mayhap it simply needs to be rewrapped."

Veronica was more than willing to do that. As he sat there on the bench, stripped to the waist and with a big dog head on his lap, Veronica went about finding more bandages. She'd put the boiled linen aside when Westley didn't use it, so she bent over to pull it out of a cabinet in the corner of the carriage.

"What did de Correa say?" she said as she organized the wrappings. "Did you see him? What is he like?"

*Tell her gently.*

That was what Douglas had advised, so Myles struggled to figure out what, exactly, that meant. He had to tell her the truth, and he wasn't sure how he could gently tell her such a thing. There was the truth, and that was that. She needed to know, especially if she was asking him a direct question.

Still, he tried to proceed carefully.

"It is an interesting story, in truth," he said as she came over to him and poured a little of the remaining ale on the boiled linen before putting it against his wound. "It seems that Abner de Correa had meant the betrothal to be between you and his son, Enos. It wasn't meant for Abner himself."

Veronica paused in her duties, looking at him with surprise. "His *son?*" she said. "My father never said anything about a son."

"It is possible your father did not know Abner's intentions," Myles said. "But I was informed that the original purpose was for you to marry his son."

Veronica's surprised gaze rested on him a moment before she slowly continued her duties. "His son," she repeated as if forcing herself to become accustomed to the idea. "Did you meet this son?"

"I did," Myles said, flinching a little when the ale stung the wound. "The story, my lady, is this—Abner is dead. He died seven years ago. His son, Enos, is now in command of Adlington Castle, and Enos married a few years ago against his father's wishes. He already has a wife. But, legally, he owns the betrothal contract. He can do with it as he pleases."

Veronica stopped wrapping. She looked at Myles with such trepidation that he could literally feel her fear. She was struggling very hard not to appear terrified but couldn't quite manage it.

"My God," she breathed, taking a step back from him, bandages in hand. "What does that mean? What is he going to do?"

"Sell it."

She gasped, sucking in a ragged breath, before sitting heavily on the bench behind her. "He is?" she asked, her voice quivering. "Did he tell you that?"

"Aye."

She hung her head and the tears began. Myles realized he hadn't been gentle enough, and he came off the bench, going to his knee in front of Veronica and wanting desperately to comfort her. He hadn't meant to make her cry.

"Veronica, listen to me," he said, his voice soft but firm. "Do you truly think I would allow anything unpleasant to happen to you? Do you honestly believe I would simply leave you off here and let a man like Enos de Correa sell you to the highest bidder?"

Veronica was trying hard not to cry, but she couldn't manage it. "I… I do not know," she said. "You are only my escort, Myles. What could you possibly do to prevent it?"

"Buy your betrothal."

That brought everything to a halt. Breath, movement, and time. Time itself seemed to stop. Veronica's head shot up, and she paused mid-sob as her wide eyes fixed on him. For a moment, she simply stared at him, absorbing what he'd said.

She could hardly believe it.

"Y-you?" she finally said. "*You* bought it?"

"I did."

Her face began to crumple. "So *you* can sell it?"

He couldn't help it; he broke out into a grin, shaking his

head as he did so. "Sweetheart, I bought it for me," he said. "I bought it because a woman—*you*—is the most glorious creature God has created. You are an angel of wit and charm and beauty. I exchanged my new colt for a wife because I exchanged one glorious creature for another."

Veronica heard his words, words he'd spoken the night he became drunk on the hard cider. They were words that, at the time, she'd thought were quite clever, but hearing him speak them now, she wasn't sure what she thought. She was still wallowing in a world of shock.

Utter and complete shock.

"You bought the contract with a horse?" she finally said.

Myles nodded. "The most beautiful animal you have ever laid eyes on," he said. "I offered it for the most beautiful woman I've ever laid eyes on. That and eighty pounds. He accepted."

Her wide eyes widened further. "Eighty pounds?

"Gold."

"Gold?" she repeated, stunned. "Myles… that is an incredible sum."

"I know."

"But *why*?"

He wasn't sure if she was pleased or not, which shook his confidence a little. Now that she was calm, he went back to the bench and sat down opposite her, studying her in the faint light. It seemed that there were a few things that needed to be said, and he summoned up the courage to say them.

"Because you are worth all of that and more," he said quietly. "Veronica, I am fully aware that you may not be feeling what I'm feeling, but ever since I met you, there is something about you that I have found both fascinating and endearing. We have already established that I am not a man of charm or flattery. I fully admit that I know nothing about women, so I have nothing to lose by telling you this. I have spent my life being pursued by highborn, shallow women who merely wanted a handsome husband. I am aware of my appearance. I've had married women, unmarried women, nobles, and royalty alike pursue me because they wanted something handsome to play with. That is all I ever meant to them. You are the only woman I've ever met who treated me as if I was something more. You see the man, not the appearance. I've known that from the start."

Veronica's tears were gone as she listened to what was, inarguably, a sad speech. It must have been difficult for Myles to say such things about himself, but as she'd seen from the beginning, he was a man of honesty. Brutal, straightforward honesty.

Perhaps it was time to give her some of her own.

"That is because you *are* more," she said softly. "You have told me that women are a mystery to you and that you cannot communicate with them, but that is not true. You have communicated with me with astounding clarity since the moment we met. And I've found you to be kind and under-standing. Does that surprise you?"

He smiled faintly. "It does, a little," he said. "You are the only woman who has ever told me that, but it is something I have felt between us from the start. You understand me. You do not treat me like an object or a prize. That is why I bought your betrothal contract—because you told me once that I would find a worthy woman someday. Do you recall? Well, I have found her. I have found *you*."

Veronica's bright blue eyes were blazing at him. "Oh... Myles," she breathed. "That is the sweetest thing anyone has ever said to me."

It was perhaps the sweetest thing Myles was capable of saying, and he was both uncomfortable with it and pleased with himself. He only knew that he had opened himself up in a way he'd never done before.

Nervously, he averted his gaze.

"Of course, I understand you may not feel the same way, as I've said," he said. "If that is the case and you do not wish to marry me, then I will not force you. I will return you to Cradley Heath and you may live out the rest of your life there, free and happy in the knowledge that I hold your betrothal contract and will never sell it. You will never be forced to marry anyone you do not wish to marry. But I will also chase Gregor away from Cradley so you may live in peace. If this is what you wish, I will do it. All you need do is simply tell me, and that will be the end of it."

He was looking at his feet at that point, waiting for the words coming from her lips that would change his life forever. He realized that if she did not want to marry him, he would be extremely disappointed. Sad, even. He held his breath as the seconds ticked away. The more time passed and the more she didn't say anything, the more his heart sank.

Then she moved.

Myles could see her feet in front of him, and by the time he looked up, she had reached out to cup his face with both hands. He found himself gazing up into that astonishing face and those glowing eyes, feeling more vulnerable than he'd ever felt in his life. As he watched, she leaned over and kissed him gently on the forehead.

"While I am not thrilled you have paid for me with a horse, I understand why you've done it," she said, a smile tugging up the corner of her mouth. "That horse had better be more magnificent than Pegasus, Myles. Otherwise, people might point at your wife and laugh when they find out you traded an old nag for her. Is that what you want? To shame me so?"

He was coming to realize that she was agreeable. *Agreeable!* He shook his head, an expression of utter joy washing over his features.

"I swear to you that the horse is the most splendid creature in the world," he said. "But it is not more splendid than you. And I will part with him willingly if it means you will be by my side, for always. Will you?"

Veronica's smile broke through as she looked down at the man. "I will," she said. "But what about Aviara? You seemed very upset about losing her only a few days ago. Can you truly forget her so quickly?"

Myles sighed so heavily that it was as if his entire body deflated. "This is going to sound banal, but I have come to realize she never really meant much to me," he said. "You have made me realize that, even in the short time I have known you. My father said it best... Aviara was a prize. She was a victory. She was never anything to me beyond that. I understand that because she could not have brought me the joy I am feeling right now. Only you, Veronica. I swear... only you."

Veronica's smile broadened, and she lowered her head, gently kissing his lips as Myles' head swam. He actually felt faint. Her touch was tender and warm, unlike anything he'd ever known, and his heart was thumping madly against his ribs. *Is this what it means to feel adoration?* he thought.

*Is this what love feels like?*

He reached for her, pulling her down to him as he kissed her deeply. Veronica collapsed against him, clutching him against her just as he was clutching her against him. He'd had his tunic off, and her hands were against his warm flesh, smooth and soft, and it was the most intimate thing she'd ever experienced. Everything about the man was intimate and sensual, heated and raw, and when his mouth left hers and began suckling down her neck, she laid her head back to enjoy the experience. She could hardly believe it was real. But his right shoulder was against her cheek, and she turned her head slightly, sinking her teeth into the skin of his shoulder.

That brought a growl from Myles.

Suddenly, his mouth was on hers again and he was laying her back on the bench, ravaging her with his mouth as she gasped for breath beneath him. His arms were around her, so his hands never wandered. Veronica had never felt warmer or safer or more thrilled in her entire life, with a kiss that was sucking all of the air out of her. But she hardly cared. Myles could kiss her like this for eternity and she wouldn't care. It was as if all of the hopes she'd ever had about a husband had come to fruition in this awkward, beautiful soul.

She had the man of her dreams, and she wasn't going to let him go.

"Am I to take it that you agree to everything, then?" he asked huskily as he paused in his onslaught.

Before she could answer, Mud climbed off the other bench and began licking Myles' face, bringing peals of laughter from Veronica. Myles took it stoically, closing one eye as the dog licked his eyebrow.

"That means we both agree," she said, finally pushing the dog away. "If Mud approves, then so do I."

Myles had to wipe the saliva from his eye before he opened it. "I am grateful," he said, focusing on her. "Truly, my lady... I am more grateful than you'll ever know. I feel as if I am living a dream. A most wonderful dream."

Reaching up, Veronica stroked his stubbled face. "It is our dream together, I suppose," she said. "I never thought… Myles, how are your parents going to react to this? You are the son of an earl, and you probably have titles yourself that I do not know about. I am the daughter of a simple cartographer. I am not nearly of your station."

Myles snorted softly. "You are perfect," he said. "You could come to me with only the clothes on your back and you would still be perfect."

She lifted a well-shaped brow. "I do have twenty-four thousand pounds to bring to the marriage," she said. "Mayhap that will make me more attractive to your parents."

He gazed down at her, tucking a stray piece of hair behind her ear in a gentle gesture. "My parents will love you no matter what you bring," he said. "As for titles, I am a middle son. I will not inherit. But my father has told me that he will give me some property he acquired years ago. Monnington Castle is on the border of his property with Wales, and it comes with the lordship of Doré. I have spent a good deal of time there, as garrison commander, so my father told me that he will simply give it to me at some point. Mayhap as a wedding gift."

She smiled at him, her hand still on his face. "And this pleases you, Middle Son?"

"It does. I have earned it."

"Then I am happy for you, Middie."

He eyed her, chuckling, as he sat up and pulled her with him. He still had his arms around her because he couldn't seem to release her. He didn't *want* to release her. All he could do was gaze at her as if looking into a corner of heaven he never knew to exist.

And she belonged to him.

"As much as I would like to stay like this all night, I have duties to attend to," he told her. "I must get de Correa's agreement to sell me your betrothal, so I will remain here while I send you with West over to the village for the night. I do not want you anywhere near this place in case de Correa decides he wants to take a look at what he has given up. I do not want to chance his going back on his bargain."

The warm expression on Veronica's face faded. "Do you think he might?"

Myles released her. "I do not know," he said. "But I do not wish to chance it. Will you replace the bandage on my shoulder so I may dress?"

Veronica jumped up and went to gather up the bandages that had fallen away when she and Myles became amorous. As he sat still, she carefully bandaged up his shoulder wound, and he thanked her by kissing both of her hands and finally her lips. She tasted so good that he swooped in for more of a kiss, and they ended up in a tight embrace again. But he was forced to release her because he truly did have things to attend to, and, more than anything, he wanted her away from Adlington.

There would be more time for kisses later.

After pulling his padded tunic over his head, followed by his mail coat and de Lohr tunic, he strapped on the smaller pieces he usually wore while Veronica watched him closely. She'd never been around a knight before, so it was all new to her, and she very much wanted to learn. She asked a few questions about certain articles of clothing, about his sword, and he was happy to tell her. As he'd seen from the beginning, she was interested in the man more than his appearance.

It was an acceptance he knew he could grow to love.

As he headed for the carriage door, he paused.

"Before I go, I want to tell you something," he said. "My parents always thought there was a hardness about me. I have a warm and loving family, but somehow, I never fit in to that. My mother told me once that she thought I kept my heart hidden because it was more vulnerable than the others. It has occurred to me that you may have just found a path to it, my lady."

Veronica smiled at his very sweet sentiment, putting her hand against her heart in response. "I will guard it with my life," she swore softly. "My heart is not so difficult to find. I am certain you are very close to finding it already."

Myles liked the sound of that. In fact, he liked the sound of everything. Winking at her, he left the carriage, shutting the door behind him and heading off to find Douglas.

But he would swear, until the day he died, that he was walking on clouds.

# CHAPTER FOURTEEN

*Lioncross Abbey*

"A ND THAT IS why we've come, my lord. We have made a terrible mistake."

Christopher had just listened to what was more than likely the most pathetic swill he'd ever heard come out of one man's mouth. And he knew the man very well—Bertrand de Serreaux. A man he'd always considered to be stable and responsible, but after what he'd just heard, he had his doubts about the man's sanity in general.

He was having trouble swallowing it.

"Forgive me, Bertrand," he said. "I will have you repeat what you just told me so I may understand it more clearly."

Bertrand was more than willing to do so. Having just arrived at Lioncross Abbey, the end of a seemingly hurried journey from Aldsworth Castle, he had been ushered into Christopher's lush solar like a long-lost friend. Together, they had shared some of the earl's fine wine all the way from Madrid and discussed mundane things until Bertrand confessed the reason for their visit—he'd brought Aviara with him, and now, Christopher knew why.

But he still couldn't believe it.

Bertrand was more than happy to repeat himself.

"As you know, my daughter married your cousin, Oliver de Grey," he said patiently. "I sent you an announcement of their nuptials."

Christopher was sitting at his table, a look of confusion on his face that threatened to morph into one of disbelief. "We received it," he said. "Go on."

Bertrand did. "I will not pretend to be oblivious to the situation between my daughter and your son, Myles," he said. "I will address that immediately, my lord. My daughter and Myles shared an affectionate relationship for the past two years, but she was also much pursued by Oliver. You know this."

"I do."

"And it is established that my daughter ultimately chose Oliver," Bertrand continued. "I have wanted to visit you since the decision was made to ensure there are no hard feelings between you and me. But women are fickle creatures. My daughter is, and her mother was as well. Myles was, in no way, deficient. It seems that Oliver simply charmed his way into my daughter's heart. That was all there was to the situation, I assure you."

"Tell me about Oliver."

Bertrand cleared his throat softly. "That is where the story turns tragic," he said. "Only a short time ago, Oliver was riding a new steed that I gifted to him on the occasion of his marriage to my daughter, and the horse threw him. Killed him instantly. But I will be truthful when I say that I was very disappointed with Oliver after he married my daughter. It seemed that when the chase was over, he no longer cared that he had won. He would go off and leave her for two, three nights in a row. What new husband would do that to his wife?"

Christopher sighed faintly as he once again heard the story Bertrand had come to tell him. It wasn't any more believable the second time around.

"I would not know," he said. "But do Oliver's parents know of his death?"

Bertrand nodded. "Of course," he said. "I sent Oliver home with an escort."

"But you did inform them first, did you not?"

"As I said, I sent Oliver home with an escort."

That drew a reaction from Christopher. "You did not send word immediately so they knew he had been killed?" he said. "You simply sent the body home and let that be the announcement?"

Bertrand could see that Christopher was outraged by that, but rather than admit he might have not handled the situation appropriately, and why, he simply grew annoyed.

"My sending him home to announce his death does not change the fact that he was, in fact, dead," he said. "My lord, Oliver had turned into a… a monster after the marriage. He was arrogant and unkind. He demanded I give him money to spend. The horse I gifted him with was a delicate animal, quite expensive, and he was very cruel to it. When it threw him, I do believe he was being punished for his offenses against the horse, against my daughter… against all of us."

Christopher scowled. "Are you saying he deserved his death?"

That brought Bertrand's tale of woe to a halt. "Nay, not at all," he said quickly. "I am simply saying that he was not innocent. He contributed to it. And that is why my daughter and I have come, my lord. We have come to beg Myles' forgiveness."

Christopher hadn't heard that part yet. He'd only heard the part about Oliver's death. Sending the body back to his family without sending word ahead and coming to Lioncross to beg for Myles' forgiveness was new information.

But Christopher was on his guard.

He kept falling back on what Dustin said, how Bertrand was pliable to his daughter's whims. Christopher had always believed Bertrand to be a reasonable man, but the behavior he was exhibiting at the moment wasn't reasonable. It was suspicious. Was Bertrand only repeating what his daughter had told him, or was this something he'd experienced, and decided for, himself? Moreover, *why* did he feel the need to apologize to Myles?

Something didn't feel right.

"Bertrand, you and your daughter are always welcome at Lioncross, but apologizing to Myles is unnecessary," he said. "He knows that Lady Aviara has married Oliver. He has accepted that. There is no need for apologies."

"But there are," Bertrand said, rather strongly. "Aviara feels that she has offended Myles because of her marriage to Oliver, and it is important to her to mend the relationship. She is quite fond of him, you know. She wants to ensure that things are well between them once again, as do I."

There it was. It occurred to Christopher why Bertrand and Aviara had come. She'd just lost her husband and now she was looking for another. Oliver and Myles had been in competition for her affections, so with one gone, she was falling back on the other. She was hoping she had a de Lohr son waiting for her, and that was why they'd come to Lioncross.

That realization infuriated Christopher.

"You did not have to come all the way to Lioncross," he said, moving to pour himself more wine, but he made no move to pour any for Bertrand. "You could have simply sent a missive."

"It was barely a two-day journey," Bertrand said. "Aviara wanted to apologize in person."

"Then you have wasted your time," Christopher said, looking at the man. "Myles is not here, and I do not know when he will return."

Bertrand's expression was filled with both disappointment and surprise. "I am sorry to hear that," he said. "Where has he gone?"

"On business for me," Christopher said vaguely. "He could be away for weeks, and certainly, you do not want to stay here that long. You would do better to return home and send him a missive."

It was clear that Bertrand was disheartened by the news. "Aviara will be disappointed," he said. "She was so looking forward to seeing him."

Christopher looked at the man. "Bertrand, it seems to me that you do not realize that your visit here is completely transparent," he said. "Do you really expect me to believe that your daughter, who is supposed to be a grieving widow, is so focused on Myles that you've crossed Gloucestershire so she could apologize to him for not marrying him? You must think I'm as stupid as a goat."

Bertrand sat up in his chair, greatly concerned. "My lord?"

Christopher had had enough of the man's obtuse dealings. "The only thing you regret is that your daughter is without a husband," he said. "I will never believe that Oliver suddenly became arrogant and difficult to live with. I think your daughter realized she'd married the man out of spite, simply to punish Myles, and either you arranged for Oliver to break his neck on the back of an unruly horse or you saw an opportunity to right a wrong when he accidentally killed himself. Either way, your callous treatment of his death is appalling. I thought you were a better man than that."

Bertrand was out of his chair. "My lord, if I have offended you, then I apologize," he said sincerely. "I did not mean to treat Oliver's death coldheartedly, but—"

"Spare me your excuses," Christopher said, cutting him off. "There is no need to apologize to Myles. There is no point, and I'll not have your daughter teasing and flirting with him again, pulling him back into her web of lies and deceit. She's no good for him, Bertrand. Let her find a husband elsewhere, because it will not be Myles."

Bertrand's mouth popped open in outrage, but he kept his cool. "Clearly, I have offended you somehow," he said. "It seems that you think we are all pitiless when it comes to Oliver's passing, but I assure you that is not the case. Aviara is heartbroken over it. She only sought to mend her relationship with Myles to ease her conscience."

Christopher didn't believe him for a moment. "I realize you only have one child, Bertrand," he said. "But your daughter is not suitable for Myles. You have come a long way for nothing. Please return home on the morrow, and I will forget about this conversation in time, but make no move to contact Myles again. If you do, and I find out about it, you will not like my response."

Bertrand stared at him for a moment. "I am not sure how to respond and not make you angry," he said. "I did not come to Lioncross to annoy you, my lord."

Christopher nodded. "I know," he said. "But you came here hoping I would be oblivious to your plans. You have come for a husband for your daughter, and there is nothing you can say to convince me otherwise. Therefore, you will leave on the morrow and we will keep peace between us. You will find your daughter a husband elsewhere. Do you understand?"

Bertrand nodded, once. "As you say, my lord."

"Do not forget it."

"I will not, my lord."

"Good," Christopher said. "Now, you may go. We will feast tonight, and you and your daughter will be our honored guests. I am happy to show hospitality to an ally."

Bertrand nodded, pretending to be pleased with the offer of a feast, but Christopher knew the man was shaken. He could see it in his face. Bertrand quit the solar without another word, leaving Christopher shaking his head at such a bold scheme. He thanked God that Myles wasn't there, because if he was, Christopher might have real trouble on his hands. He had no idea if Myles had truly put the marriage of Aviara and Oliver behind him, but he hoped so. He didn't need Aviara and Bertrand stirring up problems again.

"Was that Bertrand de Serreaux I saw leaving, Papa?"

Christopher looked up from his table to see his son, Roi, enter the solar. Richard de Lohr, who had gone by the nick-name "Roi" for most of his life, was his third-born son and had been at Lioncross since yesterday, when he brought a report from Pembridge Castle on some recent Welsh activity on the border. He was only staying for a day or two before heading back to the big outpost situated in the wilds of the Welsh marches.

Roi had the distinction of being the only brother in the

family who didn't possess the de Lohr blond hair. With his crown of gorgeous red hair, Roi was a handsome lad with his father's blue eyes and his mother's temperament. He was also the only de Lohr brother who was an itinerant justice. He handled all of the legal matters for his father and was considered a rather brilliant legal mind.

Christopher waved him in.

"Shut the door," he said.

Roi did as he was told, entering the solar and shutting the door behind him. He looked at his father curiously.

"Is something amiss?" he asked.

Christopher sat down wearily. "You did, in fact, see Bertrand de Serreaux," he said. "He came earlier with his daughter, who was taken away by your mother. You haven't seen her wandering around, have you?"

Roi shook his head. "Nay," he said. "I do not know if I would recognize the daughter on sight, to be truthful. I've not seen her in years. Why?"

"Then you do not know the daughter?"

"Only by reputation," he said. "Only what Myles and Douglas and Peter have told me. Why, Papa? What's it all about?"

Christopher sighed heavily. "You know that Myles has had an eye for Aviara de Serreaux," he said. "She's been flirting outrageously with him for two years."

Roi nodded. "I've heard about it," he said. "Peter doesn't think much of her."

"Nor do I," Christopher admitted. "The woman pitted your brother against Ollie, trying to make him jealous, and Myles tolerated it. But a few months ago, Myles was on a mission with Peter, and Lady Aviara nearly interfered with it. Peter told the woman what he thought of her, and to punish Myles for Peter's interference, the woman married Ollie."

Roi gave his father a look of great regret. "I heard," he said. "Sherry told me that you sent Myles off on an escort mission to get his mind off the marriage."

Christopher averted his gaze. "I had to," he said. "The man was nearly insane with the news. He was angry, offended, and casting blame where it did not belong. I did something to him I should not have."

"What?"

"I struck him in anger."

Roi tried not to look too shocked. "God's Bones, why?"

"It does not matter," Christopher said, unwilling to divulge the truth. "Suffice it to say that he said something unkind, unkind enough that I reacted strongly. He believes Lady Aviara has been driven away from him, but that is not the case. It was best to get him away from Lioncross and focus on something else for a while."

Roi still wasn't over the fact that his father had struck Myles for something he said. It must have been horrible if it had riled their beloved father enough for him to lash out, and, given the situation, he suspected it might have had something to do with Peter. If Myles was angry at Peter, there was no telling what was said. However, he didn't press his father. He could see that Christopher felt bad enough about it.

"So he's gone," he said. "But why is Lady Aviara here at Lioncross if she is married to Ollie?"

Christopher wagged a finger in the general direction of the door, the last place he saw Bertrand. "Because Ollie was killed in an accident," he said. "A horse threw him. De Serreaux and his daughter have trekked across Gloucestershire to apologize to Myles for creating any hard feelings with her choice of husband.

What they've really done is come to Lioncross to trap Myles into a marriage. The lady has lost one husband, and now she wants another."

Roi looked at his father in shock. "*That* is why he's here?"

"He all but admitted it to me."

"What will you do?"

Christopher sat back in his chair, thinking. "What I do not want is for Myles to return while de Serreaux and his daughter are still here," he said. "I sent him on an escort mission from Worcester to Manchester. If he departed quickly, then he should already have completed his mission and will be heading for home. There is a chance they might run into each other."

Roi nodded. "Possibly," he said. "Should we send Myles word?"

Christopher shrugged. "That is what I have been thinking," he said. "While I do not want him to race back here in order to see Lady Aviara, I want him to know what has happened so he is prepared. He needs to know that Ollie is dead and that Lady Aviara is looking to trap him into marriage."

"Do you want me to go after him?"

"Do you have the time?"

Roi scratched his head thoughtfully. "A little," he said. "I told my men that I would be gone a few days, and there is nothing pressing on the marches that requires my attention at the moment."

"Good," Christopher said. "Then I would like you to find him and tell him what has happened. Roi, I know you have not been around much to know about the situation between Myles and Aviara, but suffice it to say that she is very bad for your brother. She flirts with him, teases him, and toys with his emotions. Then she runs off and flirts with someone else just to make him jealous, so believe me when I tell you that she is not good for him. I was hoping this escort mission might help clear his head a little and help him forget about the lady."

Roi knew his father didn't exaggerate, so he took him at his word when it came to Aviara. "Mayhap it would be best if he didn't return to Lioncross for a while," he said. "I can take him back with me to Pembridge."

"Or he can go to Monnington," Christopher said. "In fact, I have always intended to give him the Doré lordship and the castle along with it, so mayhap I will grant it to him now."

"You think a lordship will compensate him for losing a woman?"

"It is as good a start as any."

Roi frowned, though it was good-natured. "He'll make an even more attractive marital prospect, you know," he said. "Myles got all of your good looks. Now he gets property, too?"

Christopher grinned. "And you got all of my brains," he said. "What are you complaining about, Lord Pembridge? You have your own property."

Roi started to laugh. "I was only complaining that Myles got all of the beauty in the family," he said, even though all of the de Lohr boys were considered quite handsome. "Now you are giving him property, too. He'll be unbearable to live with."

Christopher snorted. "Do your best," he said. He quickly sobered. "Find him, Roi. If he's nearly home, tell him to stay away for a while. Take him to Pembridge if you must, and tell him I want him there. But keep him away until de Serreaux and his daughter return to their own home."

Roi nodded. Taking his leave, he quit the solar, heading out to gather his things and go in search of his brother. He happened to see Alexander as he was heading out, and, after telling him the story Christopher had relayed, Alexander decided to go with him. The fear was that Roi alone might not be able to handle Myles if he knew Aviara was at Lioncross.

Alexander had much the same opinion of the woman that Christopher had.

But Aviara didn't.

Unhappy that Lord Hereford had been unreceptive to her intent to apologize, the facts were this—she'd traveled two long days to reach Lioncross, and Myles, and it didn't matter to her that he wasn't here. As her father had told her, Hereford said that Myles could be away for weeks.

But he would come home, eventually.

And she planned to be here.

The feast that night was a lavish affair, as befitting the Earl of Hereford and Worcester, and Aviara and her father ate and drank and shared interesting conversations with the members of the de Lohr family with no hint of the conversation Bertrand had shared with Christopher. Everyone was kind and attentive, and Aviara even sang a duet with Olivia Charlotte that had the entire hall applauding. It had been a pleasant evening, but that was where the pleasantness ended.

The next morning, Aviara was on her deathbed.

Or she pretended to be.

Weak and vomiting, because she stuck her finger down her throat when Lady Hereford wasn't looking. It was Lady Hereford who advised both Bertrand and Christopher that Aviara should not be moved until she felt better. Christopher wanted her out, but he didn't want to be cruel, so he agreed. With the knowledge that she was going to be allowed to remain at Lioncross until she felt better, Aviara settled down for a nice, long stay. God only knew how long it would be.

She was in for as long as it took for Myles to return.

And Christopher knew it.

# CHAPTER FIFTEEN

*The village of Bromsgrove*
*13 miles from Worcester*

M YLES HAD NEVER seen so many people dancing around in one place.

Shocked, he paused at the head of the escort, which slowly ground to a halt behind him, and watched what seemed like half of England cavorting around the straw effigy of a horse. It was a very big horse, decorated with garlands and flowers, and the townsfolk were singing gaily.

"What's this?" Douglas asked, joining his brother as Westley came up on his other side. "A festival of some kind?"

Myles nodded, looking up at the darkening sky. "Of some kind, indeed," he said. "It will be nightfall soon. I'd hoped to stay here tonight because it will make tomorrow a very short ride to Worcester, but they may not have any vacancies in the taverns. It looks as if all of Worcestershire is here."

Douglas and Westley were looking around at the people, too. It hadn't escaped their notice that there were plenty of young women, and they passed hopeful expressions to each other behind Myles' back.

"Then let me set up the encampment on the south side of town," Douglas said. "West will help me. We'll get the tents up and the men settled, and then, I'm certain, the men would like to join the festivities—if you do not object."

Myles shook his head. "I do not object," he said. "I suppose you would like to join also."

Douglas shrugged nonchalantly as Westley nodded eagerly. "If I am not too weary, I will," Douglas said. "But only for a short while."

Myles cast his brother a disbelieving look. He knew Douglas better than that—he was a man who loved a good party more than most.

"Go, then," Myles said. "Get the escort settled, and I'll see to the lady. But get her carriage settled in the encampment."

He had to shout the last few words because Douglas and Westley were already racing back to the escort, whipping the men into a frenzy so they could set up the encampment quickly and then join the party. Myles remained in the front, parting the way through the crowd as the escort moved through the center of the village, past the straw horse effigy, past the well in the center of town. They also moved past several businesses, including four or five taverns with people spilling in and out of them. Once they reached the southern portion of the village, they moved to a field next to a blacksmith's stall and began to spread out.

Myles dismounted Tempest, slapping the horse on the neck affectionately as he led him over to the quartermaster's wagon so the man could feed him. Once the horse was tended, Myles grabbed a senior soldier and instructed the man to go to the church and find out who owned the land they were about to camp on so they could pay them for the privilege. Once that was done, he turned for the carriage, where Veronica had already opened the door and Mud had practically launched himself out. The dog ran off to find a tree to relieve himself as Veronica stood in the door of the carriage, straining to catch a glimpse of the festival going on. When Myles walked up to her, she smiled brightly.

"Greetings, Middie."

He snorted. "There is that name again."

"I think it suits you," she said, a twinkle in her eye. "But if you do not like it, I will not use it again."

"If it pleases you, call me whatever you wish."

She giggled at his quiet acceptance of what was probably an embarrassing nickname before pointing toward the center of the village. "What is all of that?" she asked. "I could see people and smell food. A wedding?"

Myles glanced off in the direction she was pointing. "A festival of some kind," he said. "Douglas and Westley are frantic to get to it, so I suppose we shall have to go as well."

He sounded as if it was the last thing he wanted to do, and Veronica looked at him, a smile on her lips. "As I recall, you like music," she said. "I seem to remember a drunken knight listening to me sing."

His eyes narrowed. "Although I fully admit that your singing enchanted me, you'd better not mention the drunken part again."

She tried not to laugh. "Why not?" she said. "It's true. Then I tried to water it down, and you accused me of poisoning you."

He grunted. "You did," he said. "I know you did. For your information, I haven't been that drunk in years, and it was all your fault."

She started laughing because he was being so serious. "Shall we see if we can find more hard cider over there?" she asked, pointing to the mass of dancing, happy people. "Surely they must have something to suit you."

"I will find my own drink, thank you," he said. "I would not trust you not to try to get me drunk again."

She was smiling openly at him, a gesture he found difficult to resist. "I would never do anything to bring shame to you," she said. "Do you believe me?"

He realized that he was being a little hard with her, and he forced a smile. "I do," he said. "Of course I do."

He was being sincere, but Veronica could see that, even so, there was a hint of doubt in his tone. She came out of the carriage, standing in front of the man and putting a hand on his arm.

"Mayhap others have tried to shame you in the past, but I will not be one of them," she said quietly. "Mayhap other women have tried to humiliate you, but that will not be me. You do recall that I tried to give you watered cider when I realized you'd had too much of it. That is because I did not want you to make a fool of yourself."

The smile on his face turned genuine. "I know," he said in a tone that sent a chill up her spine. "It seems strange to admit that I've spent my life on the defensive at times. Of course, my brothers would die for me and I would die for them, but especially when we were younger, Douglas and Westley were full of tricks. Anything to embarrass me or our older brothers. And they liked to target me in particular because I'm not quick to temper, but when I do… I do not have much control."

Veronica squeezed his arm. "I hope to never see that side of you," she said. "I will endeavor to do my best not to. But I will tell you this—if your younger brothers try to provoke you now, they will have to deal with me. I may not carry a sword, but I can find a big stick. And an even bigger dog."

He laughed softly. "You would do that for me?"

She nodded, the glow of sincerity on her face. "I would," she said. "You do not have to fight them off alone anymore, Middie. You have me now."

He sighed a dreamy sigh. "Aye, I do," he murmured, taking one of her hands and bringing it to his lips for a sweet kiss. "I can hardly believe it, but I do. But still, I suppose I must make it formal."

"What do you mean?"

He cocked a blond eyebrow. "Because we must be perfectly clear, you and I," he said. "I once asked that if you wanted a man to court you, would you tell him or would you expect him to know it?"

Veronica put a hand over her mouth, chuckling softly. "I remember."

"You told me that you would tell him."

"I also said I might have someone else do it so that I would not appear so bold."

Myles smiled, cocking his head with something in his expression she'd never seen before—impishness. On someone as serious as he was, it was adorable.

"I have good news for you, my lady," he said. "You do not have to tell me. I think I already know."

"Well done, Myles," she said, giving his hand a squeeze. "I am very glad no one had to tell you. Even though you did buy my betrothal contract."

"But that is no guarantee that you want me to marry me."

"I said I did. What more should I say?"

"Ask me to court you."

She burst out laughing again. "Very well," she said. "Myles de Lohr, will you please court me?"

"Gladly, my lady. Gladly."

Veronica watched him kiss her hand again, smiling at her but clearly uncomfortable with anything more. He simply didn't know how to show it. But Veronica didn't have such reserve—she was feeling something she could hardly begin to describe. It was joy wrapped up in excitement wrapped up in delirious delight. She'd had three days to think about the situation she found herself in, betrothed to a man she'd only just met. But, somehow, that didn't seem to matter. When there was nothing romantic between them, all she'd seen from him was honorable duty. Attentiveness. Concern. He'd left men at Cradley Heath to protect it from Gregor when he didn't have to, and he'd purchased her betrothal from a man, she learned later, was a horrific glutton and more than likely not very kind. He'd mentioned keeping her as a mistress.

But Myles had saved her.

In fact, he'd saved her in many different ways. When he could have easily consigned her to her fate with no consideration at all, he hadn't. Perhaps he was cold-hearted and stoic and even dense when it came to women, as he'd once said, but that wasn't her experience with him at all. He'd been the most generous and gentlest man she'd ever met. She wasn't hard-pressed to admit that she was looking forward to their lives together.

A future she never thought she'd have.

As she was smiling up at him, she caught movement out of the corner of her eye and looked over to see the quartermaster leading Myles' big, dappled stallion out to a tree so he could tie the animal down and have someone groom him. Myles had said that the colt he'd used in the purchase of her betrothal was the younger brother of this magnificent steed, and as she watched the horse graze, her smile faded.

"I am sorry you had to trade your horse for the contract," she said.

Myles turned to see what she was looking at, spying Tempest as the animal ripped up the grass around him. "I'm not," he said. "It is just a horse, after all."

"But you spoke so fondly of him," she said. "Do you think de Correa would simply take more money and not the horse?"

He looked at her. "I have already promised him the horse," he said. "I will not go back on my word."

"I did not mean that," she said. "I simply meant that I have the money for the cost of the horse and then some. You can give it to de Correa instead of the colt."

Myles shook his head. "While that is generous of you, I think we will leave the bargain well enough alone," he said. "I can always buy another colt. But I can never buy another you."

She looked at him, surprised. "Was that flattery, Myles?"

He appeared confused. "I do not know. Was it?"

Veronica snorted. "You'll learn," she said. "Is it possible that you've spent so much time *being* flattered that you've never had to do it yourself?"

"That is quite possible."

She continued to grin at him. "Then it will be a new world for you and for me," she said. "Now, if we're going to go to the festival, I must gather my cloak. Would you please find Mud and bring him back? I do not want him running wild at night."

It was perhaps the first husbandly duty he'd been assigned, and they weren't even married yet. *Find the dog,* she'd said. As Veronica disappeared back into the carriage, Myles dutifully went in search of Mud, who had gone through the trees and was standing in a small brook, drinking water. He knew that Veronica fed the dog throughout the day, even more now that he had wounds and was riding with her most of the time. But he no longer wore bandages, and his injuries seemed to be healing nicely. He caught sight of the dog and whistled for it, and the animal immediately ran for him. But he didn't dodge out of the way fast enough to avoid being jumped on by dirty paws.

Muttering with disgust that he had two big, muddy spots on his tunic, he grabbed the dog by the neck and headed back through the trees, where Westley was looking for him. He ran straight into his brother, who looked down his nose at the wet dog.

"Do you intend to adopt her son when you marry her?" Westley asked, pointing to the dog. "You'll make a handsome family."

Myles was still holding on to the dog with one hand, brushing off his tunic with the other. "Very funny," he said. "Once I cage this beast, Veronica and I will go to the festival. Are you coming with us?"

Westley nodded. "The tents are going up, and the men will attend the festivities in shifts so the encampment is never unattended," he said. Then he turned his attention toward the ruckus in the distance. "I seem to remember coming through this village a few days ago, and it was quiet. There was no hint of whatever celebration this is."

"Nay, there was not," Myles said as he began to walk, dragging the dog with him. "Everything was quiet."

"Things change quickly."

"They do," Myles said, seeing the carriage near the center of the encampment. "A perfect example of that is the fact that I was not a betrothed man when I passed through this burgh a few days ago. My situation has changed *very* quickly."

Westley put his hand on Myles' shoulder. "I could not be happier for you, Myles, truly," he said. "It is an amazing story to tell. I'm still astonished by it."

"I hope Papa feels the same way."

"He will," Westley said. "She seems like a very nice lady. More importantly, she seems to have a good head on her shoulders."

"She does."

"Then she'll be good for you," Westley said. "No... regrets?"

"What do you mean?"

"That other lass who escaped you not long ago."

Myles knew whom he meant. He averted his gaze, shaking his head. "It's strange," he said. "I was so convinced that she was the one I wanted. I would have sworn it. But meeting a woman like Veronica... It is astonishing how Aviara seems like a distant memory now, and nothing more. I cannot even remember feeling anything for her. Not seeing her for months... and then the marriage announcement... It has made me realize that she was never meant for me, West. I know that now."

"You're sure of it?"

"I am," Myles said firmly. "Veronica has shown me much in the short time I've known her. Mostly, she has shown me how a woman of honor and integrity behaves. She treats me like a man, not a prize. That is priceless."

Westley could see by the expression on his brother's face that he was serious. "It is incredible that it simply took the right woman to show you true happiness and not constant angst," he said. "Even if she only comes with that bare manse, she's still worthy."

Myles glanced at him. "She comes with more than the manse."

"Does she?"

Myles came to a halt and faced him. "I will swear you to secrecy on this," he said. "If anyone else speaks of it, I will know you told them, and I will never trust you again."

Westley, surprisingly, was good at keeping secrets. Like his brothers, he was an honorable man and took privileged information seriously.

"I will not repeat it," he said. "I swear. But what is it?"

Myles glanced around to make sure no one was listening. "Edgar de Wolviston saved most of what he made as a cartographer," he said. "That is why the manse is rather bare. He simply didn't see a need to spend money."

Westley was interested. "He's rich?"

"*She's* rich."

"Is that so? How much?"

"Over twenty thousand pounds."

Westley's jaw dropped. "Twenty thousand *pounds*?"

"Gold."

"*Gold?*" Westley said loudly, and Myles had to slap a hand over his mouth. Realizing he'd nearly broken his promise, he nodded quickly and lowered his voice. "Bloody Christ, Myles, you will be a rich man."

Myles nodded and resumed walking. "So it would seem," he said. "But, truthfully, the money doesn't matter. She does. She's worth more than any fortune she might bring."

Westley was still reeling from the fact that his brother would soon be extremely wealthy. "Spoken like a true romantic," he said. "When do you intend to marry her?"

They were nearing the carriage now, and Veronica opened the door, emerging with the dark blue cloak she'd brought from Cradley Heath. With her dark hair and bright blue eyes, Myles couldn't take his eyes off her. He let go of the dog, who ran to her. As she pushed the dog into the carriage, Myles spoke softly.

"As soon as I can," he said quietly. "As soon as we get home and I announce to Papa what has transpired. I will not wait to begin my life with her, West. She has shown me something… something very good. It is the life I want."

With that, he stepped away from his brother and walked toward Veronica, who was still trying to stuff the dog into the carriage. But Mud had other ideas and stuck his head out, a few times, until Myles pushed the dog's head back into the carriage so Veronica could close the door. As Mud scratched at the door and whined, Myles extended his elbow to her.

"Would you like to go find food and drink now?" he asked.

Veronica clutched his elbow tightly. "I would, thank you."

Smiling at her, Myles led her and Westley off toward the village center and the enormous celebration going on.

Little did he know that it would be a night to remember.

&#x2CF;

IT WAS THE feast day of St. Mary Magdalene and also an anniversary of a legend about a white horse who used to wander these lands, bringing fertility and good fortune with him. Evidently, the villagers had been celebrating for two straight days, so the village center was something of a mess. Most people were terribly drunk, and exhausted, but there were rows of tables still laden with food. Good food.

That was where Myles, Veronica, Westley, and finally Douglas went first.

The people of the village had spared no expense for the celebration. One of the village elders had a daughter who had recently married, so he and his wife in particular went all out to celebrate the festival of fertility and good fortune. They surely must have spent a small fortune on the food they'd had prepared, because it included small cakes made from precious white flour, honey, and wine. There were also almond-milk pies, cheese tarts, beef prepared several different ways, beans with onion and garlic, and fish in several different dishes.

It was a veritable feast.

Veronica turned her nose up at the fish, but she wanted some of the beef dishes, the tarts, and the white cakes. Small, flat discs of stale bread were provided for guests to put their food on, and she loaded up one of those as the de Lohr brothers loaded up three and four each. There were tables to sit at, so they found their places and settled down to an unexpected banquet.

The food was surprisingly good. Douglas managed to track down the wine, kept near the entry to the small church in town, and brought back cups and a big pitcher. In contrast to the good food, the wine was cheap and it was strong, but they were thirsty, so they drank it down as they enjoyed beef in garlic sauce and cheese tarts that were quite cheesy and salty.

For Veronica, the meal itself was an eye-opening experience. Her only supper companion, over the years, had been her father and an occasional guest. She certainly hadn't spent her time with three knights, brothers, who had seen much of the world and fought in many battles. Their conversations were quite worldly. Even Westley, who was just a couple of years older than she was, had far more experience in life in general than she had. He spoke of a street in Paris that was small and crowded with stalls that produced perfume with ingredients from all over the known world. But it also happened to be near a brothel, and he laughed about that until Myles shot him a quelling look and he realized that he was speaking of something vulgar in the presence of a gentlewoman.

But Veronica didn't mind.

She was fascinated.

"I suppose you would like to go to Paris someday, my lady?" Douglas asked her, his mouth full. "Every young woman should go to Paris at least once in her lifetime. Make sure my brother takes you."

Veronica looked at Myles, who nodded. "I will take you if you wish to go," he said. "Douglas is right—everyone should travel. It expands one's views on the world."

Veronica shrugged. "I've not thought on it much," she said. "It would be lovely to go to Paris and see the great cathedral and listen to the musicians. I've heard that the musicians in France are the very best in the world."

"Many things there are the very best in the world," Myles said. "Paris is a glorious and colorful city, but it also has its darker side. Every city does."

"I suppose."

"If you'd like, I will take you there for our wedding trip."

She smiled at him. "If you think it is the right thing to do, I would be happy to go," she said. "But I am equally happy not to go. I do not need a wedding trip."

"Why not?"

"Because the wedding will be enough, as it will be with you. I do not need anything more."

"Ah," Douglas said, putting his hand over his heart. "A lady who flatters. How fortunate you are, Myles."

Myles was close to blushing. He took a long drink of that cheap, strong wine to fortify himself before answering. "I am the most fortunate man in all the world," he said before returning his focus to Veronica. "As for the wedding trip, we do not have to decide now. You may want to think about going to other places, so there is no hurry."

"When will you marry?" Douglas asked.

"Soon," Westley answered for him, mouth full. "I asked him already. He says soon."

"Mama might have something to say about that," Douglas said. "You remember how she took control of Christin and Brielle's weddings. She wasn't at Curtis' wedding and it crushed her, so she compensated by making Roi's marriage to Odette a monumental thing. And with you—she will do the same thing."

Myles looked at Veronica, a hint of remorse in his expression. "I hope you do not mind," he said. "My mother is a wonderful woman and we love her dearly. I know you will, too. But she is… strong-willed."

Veronica didn't seem troubled by it. "My mother died when I was very young," she said. "I do not even remember her. It would be good to have your mother help with the wedding, since I do not have a mother of my own."

"God," Westley muttered, mouth full of more food. "With that kind of attitude, Mama will love her more than you, Myles. A perfect daughter."

Myles grinned, looking at Veronica with an expression neither brother had ever seen before. Something between joy and anticipation. They passed amused glances between each other but didn't say anything. They continued with their food and drink as Myles and Veronica became lost in each other's eyes.

"Have you eaten enough?" Myles asked. "Do you want to dance now?"

Veronica had eaten her share, and the strong drink was making her head swim a little. She could see people dancing around the straw horse, but she didn't leap to Myles' invitation.

"You are forcing me to make a confession," she finally said. "I do not know how to dance. I never learned. Therefore, I do not think I wish to dance, but I thank you for the invitation."

Myles picked up her hand. "You may not know this about me yet, but you will learn," he said. "I happen to like dancing. I'm very good at it and I can teach you, I promise."

"It's true," Douglas said, nursing his third cup of the strong wine. "Myles is an excellent teacher when it comes to dancing. You should let him show you."

That was a surprising bit of information about her future husband. Given what she knew about the man, she would never have guessed it. Still, she was nervous about it.

"Mayhap another time, when there are not so many people around," she said. "I do not wish to make a fool out of myself in front of all of these people."

Myles stood up. "You will not."

He pulled Veronica to her feet, took the cup out of her hand and set it back on the table, and then lifted her up so that she was sitting on his broad right shoulder. She squealed with terror and delight as he rushed over to the crowd and began dancing with them, spinning her around to the point where she nearly fell off his shoulder. But she was having a marvelous time doing it as Myles danced with the villagers, going through the steps that he would teach her at some point.

That brought Westley and Douglas.

They, too, began to dance with the villagers, making sure to pick out the prettiest girls. Myles followed them, twirling a jig. For such a big man, he was surprisingly light on his feet, but Veronica eventually lost her balance on his shoulder and ended up in his arms. He simply carried her around, dancing to the music, whirling her about until she screamed.

"You are going to make me swoon," she said, wrapping her arms around his neck as he carried her from one dancing circle to the other. "My head is swimming with drink!"

He wasn't even out of breath, but he was clearly having a good time. "Are you at least enjoying yourself?"

"I am."

"Then that is all that matters."

He spun her around again, and she squealed, holding him fast so she would not lose her grip. When he slowed, she spoke again.

"May I ask you something?" she said.

"Anything."

"Would it be possible for me to stay in a tavern tonight?" she asked. "I do not mean to be trouble, but the benches in the carriage are extremely uncomfortable. I would do better sleeping on the floor, and I have for the past two nights, but I also know that if you discovered that I slept on the floor and did not tell you of my discomfort with the benches, you might become angry with me."

He was momentarily distracted from the dance. "You are correct," he said. "I *would* become angry with you, and you should have told me sooner. I can send men to the taverns in town to see if there are any available beds, but you can see that the village is full. I suspect the taverns are, too."

"But will you try? I will be happy to pay for it myself."

He frowned at her. "You will do no such thing," he said. "I

will send men to see if there is anything available."

True to his word, he danced over to a group of de Lohr soldiers as they cavorted with some of the women in town. He spoke to three of them, asking them to find a room for Lady Veronica and instructing them to offer to pay handsomely for it, because it would be an incentive to some tavernkeep to kick a lesser-paying customer out of a chamber.

As the men fled, Myles took their place in the circle and, still carrying Veronica, followed all of the dance steps with his future bride in his arms. Her closeness, her body against his, fed him with a sense of euphoria. Was this what it meant to be happy, he wondered?

*Is this what my life will be like from now on?*

It was one of the better moments he'd ever had.

Night finally fell, and the villagers lit the straw horse effigy. Flames reached for the sky, sending sparks up into the heavens. Myles stopped dancing and set Veronica to her feet, and together they watched the bonfire as villagers threw flowers into the blaze. They heard someone say that the flowers were an offering for good luck, so Myles found a flower on the ground and handed it to Veronica. With a grin, she went to the bonfire and tossed it in. As Myles watched, a young woman grabbed her by both hands and began twirling with her in front of the fire. He smiled as he watched her laugh, spinning out of control in front of a pagan fire.

He could have watched her all night.

"Myles?"

Hearing his name, Myles turned around to see Roi and Alexander standing behind him. Shock rippled across his features.

"Roi?" he said. "Sherry? What are you doing here?"

"I was going to ask you the same thing," Roi said. "Since when do you stand in the middle of peasants and worship a pagan bonfire?"

Myles ignored the question, looking between them, knowing their appearance wasn't by chance. Immediately, his good feelings fled and he was all business. It happened in the blink of an eye.

"What is wrong?" he asked. "Why are you here? Are you looking for me?"

Roi nodded. "We are," he said. "Papa sent us. Let us go somewhere quiet where we can talk."

He started to move, but Myles stopped him. "Wait," he said. "Roi, what is happening? Can't you tell me?"

Roi paused, looking his younger brother in the eye. "Aviara and her father are at Lioncross," he said. "Papa sent us to find you and warn you."

Myles scowled in disbelief. "*Aviara* is at Lioncross?" he said. "Why?"

"That is why we need to speak with you," Roi said. "Come."

Still, Myles wouldn't move. "Wait," he said. "I cannot leave without Lady Veronica."

Roi shook his head. "Who is that?"

"The lady I was sent to escort," Myles said. "The daughter of Edgar de Wolviston."

"Ah," Roi said. "Very well. Collect her and secure her for the night while we speak. Where are you staying?"

Myles gestured toward the southern side of the village. "Down there," he said. "Did you not see the encampment?"

Roi shook his head. "We did not come from that road," he said. "Where are Douglas and Westley?"

Myles looked around. "Somewhere," he said. "The last I saw

them, they had a woman on each arm."

"Typical," Roi muttered. "Well, find the lady and let us get on with it."

Myles nodded, but he hesitated a moment before speaking. "There is something you should know," he said. "There was a problem with fulfilling the betrothal. I—"

"Middie!" Veronica was suddenly in their midst, coming up behind Myles and grabbing him around the waist to stop her momentum. She was laughing and breathless, having pulled away from the women who were forcing her to dance. "God's Bones, those women are boundless. I thought they were going to try to dance my legs off!"

She continued to giggle, but Myles wasn't laughing. The business-minded knight was back, especially in the presence of his older brother and brother-in-law. In fact, he was feeling increasingly uncomfortable with the fact that he hadn't had the opportunity to tell them what had happened, yet Veronica was showing obvious affection toward him. She still had her hands on his waist as he forced her to face Roi and Alexander.

"Lady Veronica de Wolviston," he said evenly. "This is my brother, Richard de Lohr. He was named for King Richard, a personal friend of my father's. Everyone calls him Roi. And the black-eyed knight next to him is Sir Alexander de Sherrington. He is married to my eldest sister, Christin."

Veronica stopped laughing. In fact, she looked at Roi and Alexander with a little fear, startled at their appearance and more than embarrassed that she'd been caught laughing and gasping. Not only that, she'd grabbed Myles in a very familiar way.

Quickly, she dropped her hands.

"My lords," she said, curtsying politely. "It is an honor to meet you."

"And you, Lady Veronica," Roi said, though it was clear that he was puzzled. "I… I hope your trip has been pleasant so far?"

Veronica didn't know what to say. "It has been… eventful," she said. "But the weather has been pleasant. That makes it all the more bearable. And this festival was an unexpected treat."

Roi glanced at the festivities going on around them. "It looks quite… loud," he said, chuckling, before he focused on her again. "May I offer my condolences on the passing of your father. Though I did not know him well, I met him on a few occasions. I know that his maps are without equal."

"Thank you, my lord."

"Did you inherit his talent?"

Veronica grinned, shaking her head. "My father could draw most anything with incredible precision," she said. "Unfortunately, I did not inherit his talent for drawing."

"But she can do other things," Myles said. "She can sing like an angel. She was gracious enough to entertain us when we arrived at Cradley Heath."

"Oh?" Roi said, seemingly impressed. "That takes a good deal of skill."

Veronica was modest. "It takes hours of a young girl fooling with a harp and pretending she has some idea of how to play it," she said, watching them smile. "Your brother is very kind in his praise, even if it is not true."

Myles cocked an eyebrow. "It is true," he said, but he would go no further, not until he'd told Roi and Alexander what had transpired over the past week. "My lady, my brothers have business to discuss with me, so I can leave you in the care of Westley and Douglas, or I can return you to the carriage for now. What is your choice?"

Veronica looked at all of the dancing going on, and as much fun as it had been, it had really only been so because Myles had been there. She didn't want to dance and celebrate without him.

"I think I will return to the carriage," she said. "It has been a long day, and I am weary."

"Then I will escort you back to the encampment," Myles said as he grasped her elbow, then turned to Roi. "Where shall I meet you?"

Roi pointed at a smaller tavern across the road where people were milling about in the doorway and warm light streamed from the interior. "We have a rented chamber over there," he said. "We'll wait for you in the common room."

That brought Myles pause. "You have a chamber?"

"Aye."

He looked at Veronica. "Would you mind if the lady took your chamber?" he said, returning his attention to his brother. "The lady has been forced to sleep in the carriage for most of the journey, and I think you know how uncomfortable the benches are. I told her I would find her a room tonight, but with the village full of revelers, I suspect all of the rooms are gone. You two can sleep in the encampment in my tent if you wish."

Roi didn't seem troubled by it. "If she would get good use out of the chamber, I am happy to surrender it to her," he said. "But I am sleeping on your bed, Myles. Do not try to put me on the ground."

Myles waved him off. "Sleep where you will," he said. "For giving the lady your rented chamber, you can sleep anywhere."

As Roi and Alexander resigned themselves to sleeping in an encampment and not a warm chamber, Veronica ran off to collect her things while the men waited around. She also had a dog to collect, who would appreciate sleeping before a hearth. It took her just a few minutes to gather her things, and her dog, before they were heading over to a tavern called The Pig's Ear.

With a lingering glance at the dancing still going on over in the village center, Veronica couldn't remember such a lovely day. A lovely day and a lovely evening, and all of it was because of Myles. If this was what her life was going to be like from now on, she would gladly give herself over to it. From the relatively uneventful life as the daughter of a cartographer to the worldlier and busier life as the wife of a knight, she was ready.

With all of her heart, she knew she'd never been so happy.

Looking at Myles, she had a suspicion that he felt the same way.

# CHAPTER SIXTEEN

"SO THAT IS her scheme, is it?" Myles said, shaking his head in disgust. "All I can think of at this moment is poor Ollie. The man suffered the fate that more than likely would have happened to me, too. I do not think his death was an accident, not for one minute."

The Pig's Ear was loud, hot, and smoky on this evening as the common room was near capacity. People were wandering in from the festival outside, demanding food and drink and a place to sit, but Myles, Roi, and Alexander were at a table in a small alcove next to the rented chamber that they'd given over to Veronica. There was a heavy curtain that separated their table from the rest of the common room. It gave them some privacy, but it didn't stop the noise. It was still as loud, but not as loud as Myles' reaction to what Roi had just told him.

The story of Aviara's return and Ollie's death was still ringing in his ears.

"Damnation," he muttered. "Poor Ollie. He did not deserve that."

Roi grunted. "Even after he stole Aviara away from you?" he said. "Papa told me everything. Unless you have a different version of the situation, it seems to me that Ollie stepped into it with his eyes wide open."

Myles wasn't hard-pressed to agree. "He viewed her the way I did," he said. "As a prize. When I first heard about their marriage, I thought he might have coerced her into marrying him. I admit that I did not believe it. But I've had time to think on it. Mama, Papa, and those who knew Aviara have been trying to convince me that she was no good for me. Especially Peter, who stood up to her. I realize now that I should have listened to them."

Across the table, Alexander was nursing a large cup of ale, now half gone. He was the observer, perhaps the wisest man in the family next to Christopher. Alexander's life and exploits were legendary. He knew a little something about love and manipulative women. He'd experienced them before. He'd watched Myles deal with Aviara over the past couple of years and, like the rest of the family, thought she was poison. If Myles was sincere that he was now starting to see reason, then Alexander couldn't be happier.

But he wasn't sure he was convinced.

"Why are you listening to them now, Myles?" he asked. "It seems like a drastic change."

"I know. But it is true."

"What has changed that you would see reason?"

Myles knew the question would come, but he didn't think it would come so soon. In truth, he was a little nervous to answer, but he had no choice. They deserved to know.

"I'm truthfully not sure where to start," he said. "Many things have become clear since Papa told me about Aviara and Ollie. The best thing Papa did was send me on this escort mission, because I met someone who was unlike anyone I ever knew before. A woman who spoke to me as if I was a man to be respected, not an object to toy with. A woman who respected my judgment, my actions, and my mind. She saw the man, not the de Lohr name. Not the physical features. She has made me see a lot of things I've never seen before."

Both Roi and Alexander were listening with interest, and perhaps some suspicion, and it was Roi who finally spoke.

"Lady Veronica?" he asked.

Myles nodded without hesitation. "It is," he said. "But that was obvious."

Roi conceded the fact. "She's the only woman you have been around since leaving Lioncross, so it wasn't difficult to determine who it was," he said. "And she did seem quite... familiar with you earlier."

Myles couldn't deny it, so he didn't try. "She's not a high-born, petty chit like so many of the noblewomen are," he said. "All I've ever known about those women are their games and their objectives. How they want to marry a de Lohr. Papa's position in England has made it so that his sons are highly prized, and I seem to attract the worst of them. The ones looking for a handsome husband, regardless of what I think or feel. Veronica isn't like that."

"Then if she has helped you see that all women are not like Aviara, I am happy for you," Alexander said, finally speaking up. He leaned forward, folding his hands on the table as he looked at Myles. "We've all seen how highborn women can be, but fortunately, I did not marry a woman who behaved like that. None of your sisters are like that, nor is your mother. Roi's wife is not like that. But sometimes it is more important to find proof of such a thing outside of the family, so if Lady Veronica has done that for you, then I am glad. This will be a pleasant journey for you to Manchester if the lady you are escorting is pleasing."

Myles looked at him. "We *have* been to Manchester," he said. "We are returning."

Both Alexander and Roi appeared confused. "They why—" Alexander began.

But Myles wouldn't let him finish. The time had come for him to lay out the situation for them so there was no mistake. Dragging it out wouldn't do him any favors. He held up a hand to silence Alexander, and even Roi when the man opened his mouth. With both knights shut down, Myles cut to the crux of the situation.

"The circumstance is this," he said, lowering his voice. "Believe me when I tell you that it is confusing, and possibly shocking, but this is what happened. I went to Cradley Heath, on the orders of my father, over a week ago. When I arrived, I was met by a man who identified himself as the brother of Edgar de Wolviston. The man's name was Gregor. Gregor de Wolviston told me that Edgar's daughter was violently opposed to being escorted to her betrothed, so I would have to take her by force. After a struggle, during which both Douglas and Westley were injured, I finally subdued Edgar's daughter, Lady Veronica."

Roi and Alexander were hanging on every word. "And?" Roi said.

"*And*, as it turned out, she was not opposed to being escorted to her betrothed," he said. "Gregor had lied to me because he wanted her forcibly removed from Edgar's home so he could strip it of anything of value. Evidently, he came to Cradley after his brother died with the intention of doing just that. The only thing preventing him from doing it was, in fact, Veronica.

Therefore, he sent for a de Lohr escort to get her out of the manse. Once the lady and I realized that, things went smoothly."

Roi was frowning with the extent of Gregor's deceit. "Was there even a betrothal contract?" he asked.

Myles nodded. "There was," he said. "One that had been secured about ten years ago. Somehow, Gregor knew about it, and he made the decision that it was time to be fulfilled."

"To get her away from the manse."

"Aye."

"Then what?"

Myles continued. "The betrothal contract called for her to be delivered to Abner de Correa," he said. "According to the terms of the contract, she was to marry him when she came of age, which is next month."

"Coincidentally."

"Exactly," Myles said. "There was no need to delay. But the lady had a plan in mind. She agreed to go to Manchester and marry de Correa, because once she did, de Correa would inherit Cradley Heath by marriage and more than likely throw Gregor out on his ear."

That made sense to Roi and Alexander, who shook their heads in disapproval of Gregor's actions. "So a greedy uncle tried to get rid of her," Alexander said. "But it would come back on him in the end when de Correa threw him out of Cradley Health."

Myles nodded. "Precisely the point," he said. "I, therefore, escorted her north. By necessity, we were together the entire time, and we had deep and enchanting conversations. I enjoyed coming to know her immensely, and I will admit that I was sorry she was betrothed. By the time we reached Manchester, I was *deeply* sorry. But I delivered her to her betrothed, as ordered—only when we arrived, we were informed that Abner was dead. His son is now Lord Adlington and has been for several years. Moreover, the son is already married, so he could not marry her. Trust me when I tell you the man is a slovenly pig, the vile sort. Since the betrothal legally belongs to him, he thought he might take Veronica as his mistress. But then he decided it would be worth more to him to sell the betrothal, so he did. He sold it."

That also made sense to Roi and Alexander. "It belongs to him," Roi said. "He had every right to sell it."

"I know."

"And that is what you are doing now? Escorting her to her new betrothed?"

"*I* bought the betrothal, Roi."

Roi's eyebrows lifted in surprise. "*You* did?"

"I did."

There it was. The entire situation laid out and explained. The more the news sank in, the more shocked both Roi and Alexander became. Roi's mouth fell open as he looked at Alexander, who was gazing at Myles as if completely dumb-founded.

"*You* bought the betrothal?" Alexander said incredulously. "But why? What are you going to do with it?"

"I'm going to marry her."

That clearly hadn't been on either Roi's or Alexander's mind. Myles had a head for numbers, so they were thinking he'd bought it to make money from it. To realize he'd bought himself a bride brought astonishment and disbelief.

"You cannot be serious, Myles," Roi finally said. "You are actually going to marry this woman?"

"I am."

"But… you do not even know her!"

"I know enough," Myles said calmly. "Before you chastise me for it, know this—I've spent over a week with her. So have Douglas and Westley. If you'd like to get their opinion on this woman, I would encourage you to do so. She is kind, resourceful, respectful, and wise. I told you before that she does not make me feel like an object to be won. She makes me feel like a man. That is something that I've not experienced much of from the women who have chased me."

Roi started to speak, possibly to scold him, but Alexander held up a hand to silence him. "Myles, no one is questioning the lady's virtues," he said, quickly coming to realize this was an extremely touchy situation. "But the truth is that you've never been a very good judge of a woman. You've admitted that yourself, many times. Do you not think this was done rather impulsively?"

"I do," Myles said honestly. "But Aviara and I toyed with each other for two years, and that ended in disaster. The length of time you know someone does not matter, does it? It's the feeling you have when you look at them. It's how they make you feel when they speak to you. It's learning about them and appreciating their good qualities. All I know is that marrying Veronica feels right, and that is all that matters to me. Nothing that makes me feel this happy can be wrong."

After hearing that, Alexander was willing to go on a little faith, but Roi was watching his brother as if the man had lost his mind. When both Myles and Alexander looked at him for a reaction, he rolled his eyes.

"Myles," he said. "I hope you know that I love you. You are my brother and I adore you. I would never say anything to you that I did not feel deeply, so forgive me if I am going to be blunt about this, but you are behaving stupidly. Absolutely stupidly."

Myles tried not to become offended. "Why?"

Roi threw up his hands. "*Because* you have been toying with Aviara for two long years," he said. "Not two weeks ago, Papa received word that the lady had married Ollie, and you nearly lost your head over it. Clearly, the woman is under your skin, deep enough that you and Papa fought over it."

Myles was struggling not to react to Roi's condemnation. "Did he tell you that?"

"He told me that he struck you in anger, but he did not tell me why."

That was news to Alexander, who looked at Myles in disbelief. "He *struck* you?" he hissed. "Christ, Myles, what on earth did you say to make him strike you?"

Now it was both of them piling on, and Myles was trying very hard not to go on the defensive. "It does not matter," he said. "It was something I should not have said, and he was right to punish me. But the truth is this—I am going to marry Lady Veronica. She makes me very happy. If you two think it is a ridiculous thing to do, then that is your opinion. It is not mine. You have not been on this escort. You do not know the lady. She makes me feel *good*."

"So does a whore on Candlewick Street, but that does not mean you marry her," Roi said in an uncharacteristically low blow. "Has this woman seduced you, Myles? Is that what has happened here?"

Myles stiffened. "You are dangerously close to insulting me," he growled. "I know you are concerned for me, Roi, but you do not have any right to accuse me or the lady of vulgarity. She is a proper lady, and if you speak poorly of her again, then you and I will have a problem."

Roi put up a hand to ease him. "I am sorry," he said. "I am not trying to anger you, but I am trying to understand what has happened. Are you truly so shallow that you can transfer your affections from one woman to another within a few days? How do you even know these feelings for Lady Veronica are real? How do you know that if you see Aviara again, you will not rush into her arms and Veronica will be a distant memory?"

Myles was finished being scolded. He braced himself for the fight to come. "You should talk," he said, jabbing a finger at Roi. "I seem to recall a certain earl's daughter who threw you over for another suitor, and within two weeks, you had met Odette. You married her fairly quickly. So do not speak to me about transferring affections from one woman to the other when you have done the same thing."

Roi's jaw flexed. "That was different."

"Of course it was," Myles said sarcastically. "Because it happened to you and not to me, and evidently, I'm as stupid as sin when it comes to knowing my own feelings. Is that what you're telling me?"

Alexander put his hands up between them, trying to prevent a full-on fight. "This is not going to get us anywhere," he said steadily. "Myles, the only reason Roi is speaking bluntly is because he is new to the situation. He is seeing it from a logical standpoint. He does not want to see you make a mistake. Would you not agree that Roi simply wants to protect you?"

Myles' jaw was twitching as he sat back in his chair, his enormous arms folded angrily across his chest. "He is not protecting me," he said. "He is criticizing me. But you are correct on one thing—he does not know the situation. He does not know Veronica. Why must I justify my feelings to him or you or anyone else? I am telling you that I lusted after the wrong woman. I can admit that. Now, I've met the right woman, and whether I met her a week after Aviara married, or a year after she married, I would still feel the same way. Time does not change what I *feel*."

Roi was having a hard time understanding everything. He couldn't accept it. He shook his head because he was afraid his brother was jumping from one woman to the next, trying to ease the pain of losing one by focusing on another. Myles wasn't usually so emotional, which made the entire situation that much more shocking. Roi just didn't want to see the man make a decision that would adversely affect him for the rest of his life.

"Did you buy the betrothal because you were seduced, Myles?" Roi said, unable to let the subject ease. "Is that what truly happened? Did she seduce you and now you feel pity for her?"

Myles was starting to turn red around the ears, a sure sign that his slow temper was about to explode. "That is a terrible thing to say," he said. "Is it because you fucked Odette first and then decided to do the honorable thing by marrying her? Are you assuming I've done the same thing? I haven't, you know. I have more restraint than you do."

Roi had had enough. He was about to get physical with his brother, but Alexander managed to grab him before he could launch himself. As Alexander tried to cool the situation, the curtain was yanked back to reveal Douglas and Westley. They were mildly drunk, having just come in from the festival outside. Westley went to embrace Roi but ended up falling on him as Alexander stood up and pulled the knight into a chair. Douglas, however, made it to his own chair next to Myles unassisted, pulling off his gloves and laying them on the table in front of him.

"What is all the shouting about?" he said. "We could hear you when we came in."

Myles was still furious with Roi. "Our older brother seems to think I am foolish when it comes to Lady Veronica," he said. "I told him about the betrothal, and he thinks I am stupid."

Douglas looked at Roi. "Did you tell him that?"

Roi wasn't going to back down. "Not two weeks ago he was longing for Aviara, and now he is getting married to another woman?" he said. "I told him that I thought he might be transferring his feelings from one woman to ease the loss of the other. Lady Veronica must have seduced him somehow."

Douglas shook his head. "It is not like that, Roi," he said. "Forgive me, brother, but you do not know what you are talking about. You've not been around the lady and Myles. You do not see how good they are for each other. She's a lovely woman."

Roi frowned. "God, not you too," he said. "You are under her spell too?"

"It is no spell, I assure you," Douglas said. "She is kind and thoughtful. She seems to think a good deal of Myles, and I, for one, am very happy for him. You should be, too."

Roi shook his head in disbelief. "So you do not think this is happening quite fast?"

Douglas looked at Myles, who was considerably down in the mouth. "I'll tell you what I told Myles," he said. "Love is not always about timing. Sometimes, it is about opportunity. Myles has a glorious opportunity in front of him, someone who has already helped him heal some of the damage done to him by Aviara, so stop giving the man grief. Be happy for him."

Roi wasn't so sure. It wasn't that he didn't trust Douglas, because he did. The man had their father's wisdom, something unusual in one so young. But he simply didn't like the sound of all of this.

"I suppose we'll find out just how serious he is about Lady Veronica, because Aviara is at Lioncross," he said. "The true test will come."

Douglas frowned. "What is she doing there?"

"Ollie is dead," Roi said. "Papa thinks Aviara has come to claim Myles as her next husband. As I said... give him a few days to think on that, and we'll see if he's serious about Lady Veronica's betrothal or not."

Douglas looked at Myles with some apprehension before returning his focus to Roi. "Why are you so concerned about this, Roi?" he said. "It's Myles' life, not yours."

Roi knew that. He also knew he'd been rather hard. "I just do not want to see him make a mistake," he said quietly.

"That may be, but it would be *his* mistake," Douglas said. "Leave him alone."

That seemed to settle it, at least for the moment. As Myles and Roi refused to look at one another, each convinced they were correct, they failed to see the chamber door open next to their alcove. The curtain had closed again, so no one noticed the cloaked figure slipping past them, pulling the dog with her. They were still wrapped up in the subject of Myles buying a betrothal, perhaps heading into a second round of arguments. But Alexander tried to direct them onto another subject, so they were occupied and not particularly interested in the world around them. Therefore, no one noticed when the cloaked figure and the dog blew out into the street beyond.

Swallowed by a festival and the dark, starlit night.

# CHAPTER SEVENTEEN

S HE'D HEARD IT all.

Unfortunately, the walls of The Pig's Ear weren't very thick. Veronica had felt very safe in her little room that faced the main road, and from her window, she could see the continuing festivities. There was already a fire in the small hearth, and Mud had gone straight to it, stretching out on the warm stone, while Veronica pulled off her cloak and began to prepare for a bed she was incredibly grateful for.

She didn't have to sleep on the rock-hard benches of the carriage again.

Checking the bed didn't turn up any vermin, which made her doubly grateful. She'd brought her satchel with her, so had soap and a comb, but she didn't have any water. She knew that Myles and his brothers were in the alcove right next to her room, and she could hear their voices through the wall. Sounds, but not the words. Not wanting to trouble Myles for something as mundane as water, she thought to hail a serving wench herself.

Carefully, she opened the door.

The common room was full. And loud. She took a few steps

out of her chamber, looking for a serving wench and seeing one who was moving among the tables about twenty feet away. She tried to catch the woman's attention, but she failed. As she tried again, she began to hear raised voices behind the curtain, and she could hear what, exactly, Myles and his brothers were speaking of. They were becoming louder.

Clearly, someone wasn't happy.

Hearing her name, Veronica forgot about the serving wench and backed up near her door, at the seam where the curtain met with the wall. Perhaps she shouldn't have listened, but when her name was mentioned, she couldn't help herself. She listened to Roi speak of Aviara's return and how the woman was waiting at Lioncross for Myles' return. Shocked, as well as concerned, she heard Myles explain their journey to Manchester and how it had affected his outlook on life in general. His sweet words praised her for helping him understand a different perspective when it came to women, and she smiled as she listened to that, but quickly, the conversation deteriorated.

Roi didn't have anything good to say.

It was increasingly distressing to listen to Roi lambast Myles for being "stupid," in his words. He called Myles stupid for buying her betrothal. He was angry about it. He also accused Myles of being shallow for transferring his feelings so quickly from one lady to another, something that had also concerned Veronica. She had even asked him about it. Evidently, Roi had the same concerns, but Myles was convinced his brother was wrong.

And that was where the problem started.

As much as she hated to admit it, Roi was voicing some of Veronica's own concerns. Things she'd secretly kept tucked away. The first night she met Myles, he'd spoken of Aviara and his attachment to her. He'd never kept that from her. But hearing the situation through Roi's eyes made her see another side of it, something Myles hadn't conveyed. He had spent two years engaging in some kind of romantic game with Aviara, enough that he wanted to marry her, but he refused to admit that anything he was feeling for Veronica was tied to Aviara.

Roi had called him stupid.

Maybe it wasn't stupidity as much as it was denial.

Myles sounded like a man in denial.

Roi seemed convinced that Myles was simply exchanging one lady for another, again reinforcing Veronica's own fears. When he accused her of seducing Myles, it was enough to drive her to tears. She was embarrassed and horrified to see her budding relationship with Myles through his brother's eyes. It looked like something superficial and impulsive. Perhaps the entire family would look at her and think she had seduced Myles in a weak moment as he was reeling from the loss of Aviara.

She knew she hadn't seduced him.

But she certainly hadn't stopped him.

The voices were growing louder, and some nasty things were said. She wasn't going to stay there and listen to Myles' brother beat him down and accuse her of things she hadn't knowingly done. She'd never meant to prey on Myles in his weakened state. He'd said so many wonderful things to her, and he'd treated her with such care, but she'd naturally fallen for him. She couldn't help it. But now, Myles' brother was laying out the reality of the situation.

Maybe he was right.

God help her… maybe he was.

She stumbled back into her rented chamber and shut the

door. Tears trickled down her cheeks and her hands were shaking. Everything was shaking. Fighting back sobs, she knew she had to leave. She couldn't face Myles and she couldn't face his brothers, not after what had been said. She stuffed her possessions back into her satchel and swung her cloak around her shoulders. She roused Mud, who was unhappy at being awoken, but he dutifully stood up and stretched as Veronica grasped him by the hair on his neck and cautiously opened the door.

The common room was still loud and full of smoke and people. As she stepped out of the door, she could hear Douglas talking. Realizing he must have joined his brothers in the past few minutes, she quickly directed the dog out of the tavern, moving as fast as she could. No one seemed to bother her, thankfully, so she was able to depart unmolested.

Out in the night air, she took a deep breath and came to a pause.

The festival was still going on all around her. All of that happiness when her world was in turmoil. She didn't want to go back to the de Lohr encampment. Truth be told, she simply wanted to go home. She didn't want to be around Myles and his brothers who thought so poorly of her—and, quite frankly, she realized that she'd given them every reason to. Myles had left men at Cradley Heath to keep Gregor out, so she was certain she wasn't going back home to face her uncle again. He was probably long gone by now. She would have to face Broden, and the de Lohr soldiers, but she was confident that they would leave if she asked them to.

She didn't want any remnants of the de Lohr escort around.

She just wanted to forget everything, including her feelings for Myles.

God help her, she was falling in love with the man. She knew she was. But given what she'd just heard, she could see how foolish it was. Being relatively naïve when it came to men, and having never even been kissed until she met Myles, she'd let herself become upswept in the dream. That hurt her more than anything.

How she wanted that dream to be her reality.

With Mud trotting after her, she made her way toward the south end of the village, which was still crowded with people. There were horses about, however, tethered in groups and sleeping standing up for the most part, so she did something she wouldn't have done under normal circumstances—she took one. The beast was hairy and round, and she was able to climb on its back easily. When she turned it around for the road and gave it a kick, it took off at a quick trot.

Mud followed.

Fortunately, Veronica knew where she was. She and her father had traveled to Bromsgrove several times, so she knew that the road south would take her right into Worcester. It wasn't very far away, either. She'd easily make it by morning, even though there was only a half-moon in the sky, making the landscape fairly dark. But she didn't much care.

She was going back where she belonged.

Myles still owned her betrothal contract, but he'd already told her once that if she didn't wish to marry him, he'd simply take her home and let her live out her life in peace. Given everything she'd heard from Myles' brother that night, perhaps that was the best thing for both of them.

But it was breaking her heart every step of the way.

*Farewell, Myles...*

# CHAPTER EIGHTEEN

*Worcester*

I T WAS DAWN on a surprisingly clear morning as Gregor emerged from a business on Wyld's Lane, chewing on a piece of bread as cries and grunts echoed behind him. The four men he'd brought with him to Cradley Heath followed him from the business, one at a time, carrying armfuls of bread and, in one case, a silk scarf. The proprietors of the bakery had given them anything they wanted, including the protection money they demanded, if they would simply leave them alone.

And Gregor would, for about a week, and then he would visit them again.

That was how he made his money these days, by rousting local business and demanding money or he would tear their establishments to shreds. He only targeted businesses on the south side of Worcester, where they didn't fight back much. He'd tried his tactics on the Street of the Jewelers, only once, because the jewelers usually employed armed men to protect their stock. He'd been hit in the head by a club from one of the armed men, a blow that set his world upside down for a day, so he never went back there again.

These days, he only struck the weak and the afraid.

But he was having a good time doing it.

On this bright but cold morning, he'd managed to procure food to break their fast by harassing the baker. They had fresh bread in their arms as they wandered down the street, shoving the food into their mouths as they laughed about the old man they'd just roughed up. There was a tavern toward the end of the road, and beyond that stood Cradley Heath.

The apple of Gregor's eye.

Every morning, he watched the manse to see if anything had, or would, change. Perhaps the de Lohr soldiers would leave. That was always the hope. But every morning, he was disappointed, so he wondered about staking out the manse even now. Nothing had changed over the past week. No one had come or gone. He saw servants leave to go about their daily business, but they always left with a couple of soldiers. There was no opportunity to abduct or harass one of them. But still, he watched.

It had become his routine.

This morning, he sat at the corner of The Bull and The Buck, which had been his home since he'd been denied entry to Cradley Heath. He chewed the bread in his hand as one of his companions went inside to demand hot wine from the tavernkeep, who took a big stick to the man and threatened to hit him if he didn't pay for it. That drove the companion back outside, where he ate bread with the others.

It was the start of another uncertain day.

"Are we going to stand here again today?" A man with a huge scar down his left cheek, known as Biddy, didn't seem terribly happy with their current activities. "Why not go into Bransford? I told you that I heard about a place where there is gambling. We've got enough money to play and win."

Gregor was still watching the front of Cradley Heath. He could see the de Lohr soldiers on the walls. His mind began to wander, thinking of that lovely pewter plate in the great hall still waiting for him to take it. He couldn't even get into the postern gate dressed as a servant because the soldiers were checking everyone who did business with the manse.

"Nay," he said. "I will not go. But if you want to gamble, go ahead. Just come back by the morrow."

Biddy and the others all thought that was a stellar idea. The truth was that they only knew Gregor from his own visits to a gambling establishment in Lincoln. They weren't servants at his shabby cottage, nor were they men with any vocation of Gregor's social status. They were, quite simply, gamblers and mercenaries, and they went where the money was. Because Gregor owed them money from his years of gambling with them, he had promised them the repayment of his debts when his brother died, which was why they'd come with him to Cradley Heath. When de Lohr took over the manse, they'd turned into petty criminals.

That was all they were good for.

At the prospect of going to a gambling establishment, they began pulling coin out of their pockets, the coin they'd stolen from businesses or that were given to them simply to make them go away. Between the four of them, they had quite a bit of money to spend, and Gregor's suggestion that they go without him had them planning that very thing. They remained with Gregor while they finished their bread before finally departing for Bransford and the lure of more ill-gotten gains.

But Gregor didn't much care.

He knew they'd be back.

Usually, he was very much in the mood to gamble. That was how he'd lost everything he had inherited. With his companions off to piss away the money they'd received from frightened shopkeepers, Gregor was thinking about going inside the tavern and having more than bread to break his fast. They'd had boiled beef last night, and he was certain that there was some left over for a morning meal. He'd have to pay for it, because the tavernkeep wasn't afraid to use a club on those who tried to cheat him out of paying, so Gregor was resigned to the fact that he'd have to part with some coin. Just as he stood up from the old stump he'd been sitting on, he caught sight of a dog.

Not just any dog.

A dog he'd seen before.

*Mud.*

Startled, Gregor watched as Mud preceded a figure wrapped in a cloak astride a fat, hairy pony. Both the dog and the figure were heading for Cradley's gatehouse, and it didn't take a genius to figure out that the person on the pony was none other than his niece, Veronica. He caught a glimpse of her profile, so there was no doubt.

And she was alone.

Gregor's mouth was open in shock as he watched her plod along, coming in from one of the smaller north-south roads. She couldn't see him because she was facing away from him as she moved, but he could most definitely see her. Quickly, he slipped behind an old yew tree growing next to the tavern and strained to catch a glimpse of the road behind her. He was looking for the de Lohr army she had left with.

But there were no signs of anyone.

Especially not those big knights.

*She's alone!*

Gregor was a fast thinker. That was a trait that had always come in handy. His thoughts were never kind or generous, but they were quick, and in this case, he was thinking about the possibilities of a lady with no guards. No guards meant no protection.

He could force her to order the de Lohr soldiers to open the gate of Cradley Heath.

But he had to do it before the gate guards saw her.

He had to move.

Tossing aside the crust of the bread he still held, Gregor raced after Veronica as she plodded toward the manse. She needed to turn a corner and then she would be in full view of the gatehouse, so he had to get to her before she made that move.

He ran faster.

Just as Veronica was about to make the turn that would put her in direct line of sight for the gatehouse, Gregor hit her from behind and knocked her off the pony. Startled, the horse bolted as he dragged her to the ground and collared her around the neck, putting a dirty hand over her mouth so she couldn't scream. As Veronica put up a good fight, Gregor dragged her into a small alleyway between two businesses. But she kept fighting, so he squeezed her neck with his arm, choking off her air supply. She fought hard until she couldn't breathe any longer, and when she finally went limp, he let her fall onto the ground, where she smacked her head on a rock.

And then she lay still.

Quite pleased with himself, Gregor stood over Veronica, smiling at her unconscious form. Now he had her exactly where he wanted her, and he began to think of all of the wonderful things he could do with her. How he could force her into admitting him entrance into Cradley Heath. How he could force her to give him the plate in the great hall. Certainly, there had to be more that he could force her to do, but he couldn't think now.

All he knew was that there were… possibilities.

And he was going to explore them.

But that was his last clear thought before he heard growling. By the time he turned around, that ugly, dirty dog had launched himself in Gregor's direction, and Gregor soon found himself fighting off a very big, very angry mutt. The dog bit him, twice, and forced him to back away from Veronica.

As Gregor found himself bleeding from one of the bites, he furiously collected several rocks and began tossing them at the dog. He hit him more than he didn't, but Mud wouldn't back away. He charged Gregor again, and the man was forced to run in circles because the dog was intent on carving him up with his big teeth. Gregor managed to dodge the dog at one point, and he was able to pick up a big stick that was lying near the yew tree. When the dog came at him again, he swung the branch and caught Mud in the head.

With a yelp, the dog backed off.

But not for long.

The fight for Veronica continued.

CB

SHE HAD RUN.

Quite honestly, it hadn't taken Myles long to discover Veronica had left once he started looking for her, and that had been after midnight when he and Roi were finally separated because Myles had thrown a punch at his brother's head. He was tired of being called stupid and impulsive, and he'd simply had enough. Roi was genuinely trying not to be cruel, but the honesty he was projecting was coming across as judgmental, and Myles was finished with it. Right or wrong, he didn't want to be judged. It was *his* life.

And he wanted to live it with Veronica.

Therefore, Douglas and Westley dragged him away from Roi and Alexander, but Myles wouldn't leave the tavern without making sure Veronica was settled for the night. He'd hoped that the sight of her, the sound of her, would calm him down, but after knocking at her door for a ridiculous length of time, he opened the panel cautiously to find the chamber empty and her things gone.

Everything was gone.

Startled, he entered the room as if to convince himself she wasn't hiding in a corner or under the bed. In fact, he tore the place apart looking for her, but still no Veronica. By this time, Douglas and Westley were in the chamber helping him as Roi and Alexander stood in the doorway, concerned. The lady had gone, and it was Roi who started the mad dash back to the encampment to see if she was there, but they found it empty except for a few de Lohr soldiers. Still, quiet... and no lady.

That was when Myles threw another punch at Roi that made contact.

This was all his brother's fault. Peter had ruined it with Aviara, and now Roi was doing the same thing with Veronica. Myles knew she'd heard the arguing because they'd been loud, as the de Lohrs usually were, and her rented chamber was next to the area where they had been sitting. There was no way she couldn't have heard them, and all of the cruel things that had been said, and Myles was convinced that she'd run away because of it. She'd fled the room, but she hadn't gone back to the encampment. In fact, her cap case was still in the carriage. It was Roi, wiping away a streak of blood from the corner of his mouth, who suggested she might have very well gone back to Worcester, since they weren't far from it.

Perhaps she'd simply gone home.

That was something Myles had clung to.

Without any clear idea as to where she had gone, it seemed to make sense to return to Cradley Heath. There was literally nowhere else she could go. Unless she'd been abducted, of course, but they would have heard a struggle if that was the case, and her chamber had been perfectly neat. No signs of a fight. Myles gave up on that hypothesis purely based on that logic, but if he didn't find her at Cradley Heath, then he was going to return to Bromsgrove and tear the place down to the ground in his search for her.

He wasn't going to give up.

He was going to find her.

So, he and his brothers and Alexander mounted their steeds and headed south in the dead of night. Fortunately, the road was straight and in good condition, and they'd brought three torches with them that helped light the way as the moon sank lower in the sky. By the time it hit the horizon, the sun was starting to come up in the east.

Onward they pressed.

They started passing farmers on the road who were heading to market in Worcester, and the smell of morning fires filled the air as they drew closer to the city. They slowed the horses a little because they'd all been traveling quite a lot over the past several days, so the closer they drew to Worcester, the more Myles slowed the pace. Tempest had quite a bit of endurance, but even he was showing some signs of fatigue. On the main road, they entered the northern section of the city, heading for the southern end, where Cradley Heath was.

Myles, who had managed to control his anxiety for the ride south, was now exhibiting symptoms of stress. He sped up as they passed into the town, forcing those with him to pick up the pace as well. The city of Worcester was coming alive as the day dawned, and by the time he reached the city center, with the cathedral to the south, stretching to the sky with bones of sand-colored stone, he was forced to slow down because of the wagons and people on the road.

Then he simply went around them.

He had to get to Cradley Heath.

Finally, they managed to move through the bulk of the city bustle at that hour. Cradley Heath was just out of his sight. Another block and he'd be able to see it. He spurred Tempest, and the horse snorted, moving faster as they thundered down the road.

And then he saw it.

Cradley Heath.

It was surprisingly quiet, not at all what he'd expected, though he wasn't really sure what he had expected. Maybe he'd expected more hustle and bustle with the return of Veronica. Men shouting and people cheering. God, he didn't know what he had expected, but the silent-as-a-tomb scenario didn't sit well with him. Something seemed... wrong. As he pulled Tempest to a halt, looking at Cradley as if expecting to see Veronica through the stone walls, he began to hear growling and barking off to his left.

There was an angry dog down the road as the road continued through some businesses. He almost didn't care until the dog began barking again, almost frantically, and it occurred to him that he'd heard that bark before.

"You damnable beast!" someone was shouting. "I will kill you!"

Douglas, Westley, Roi, and Alexander heard it too. They all looked at one another in confusion until Myles, lured by a suspicion, dismounted and unsheathed his broadsword. That had Douglas and Westley following. Even Roi and Alexander followed. But Myles was the first one to see Gregor fighting off Mud, who seemed to be tearing at the man. A few more steps toward him and Myles caught sight of feet in an alleyway. He realized, with horror, that he was looking at Veronica.

And she was unconscious.

That spurred Myles after Gregor.

Unfortunately for Gregor, he saw five very big knights heading toward him, and one in particular who had his sword in an offensive position. He recognized him as one of the de Lohr knights he'd spoken with when he left Cradley Heath several days ago, the same man he'd instructed to take Veronica by force. But the man was bearing down on him with his broadsword wielded, and Gregor had no idea why. He only knew that his life was in danger for some reason. He panicked and grabbed Mud by the ear, lifting the beast with the intent to use him as a living shield against the incoming knight.

"Stop!" he said. "Stop this instant, do you hear?"

Myles had to hold position because Gregor had Mud in such a way that it would be difficult to get a clear shot at him.

"What did you do to Veronica?" Myles asked through clenched teeth. "Why is she on the ground?"

Gregor was still puzzled by the appearance of the knights. He had no idea why they'd come, or even how they had seemed to appear out of nowhere. Behind the knight who was threatening him, he could see two of the man's companions pulling Veronica into a sitting position as she began to come around.

But that still didn't clear up why these men were here.

Only that they were not supposed to *be* here.

And neither was Veronica.

"Where have *you* been?" he demanded. "I told you to take her to de Correa. I told you that she did not want to go. Why is she back in Worcester?"

Myles' eyes narrowed. "The last I saw of you, you were leaving town," he said. "You should have stayed away."

Gregor stiffened. "Cradley Heath belongs to my brother," he said angrily. "He asked me to manage his estate. You know this. I have every right to be here, yet the de Lohr men at the manse will not admit me. Why not? What did you tell them?"

"I told them not to let you in."

Veronica was walking up behind Myles, blood on her left temple. She looked pale and strained and exhausted, but the fire in those bright eyes was focused solely on Gregor. Myles heard her voice, but he didn't take his eyes off his prey. He'd already made up his mind that Gregor was not going to survive the hour, but he had to wait for the right opportunity. Yet the fact that Veronica was awake and talking relieved his heart in a way he'd never known before. If he had any less control, he probably would have wept with joy.

But that would have to wait.

He had a man to deal with.

"You?" Gregor said when he saw Veronica coming toward him. "Why would you do such a thing? It is my right to be at Cradley Heath! Until you marry, it is mine!"

"It is *not* yours," Veronica said, raising her voice. "It belongs to Sir Myles."

"Who is that?"

Veronica pointed to Myles. "Him," she said. "He holds my betrothal contract. De Correa sold it to him. Now, put my dog down or I will kill you myself."

Gregor could see the situation slipping away from him. He was holding Mud against him, with his hand clamping the dog's jaws shut, but that wouldn't last forever. Mud was getting panicky, and he was a big dog, so he began to squirm and twist. Gregor eventually lost his grip, and Mud slipped to the ground, and then the dog came up and clamped his jaws on Gregor's left hand. Gregor screamed and grabbed the dog around the neck with his free hand, squeezing as hard as he could. His intent was clear—he was trying to strangle the dog. As Veronica gasped and rushed toward him, grabbing Mud's hind leg to pull him free, Myles used the distraction to come around on Gregor's left and plunge his broadsword into the man's chest, straight through the armpit.

The dog was released and Gregor fell to the road, screaming in agony.

As Veronica grabbed her dog and pulled him away from the battle, Myles swung his sword in a skilled maneuver and brought it down again, slicing Gregor's head clean from his body. As the man immediately stopped moving, Myles hardly gave him a second look before he was turning to Veronica as she continued to drag the dog away from the fight.

"Stop," Myles commanded softly, but she kept dragging. "Veronica, please stop. Gregor will not be a threat any longer. Let me see what he's done to you."

He was referring to the blood on her temple, but Veronica didn't know that. She came to an unsteady halt and let go of Mud, backing away as Myles came closer. That caused Myles to stop, looking at her with a pained expression. He'd been fully prepared to scold her for riding alone from Bromsgrove, but he just couldn't manage it.

There were more important things to say at the moment.

"You are injured," he said, gesturing to the left side of her face. "Let me tend your head."

She refused to look at him. "Nay," she said. "I… I will do it. You needn't bother."

"Needn't *bother*?" he repeated, pain in his voice. "Christ, Veronica, what is it that I have done to make you run from me like this?"

Veronica's head was killing her, and she was feeling sick and disoriented from her fight with Gregor. She could see her uncle's body several feet away, could see the copious amounts of blood pooling, but it did not distress her. If anything, she felt relief. Relief so great that she could hardly believe it. But she could also see Myles standing in front of her, absolutely distraught. He looked the way she felt.

*Heartbroken.*

She broke down in quiet tears.

"I… I had to come home," she wept.

"Why?"

"Because I had to."

Myles sighed faintly. "Why?" he said. "Because you heard our argument back at Bromsgrove? Do not deny it, because I am certain that you did."

She couldn't look at him, wiping away the tears as fast as they would come. "It does not matter."

"Of course it matters," he said with more emotion than he could control. "You heard us arguing and you ran. Not that I blame you, but I am so very sorry you had to hear that. Please know I would not have hurt you for the world, not intentional-ly."

She sniffled. "I know," she said. "But I did hear everything. I had to come home. I had to… think."

Myles closed his eyes regretfully. Think about what, he wondered? Their future together? He looked over at Roi, who was standing several feet away. Their eyes met, and it was all Myles could do to not erupt at his brother. *Again*. He and Roi had always gotten along, so the animosity he was feeling wasn't normal. But he was furious with the man.

Now, he had to convince Veronica that the argument meant nothing.

He'd never felt more desperate in his life.

"Sweetheart, listen to me," he said quietly. "Roi was simply voicing his concerns. He is a man of logic. It is difficult for him to understand our situation, but it does not mean it is wrong. It just means he has an opinion, but I do not share it."

Veronica sniffled. "But he is right," she said, finally gazing up at him with watery eyes. "He is right when he says it has all happened very fast. And I suspect he was right when he voiced his concern that you might possibly be using me to ease the loss of Aviara."

"I am *not* using you to ease the loss of Aviara."

"How do you know?"

Myles looked at her seriously. "Because I never felt for Aviara what I feel for you," he said. "My father once said that he thought I viewed her as a prize to be won, not a woman of flesh and bone. In a way, I suppose he was correct. Aviara pitted me against my cousin, Ollie, and I was determined to win the competition. That was all it ever was—a competition. That was all it could ever be."

Veronica was still weeping, still wiping at her face. "Mayhap that is true," she said. "And I have no reason not to believe you. But the fact remains that this has happened very fast, Myles. We've become swept up in something exciting and new, but your brother was right when he said we are behaving stupidly."

"Why would you say that?"

She shrugged. "Because we were ready to be married after only knowing one another for a few days," she said. "And you... you had just lost a woman you thought you wanted to marry. I have had time to think on this, and I would be crushed if we were to marry and then you realized a few months later that I was not the woman you wanted. It would destroy me if you grew to resent me because of a decision made on a whim."

Myles had never been this close to begging in his entire life, mostly because she was making sense and he didn't want to admit it. Roi had tried to tell him and he refused to agree, but Veronica was telling him the same thing. And it wasn't the first time—she had asked about Aviara before the subject ever came up with Roi.

Perhaps he needed to listen.

Perhaps he wasn't going to get everything he wanted after all.

"I could never resent you," he said softly. "Veronica, I do not know if you are aware of this, but you have changed my entire life. You have changed the way I view the world. You have changed the way I feel. I told you once that you may have found the path to my heart, and I was right—you have. It's right in front of you, something I wasn't sure I even had. But I do, and it belongs only to you."

Veronica had stopped weeping, and was now looking at him with an expression of hope and longing—but also with hesitation. It was all there, rippling through her delicate features. He was being open and honest.

Perhaps she should, too.

"As mine belongs to you," she whispered. "But this must be right. It must be something we both want and not something that circumstances or lost loves have pushed us into."

That was not what he wanted to hear. She had been agreeable to marriage yesterday, but today... she wasn't. Or, at least, she wasn't sure about it.

But he was.

That stone-cold heart was in danger of breaking.

"Then what do you want to do?" he asked. "I will do anything you want to do, but please don't send me away."

She shook her head. "I will not send you away," she said. "I... I suppose I could not do that. I thought I could last night when I fled Bromsgrove. I just wanted to come home and live out my life alone. But now that I see you... I do not think I could. I would miss you every day for the rest of my life."

He was fortified by that. It gave him hope that this was salvageable after all. "Then what do you want from me?" he said. "Tell me and I will do it."

Mud, who had been over near a gutter getting his paws wet and drinking dirty water after his fight with Gregor, chose that moment to come over to Myles, wagging his tail. He bumped up against the knight affectionately, and Myles found himself looking down at that dirty, silly dog.

But one he was strangely attached to now.

Veronica was watching, too. The dog may love new playmates, but he was usually only truly affectionate with her. She could see that had changed. Mud was a good judge of character. If he loved Myles, then there was no reason for her not to love him too.

She suspected she already did.

But she wasn't ready to marry him yet.

"You promised to court me," she finally said as Myles reached down and petted the dog on the head. "Are you still willing to do that?"

He looked up from the dog. "I said I would," he said. "I said that I would gladly."

"No matter how long it takes?"

He shrugged. "A month, a year, or ten years," he said. "I will court you for as long as you want me to."

She watched him as he scratched the dog on the head, careful of his wounded ear from the fight near Macclesfield. "I should think a year would be sufficient," she said. "Long enough for us to come to know each other better and long enough for you to decide that you are not using me to replace Aviara."

He stopped scratching the dog. "I will again tell you that I am not using you to replace Aviara," he said. "But if you'd like me to court you for a year, I am happy to do that. I will do it for as long as you want, Veronica, so you can be convinced that I am completely sincere. You are the only woman for me, and it does not matter how long it takes for me to prove it to you."

She glanced at the brothers who were standing a respectful distance away. "And you will tell your brother that we will wait to be wed until we are completely sure?"

Myles, too, looked over at his brothers. Men he loved with every drop of blood in his body. Specifically, he was looking at Roi, who was gazing at him steadily. Myles could see sincerity and concern in his expression. That was the Roi he knew, a man he respected greatly.

*His brother.*

As Peter had tried to protect him once, Roi was simply doing the same thing, and with that realization, all of the anger seemed to drain out of Myles. When he smiled weakly at Roi, the man smiled back. That told Myles that everything was going to be all right between them, because he knew, in spite of their argument, that Roi would support him whatever he ultimately decided. That was never in question. But Myles' slight nod told Roi that, perhaps, he was acknowledging that Roi had been right all along.

*Would you not agree that Roi simply wants to protect you?*

Myles knew that Roi always would.

"I will tell him," he said after a moment. "Mayhap... mayhap waiting will be better for you, too. I suppose it never occurred to me that a marriage so soon after we met would make you look less than honorable, and I apologize if I overlooked that. It was not my intention. You are a woman of grace and integrity, and I want my family to know it."

For the first time that morning, Veronica smiled. "I think a courtship longer than a few days looks better for us both," she said. "We are reasonable people, after all. Let us be sure that we cannot live without one another and then prove it to the world."

"I already know I cannot live without you. But I am a patient man."

"I hope I am worth the wait."

"You are worth everything."

Her smile broadened. "For a man who claims he does not know how to flatter, you have done an excellent job with me," she said. "I think you are getting better by the day, Middie."

He had never been so glad to hear that ridiculous nickname

coming from her lips, and he laughed softly, perhaps out of embarrassment. He wasn't sure what to say to that. In lieu of an answer, he reached out to take her hand, and she let him. She let him kiss it, too, in full view of his brothers.

But it was the sweetest kiss she'd ever received, a promise of a new future.

One she was ready to face.

But it didn't stop there. Myles had one more thing to do, and he was going to make sure Veronica was there when he did. After tending the slight scalp wound on her head and apologizing, in full, to Roi, they were all heading to Lioncross within the hour.

# CHAPTER NINETEEN

*Lioncross Abbey Castle*

"H E'S BACK," DUSTIN said breathlessly as she stuck her head into her husband's solar. "Myles is here!"

Christopher, who had been reading a dispatch from London, looked at his wife in shock. "He's come *back*?" he said. "Roi and Sherry were supposed to keep him away. Where are they?"

"They're with him!"

That had Christopher out of his chair, heading for the door.

Unfortunately, others knew Myles had returned, also. News of his appearance spread through Lioncross like wildfire.

Dustin and Christopher were making their way out of the keep just as Myles, Westley, Douglas, Roi, Alexander, and a woman no one recognized came in through the main gates. Dustin stood on the steps leading into the keep, watching the situation with some concern, as Christopher went down to meet his sons.

Myles was the first one he approached.

"Welcome home," he said as the man dismounted his frothy steed. But he also looked at the men accompanying Myles, the same men he'd sent to intercept him and tell him about Aviara, and his confusion grew. "Roi? Sherry? You've all... returned. Why?"

Neither man answered him because Myles came around his horse to face his father. "Greetings, Papa," he said, seeing the apprehension on the man's face. "Is Aviara still here?"

Christopher sighed, immediately thinking that Myles had, indeed, rushed home to see her. His heart sank.

"She is," he said with regret. "She has come down with an illness and cannot be moved, or so she has informed us. But your mother thinks she is feigning illness and waiting for you to return home. I suppose we shall know for certain if she shows herself now that you have come."

Myles cocked a blond brow, an indication of displeasure. "I see," he said. "Where is she?"

"Inside the keep, I would imagine," Christopher said. "She's not come out of her room since her arrival, and Bertrand has enjoyed our hospitality every day since."

"Bertrand came, too?"

"He did."

"Good," Myles said. "I want to see them both."

Christopher thought he knew where this was leading, and he was sick over it. "Myles," he said. "Please... do not do anything foolish."

Myles appeared as if he had no idea what his father meant. "Me?" he said. "I will not, I assure you. But I want to see them both."

Christopher shook his head with sorrow. He turned to see Westley and Douglas, who greeted their father with a kiss or a hug, followed by Roi. Christopher was about to lay into Roi for letting Myles return to Lioncross when he caught sight of a beautiful woman with dark hair. Myles went to her, taking her by the arm and helping her brush off her cloak, which had become dusty from the road. It was more than a polite gesture. In fact, it was downright affectionate.

That brought curiosity.

"Papa," Roi muttered, pausing as he headed toward the keep. "It is not what you think."

Christopher eyed him. "How would you know what I think?" he said. "And *who* is that?"

He was indicating the woman that Myles had a grip on. Roi turned to watch the pair before putting a hand on his father's shoulder.

"I will let Myles tell you," he said. "Be calm, Papa. All will be well in the end."

Roi moved past him as Christopher's puzzlement grew. He was standing alone when Myles approached him with the young woman on his arm. Christopher found himself looking into the bluest eyes he'd ever seen.

"Papa," Myles said, indicating the young woman. "This is Veronica de Wolviston, Edgar's daughter."

The introduction didn't help Christopher's sense of confusion, but he smiled politely at the young woman.

"My lady," he said. "Your father was a man I admired greatly. I was very sorry to hear of his passing."

Veronica smiled at the enormous earl. "Thank you, my lord," she said. "He spoke very highly of you. His association with the House of de Lohr was highly valued by him."

Christopher smiled politely. "A sentiment I echo," he said. "You are most welcome at Lioncross."

"Thank you, my lord. I am very grateful."

Myles was about to say something more when he caught

sight of movement in the keep entry. He looked over to see Aviara hurriedly emerging with her father right behind her.

So much for being ill.

"Papa," Myles said steadily, his gaze on Aviara. "Would you please take Lady Veronica in hand? I have something to attend to, and I want you to hear it. I want you both to hear it. Follow me, please."

With that, he transferred Veronica's hand over to his father, placing it on the man's arm before heading toward the keep. Neither Christopher nor Veronica had any idea what he meant until they both turned to see people standing at the top of the keep stairs.

It was Veronica who spoke first.

"Is that Lady Aviara?" she asked quietly.

Christopher nodded. "It is," he said. Then he looked at her strangely. "Do you know her?"

Veronica shook her head. "Nay," she said. "But I knew she was here."

Christopher wasn't sure what to say to her. The appearance of his son and a woman who was supposed to have been escorted to her betrothed was all quite puzzling. But he found himself gravitating toward the keep stairs, with Veronica on his arm, where Myles was drawing closer to Aviara. He came to the top step as Aviara, with Bertrand at her side, rushed toward him.

"Myles," Aviara gasped with delight. "You've returned! The servants told us!"

Myles stood on the top step, looking at the expressions of Aviara and her father. Like predators who had finally cornered their prey.

Or so they thought.

He had a few choice words for them.

"Aye, I've returned," he said evenly. "I've returned to find you both a burden to my father's hospitality. You told him you wanted to speak with me. Well? What do you want?"

Those weren't words either one of them had been expecting. Aviara, at the very least, had been expecting something more than cold indifference. Even for Myles, the greeting had been cold. She was confused, and it was a struggle to keep the smile on her face.

"A burden?" she said, puzzled. "We... we have come all the way from Aldsworth to see you. I thought you would be pleased."

"I am not. State your business and be done with it."

That brought Bertrand forward. "Myles, be kind," he admonished. "Aviara has just lost her husband. She has come to you, an old friend, for comfort. Why would you speak so harshly to her?"

As if on cue, Aviara pretended to dab tears at the corner of her right eye. But Myles wasn't moved. He could see before him the woman that everyone had tried to warn him about. That Peter had tried to warn him about. Before him stood the woman he'd last seen at Tidworth, with her gold cap and flashing eyes, tormenting him every moment. He didn't know why he hadn't seen it then, in spite of what everyone had told him, but he saw it now. He saw before him a caricature of a woman, the very worst qualities of the human soul.

And he was going to tell her so.

Heartless, cold Myles would have his day.

"I know what happened," he said. "You married Ollie simply to spite me, and in doing so, you tormented and abused a man who would have done anything for you had you shown him the smallest measure of kindness. Instead, you used him, just as you tried to use me. You can stop with the feigned tears and the feigned illness. I might have believed you once. But I am wiser now. I can see you for what you are, Aviara, and I pity Ollie that he didn't."

Aviara's eyes widened. "Why do you speak to me so?" she demanded. "That was a horrible thing to say. I do not think I will forgive you, Myles."

Normally, a statement like that would have thrown him into confusion as to how he could possibly make amends. She was well aware of that. But this time, Myles didn't rise to the bait.

"Good," he said, making a sweeping gesture toward the gatehouse. "Then you can leave. Go back to Aldsworth and find another victim for your cruel taunts. Go find someone else who will be unable to see past your moderately beautiful appearance, which will probably fade quickly as you grow older. You see, Aviara, I have outgrown you. I've outgrown your nastiness, your pathetic attempts at manipulation, and your hollow soul. There is nothing more to you than what I see on the surface, and even that is inadequate. In short, lady, you are not welcome at Lioncross, and neither is your father, who has come here to manipulate me just as you were intending to do."

That brought Bertrand's indignance. "That is enough, Myles," he demanded. "We came here in friendship and—"

Myles cut him off, calmly but unmistakably. "Nay, my lord, you did not," he said. "You came here to secure another husband for your worthless hag of a daughter after you murdered Ollie, but I am not falling victim to your greed. You can forget about me, because I, certainly, will forget about you."

Aviara was quivering with rage. "You cannot speak to me that way," she said. "You stupid, foolish—"

Myles cut her off, too. "I could say the same about you," he said. "You *are* stupid and foolish. Instead, I will tell you and your father this once and only once. Get out. Get out and never come back. If you do not move quickly enough, I will throw you both out personally, so if you would like to risk my wrath, then by all means, ignore me. But I would not advise it."

Aviara was furious. Furious and frightened. "I will not—!"

Myles didn't let her finish. He bent over so that he was at her level and shouted at her as loudly as he could.

"Get *out!*"

His voice echoed off Lioncross' ancient walls. Aviara screamed at his booming voice, slapping her hands over her ears and running into the keep, followed by her equally furious but terrified father. Myles watched them go, feeling more relief and satisfaction than he'd anticipated. There was something hugely fulfilling in what he'd just done, something that lifted a burden from his shoulders. It was a burden he never even knew he had.

He was finally free.

"Myles," Dustin said as she came up beside him. She'd been standing at the base of the stairs, watching everything. "My dearest lad, I have never been prouder of you than I am at this very moment. That took great courage to do that."

Myles looked down at his mother, the woman he loved most in this world. "Someone gave me that courage," he said, taking her hand and gently kissing it. "In fact, I want you to meet that someone. Come with me."

He led her down the steps to the spot where a surprised Christopher was standing with an equally surprised Veronica. But Myles only had eyes for Veronica.

"Mother," he said, his gaze locked with Veronica's bright

orbs. "This is Veronica de Wolviston. I have asked to court her, and she has agreed. Would you please take her inside and show her every kindness? She has had a difficult few days and could use your gentle tending."

Dustin's eyes widened at the news and the request. "Court...?" she managed to stammer before looking to Veronica and collecting herself. "Myles is courting...?"

Douglas and Westley happened to be nearby. They'd watched the entire scene with Myles, Aviara, and Bertrand with almost as much satisfaction as Myles had felt. In their opinion, it had been a long time coming. When they heard their mother's confused stammering, they leaned over, sticking their noses in where they'd not been asked.

But they, too, had something to say.

"We approve, Mama," Douglas said, winking at Veronica. "You will too, when you come to know her."

"Me also," Westley said, kissing his mother on the cheek. "Myles is a fortunate man."

They scattered, off to tend to their duties, as Dustin watched them go with astonishment. But that astonishment was replaced by a hint of delight as she returned her focus to Veronica.

"If they approve, then so should I," she said, chuckling softly. "We are honored by your visit, Lady Veronica. Welcome to Lioncross."

Veronica, too, chuckled at the behavior of men she'd grown quite fond of. "I am very happy to know you, my lady," she said. "I am humbled to be here."

"I suspect we are going to come to know each other very well."

"I am looking forward to it."

Dustin smiled warmly, taking the woman's hand with the intention of leading her toward the keep, but she still managed to pass Myles a long look, silently conveying that she would like to know what had happened sooner rather than later. Myles simply smiled at his mother, knowing what she was thinking. As the women walked away, Christopher turned to his son.

"De Wolviston?" he hissed. "Isn't she supposed to be with her betrothed?"

Myles broke into a grin. "She *is* with her betrothed," he said. As Christopher began to puff up with confused frustration, Myles caught sight of Douglas and called to him. "Douglas! Fetch the colt! I must send him up to de Correa, so have the servants prepare him for the journey!"

Douglas waved at him in acknowledgement as Christopher grabbed Myles by the arm and forced the man to look at him.

"*What* has happened?" he demanded. "I swear if you do not tell me everything at this very moment, I will take a stick to you. You are not too old to beat, you know."

Myles started laughing. Grasping his father by the head, he kissed the man. "I will explain everything," he said. "But you will not believe it."

"Let me be the judge of that."

As the white colt with the black mane was brought out and Westley and Douglas prepared to head north again, partly to collect the soldiers they'd left at Bromsgrove, Myles told his father everything that had happened since leaving for Worcester several days ago. Every last, little detail.

Myles had been right. Christopher didn't believe it at first. But as he watched Myles glow when speaking about Veronica de Wolviston, something Dustin had said to him came to mind.

*He hasn't learned to love because the right woman hasn't*

*come along yet.*

Looking into Myles' eyes, Christopher could see that, quite possibly, the right woman *had* come along in the most unexpected of places. Perhaps it was a wild tale, but as Douglas had once said, love wasn't about timing. It was about opportunity.

Myles had found his opportunity.

And Christopher couldn't have been more delighted.

# EPILOGUE

*Lioncross Abbey*
*One Year Later*

"THE LORDSHIP OF Doré? Congratulations, old man. Well deserved."

Myles grinned. He grinned because he'd never been happier in his life, but he also grinned because his new wife had brought in barrels of the hard cider that seemed to go straight to his head. He'd had three cups of the stuff and was close to being smashed because of it. But he had a right to be smashed because he'd waited a full year for this day.

Finally, Veronica was his.

The newest Lady de Lohr, now Lady Doré, was over near the hearth, dancing an old folk dance that was only for women, but the past year hadn't seen her improve her dancing skills. She tripped more than once. She also crashed into her sisters-in-law a few times, laughing all the way. Given what a fine dancer Myles was, he found it rather humorous that his new wife was all feet and no grace.

But he hardly cared.

She had other fine qualities that he worshipped.

"I am rather pleased with it," he said after a moment. "It was very generous of Papa."

Douglas and Roi, who were also drinking that blasted hard cider, were perhaps more drunk than Myles was. The stuff was sweet, and didn't taste strong, but it had a way of going straight to one's head. Roi put his arm around Myles' shoulders.

"I'm proud of you," he said, giving his brother a squeeze. "You have a fine wife, Myles. I am delighted that your life has taken such a turn."

Myles looked at him. "There was a time when you were not entirely sure I would make good decisions about it," he said. "I'm pleased to see I've redeemed myself."

Roi shook his head. "You were never out of my good graces," he said. "I just wanted you to be happy."

"I am, Roi," Myles said quietly. "Thank you for always being truthful. Even if I did not want to hear it."

Roi gave him another hug and dropped his arm because his wife was waving at him. Odette de Lohr was a fine creature, lovely but fragile. Roi could see her and their son as the lad sat on the ground petting Mud, who was unhappy because he had been bathed for the occasion. As the dog stood up and dragged Roi's son toward the entry door, undoubtedly to find a mud puddle somewhere, Roi left his brothers to go to his wife. That left Douglas standing with Myles and watching the dancing until they were joined by Peter and Curtis. The two eldest de Lohr brothers were also a bit tipsy on the cider, which everyone in the great hall of Lioncross Abbey seemed to be drinking. There was an entire room full of drunken men and women, not the least of which was Westley, who charged into the center of the women and began dancing with them.

The four brothers snorted at him.

"He is going to hurt someone," Curtis said, watching his youngest brother twirl one of their sisters around. "He has all of the grace of a baby bull."

Myles gestured to the second woman Westley grabbed. "He has Elle now," he said. "I know that she likes to dance, but she'll throttle him if he steps on her toes."

That was true. Curtis' wife, Elle, was a Welsh-raised lass who had fought as a soldier in days past. As much as they loved Elle, as a family, she'd been known to take up a weapon or two, still. Westley was likely to find himself with a twisted ear or a bruised arm if he annoyed her too much.

But Curtis waved off Myles' concern.

"He'll have to learn the hard way," he said. "The man is taking his chances, though. She is newly pregnant, and that never bodes well for anyone. Least of all someone who frustrates her."

As they watched, Westley stumbled into Elle, and she pinched him so hard that he yelped. Shaking his head, Curtis decided to save his brother from the increasingly annoyed women. Peter, moving to the spot where Curtis had vacated, tossed back a swallow of the hard cider and grimaced.

"Christ," he muttered. "Any more of this stuff and I'll be out there getting pinched, too."

Myles laughed. "Take Liora with you," he said. "She can defend you."

Peter looked off to the northern end of the hall, where his wife, Liora, was in conversation with a few guests. A stunningly beautiful woman, she was a most gracious hostess, especially in situations like this. He smiled proudly at his raven-haired wife.

"Do not fool yourself," he said. "She pinches with the best of them."

"What a terribly slanderous thing to say about her."

Peter chuckled. "Speaking of slander, we must speak."

"What about?"

"Business," Peter said. "You know I hate to take you away from a new wife, but there are rumblings."

"What rumblings?"

Peter turned to look at him. "One of the Sussex warlords has evidently been offended by Henry through a land purchase, so I've been told," he said. "He is trying to circumvent the king's wishes by selling the land to a French mercenary who has ties to the French crown. I am trying to get more information about it, but I may have to send you and Broden south to find out what the truth of the situation is."

The Executioner Knights were never far from their tasks. Myles hadn't carried out any missions for Peter for a solid year, not while he was courting Veronica, but it seemed that was about to come to an end. Not that he really minded.

He was an Executioner Knight at heart.

"Broden has remained at Cradley Heath," Myles said. "He is my garrison commander there, and he's become fond of one of the women who serves my wife. I do not know if he will want to leave her."

Peter grunted. "I heard about that," he said. "What is her name again? Snowflake?"

"Snowdrop," Myles said. "Snowy, she is called. They make a nice couple, though she's nearly as tough as he is. She's helped the highbred, sometimes spoiled du Reims knight realize much about the world, which is good to see. But since we are speaking of Cradley Heath, we're doing more building there. Crenellations and everything. It will be a full castle before long."

"Christ," Peter said. "That's quite an ambitious plan. Who's paying for it?"

"My marriage has made me quite wealthy, so I am."

"And you are doing this with permission from Henry, I assume?"

"Our father, too," Myles said. "The Earl of Hereford and Worcester feels that another castle in Worcester would be excellent for the lawlessness that city has been experiencing. Roi will be spending more time there as the itinerant justice and Cradley Heath Castle, when it is finished, will be his administrative center as well as the jail."

Peter nodded. "That is excellent news," he said. "And you? Is Monnington Castle to become your home?"

Myles nodded. "It is," he said. "Papa has given it to me as a wedding present along with the lordship. I will be adding new apartments to that place, too. I'm looking forward to raising my family there."

Peter smiled at him. "I'm very happy for you," he said sincerely. "You deserve such joy."

Myles smiled at the man, but the praise brought about something else, something they'd not spoken of since it happened last year at Tidworth.

It was time.

"Peter," he said hesitantly. "I... I wanted to speak with you about something that has been troubling me."

"What is that?"

"I must apologize for becoming angry with you last year at Tidworth," Myles said, lowering his voice. "With Aviara, I mean. You knew better than I did when it came to her, but I didn't want to admit it. I said—and thought—things I should not have. When I thought you ruined my life, as it happens, you actually gave it back to me. I want to thank you for that."

Peter patted his brother on the cheek. "I didn't do much," he said. "But you are welcome. Sometimes others see what we do not. Especially people who love you."

"I know," Myles said, his gaze moving to Veronica as the dance ended and she refused to dance another. "I just wanted you to know that you are my brother, by blood and by name. I've never thought otherwise. But if I've ever conveyed anything contrary to you, I am sorry. I've never meant to."

Peter chuckled. "You never have," he said. "You never will. My brothers all have different traits—Curtis is the strong one, Roi is the smart one, you are the fearless one, Douglas is the wise one, and Westley is the lively one. And I love you all madly for your particular qualities. There is nothing you could ever say to make me feel otherwise."

Myles appreciated that. The past year had been such a whirlwind that he wanted to make sure Peter knew how grateful he was to him.

For everything.

"Speaking of feelings," Myles said as Veronica headed toward him. "I've waited an entire year to feel the woman I love, so if you'll excuse me, I have a marriage to consummate."

Both Peter and Douglas, who had been listening to everything said, broke down in laughter.

"That is an extremely blunt way of putting it," Peter said. "But I would expect no less from you. I suggest you take your wife now before the women get a hold of her again. She'll be dancing all night."

Myles set his cup down. "Not if I can help it."

With that, he intercepted Veronica as she headed toward the dais, whispering something in her ear that made her flush madly. But she nodded quickly, and as Peter and Douglas watched, Myles fled the hall with her.

It *was* their wedding night, after all.

It was time for them to enjoy it.

And Myles fully intended to. When he'd been young, he shared a bedchamber with Douglas and Westley, but that changed when he grew older. Since returning from fostering, he'd had a small chamber on the southwest side of the keep, on the entry level, that faced the wall and the dark mountains of Wales beyond. It was still his chamber, and it had been prepared for the new couple by Dustin and Christin and Liora earlier that day, so Myles took his wife into a chamber that was full of comfortable linens, furs on the floor, and a hearth that was burning brightly.

The moment they walked in, Veronica went straight to the bed and fell on it.

"God's Bones," she muttered, her hands to her head. "I've had far too much of the cider. Christin kept forcing me to drink it."

Myles fought off a grin as he shut the door and bolted it. "Good for my sister," he said. "Now you will be too weak to fight me off when I try to take advantage of you."

Veronica giggled. "Who says I intend to fight you off?"

"You've fought me off for an entire year," Myles pointed out with some animation in his manner. "Believe me when I tell you that it was not easy for me. The most frustrating year of my life."

"You will overcome it."

He made a face at her. "Only if you let me have my way with you now," he said. "I am your husband, after all. That body belongs to me."

He was pointing at her. With a smirk, Veronica rolled onto

her side. "I am so tired," she muttered. "I think I shall go to sleep."

She yelped when he leapt onto the bed behind her and grabbed her. "To hell with that," he growled. "Kiss now. Sleep later."

He rolled her onto her back, looming over her, as she giggled. "You are quite bold, sir," she said. "I thought we might talk all night."

His eyebrows flew up in outrage. "Are you mad?" he said. "All we've done is talk. All year, we've talked. Forgive me, but I want to see some action now."

She continued to giggle, winding her arms around his neck. "Is that all you are thinking of?"

He shrugged, his gaze moving down her neck to the swell of her bosom. "Not *all*," he said. "Most, but not all."

She couldn't stop laughing at him. "Very well," she said. "But you must be gentle with me. I've never done this before, after all."

Leaning down, he kissed her gently on the top of her shoulder. "Someone once told me that women don't always say what they mean," he said. "I hope this means you want me as badly as I want you."

She put her hands in his hair. All of that long, gorgeous blond hair, and she tugged on it, pulling his face so that it was an inch from her own.

"Worse," she whispered. "How dare you make me wait even this long."

Her mouth latched on to his, and Myles was lost. Instantly, delightfully lost. The lust that erupted so easily between them sprang to life as he pulled her against his hard body, his lips devouring hers.

The clothes began to come off.

Carefully, he untied the ties on her pale blue surcoat as his kisses distracted her from the fact that he was undressing her. As he'd discovered throughout the course of their courtship, she was easily distracted by his kisses, and he used that to his advantage. All he wanted to do was get the woman naked. He'd been dreaming about it for a solid year. A year of kisses, of intimate touches, and of a passion that threatened to set them both on fire.

But that was where it had ended.

Until now.

Before he could strip her, he began to hear yelling, realizing that people were standing below the lancet window that faced the bailey. Since the chamber was on the entry level, they were quite close. Infuriated, Myles pushed himself off Veronica and went to the window only to see his brothers standing down there, all five of them, calling up encouragement to him. Shaking a balled fist at them, Myles slammed the wooden shutters so that they had more privacy. That didn't exactly block out the shouts from below, which were turning into drunken taunts, but at least there was an illusion of privacy. Quickly stripping off his clothing until he was nude, he lay down beside Veronica on the well-appointed bed and continued.

His next goal was to have her naked as well, so he resumed his kisses as his hand snaked underneath her shift and surcoat and onto her warm, soft belly. He remembered that belly from the moments during the past year when they had become intimate with their touching, but this time, he went a step further. His hand went to her breasts, something he'd waited an entire year to do, as his mouth found a sensitive earlobe and suckled.

Veronica gasped at the overload of sensations, something that sent bolts of excitement through her body. Myles felt her relax, and he was able to lift the surcoat over her head, followed by the shift. She had hose on, however, tied to each thigh with a pretty blue ribbon, but he left them on. It was the most exciting thing he'd ever seen. With no more clothing between them, the moment had finally come.

The moment his naked flesh touched hers, he knew that he was lost.

Myles wedged his knees between Veronica's slender thighs, moving his fingers to the dark curls between her legs as his lips found a tender nipple. Veronica twitched and groaned as Myles suckled, acquainting himself with her delicious body. Now he could do anything he wanted to her, and want he did. When he slipped his big finger into her warm, wet woman's center, there was no discomfort. Her body was already primed, ready for him. Veronica had waited for this moment as long as he had.

She was ready.

Her pants of pleasure were beginning to echo off the walls. Myles inserted another finger into her, listening to her groan as she thrust her pelvis forward, seeking more of his touch. He suckled her nipples and could feel her body contracting around his fingers, a physical response to his foreplay. It was her body demanding his, whether or not she realized it, and he would answer the call.

He was ready.

Myles removed his fingers from her body, no longer able to restrain himself. He placed his heavy arousal against her and, thrusting gently, slipped in without effort. Her legs spread wider, accommodating his sheer size, her hands going to his buttocks purely out of instinct. She was moving her pelvis toward him, demanding all of him, and he kissed her deeply as he coiled his buttocks and drove his long, hard length into her.

Myles didn't wait to give her pleasure. Cupping her heart-shaped bottom with both hands, he began to move. Within the first few thrusts, Veronica realized she liked this very much. All of the touching and kissing over the past year had been a precursor to this, and she was overwhelmed with the feel of him, the smell of him. Instinctively, she began to respond to him, thrusting her pelvis up to meet his, experiencing the friction of his manhood as he penetrated deep. Pleasure gave way to a spark that grew brighter by the moment.

Veronica lay beneath him, her legs flung open as his big body pounded into her, experiencing every thrust, every withdrawal, with enjoyment she could never have imagined. There was something so deeply intimate about what they were doing, yet so deeply powerful. She was his and he was hers, and nothing could ever separate them. Myles was a tender lover, kissing her gently as he worshipped everything about her. Every time their bodies came together, Veronica could feel the spark between her legs growing into a raging fire. It was a fire that would soon burn out of control.

Myles, too, was feeling the fire as his climax approached. Veronica lit him up in ways he'd never been lit up before. He wasn't a virgin, but he felt as if he was. He felt as if this was the first time he'd ever made love to a woman. It was more than the physical—it was the emotional. She'd touched every emotion he'd ever been afraid to feel. When he finally reached his peak, he spilled himself deep, whispering her name as he did. But then whispering even more.

"I love you, Veronica. With all that I am, I love you."

Veronica felt his spasms, hearing his whispered words in her ear, and it was enough to drive her to tears. But his thrusting continued as he reached between their bodies, probing her damp curls. He found what he was looking for, and a scream erupted from her lips as he rubbed her nub of pleasure. Waves of satisfaction consumed her as her body twitched and bucked, and Veronica was vaguely aware of Myles' soft laughter.

"You like that?" he murmured, his fingers still between her legs. "I will remember that, wife."

Whatever he was doing to her caused her to release twice more, her entire body bucking with the ecstasy he was bringing her. Still embedded in her quivering body, he continued to stroke in and out of her, feeling her respond to him and loving every moment of it. It was the experience of something glorious that neither one of them could have anticipated.

It had been well worth the wait.

"I love you," he whispered again. "When the world is dust and the moon is ash, still, I will love you. Nothing will ever change that."

Veronica wrapped herself around him, her legs around his hips and her arms around his neck. She was dazed and exhausted, but in a good way. His long hair was all over her face and neck, and she pushed it back, out of the way, so she could look at his face.

"There was a time when you told me that I'd found the path to your heart," she said. "I am happy to say that you have a very big one. The biggest, in fact. And I love you for it."

He smiled wryly. "You are the only one who knows that."

"I think your parents do. Your siblings do."

He shook his head. "My love for them is different," he said. "They do not know the heart that you see. That is for you, alone."

She smiled, running her finger along his full lower lip. "I

told you once that I would protect it," she said. "It is the most precious thing you could give me, and I will cherish it, and you, always, my Middie."

That silly name again, the one he'd learned to love. It was so ridiculous, but so endearing. Leaning down, Myles kissed her gently, feeling her hands on his hair, on his flesh, and he could feel his body respond to her touch. He could feel himself becoming amorous again in spite of the fact that he could still hear his brothers, very faintly, outside the window. But it was all done out of love.

And Myles de Lohr had found it.

For a man who had used his coldness to protect the tender heart beneath, he'd found what that heart had been searching for. The love story of Myles and Veronica had been a hard-fought one, but one that would become legendary.

For the man with the heart of a lion, he'd found his heaven.

And a love that would last an eternity.

## ○3 THE END ⅋○

Children of Myles and Veronica

Sebastian

Evander

Cleo (stillborn)

Demetrius

Dustine

Anne Sophia

Lenora

Barrett

Gifford "Giff"

# KATHRYN LE VEQUE NOVELS

*Medieval Romance:*

**De Wolfe Pack Series:**
Warwolfe
The Wolfe
Nighthawk
ShadowWolfe
DarkWolfe
A Joyous de Wolfe Christmas
BlackWolfe
Serpent
A Wolfe Among Dragons
Scorpion
StormWolfe
Dark Destroyer
The Lion of the North
Walls of Babylon
The Best Is Yet To Be
BattleWolfe
Castle of Bones

**De Wolfe Pack Generations:**
WolfeHeart
WolfeStrike
WolfeSword
WolfeBlade
WolfeLord
WolfeShield
Nevermore
WolfeAx
WolfeBorn

**The Executioner Knights:**

By the Unholy Hand
The Mountain Dark
Starless
A Time of End
Winter of Solace
Lord of the Sky
The Splendid Hour
The Whispering Night
Netherworld
Lord of the Shadows
Of Mortal Fury
'Twas the Executioner Knight
Before Christmas
Crimson Shield

**The de Russe Legacy:**
The Falls of Erith
Lord of War: Black Angel
The Iron Knight
Beast
The Dark One: Dark Knight
The White Lord of Wellesbourne
Dark Moon
Dark Steel
A de Russe Christmas Miracle
Dark Warrior

**The de Lohr Dynasty:**
While Angels Slept
Rise of the Defender
Steelheart
Shadowmoor
Silversword
Spectre of the Sword

Unending Love
Archangel
A Blessed de Lohr Christmas
Lion of Twilight
Lion of War
Lion of Hearts

**The Brothers de Lohr:**
The Earl in Winter

**Lords of East Anglia:**
While Angels Slept
Godspeed
Age of Gods and Mortals

**Great Lords of le Bec:**
Great Protector

**House of de Royans:**
Lord of Winter
To the Lady Born
The Centurion

**Lords of Eire:**
Echoes of Ancient Dreams
Lord of Black Castle
The Darkland

**Ancient Kings of Anglecynn:**
The Whispering Night
Netherworld

**Battle Lords of de Velt:**
The Dark Lord
Devil's Dominion
Bay of Fear
The Dark Lord's First Christmas
The Dark Spawn
The Dark Conqueror
The Dark Angel

**Reign of the House of de Winter:**
Lespada
Swords and Shields

**De Reyne Domination:**
Guardian of Darkness
The Black Storm
A Cold Wynter's Knight
With Dreams
Master of the Dawn

**House of d'Vant:**
Tender is the Knight (House of d'Vant)
The Red Fury (House of d'Vant)

**The Dragonblade Series:**
Fragments of Grace
Dragonblade
Island of Glass
The Savage Curtain
The Fallen One
The Phantom Bride

**Great Marcher Lords of de Lara**
Dragonblade

**House of St. Hever**
Fragments of Grace
Island of Glass
Queen of Lost Stars

**Lords of Pembury:**
The Savage Curtain

**Lords of Thunder: The de Shera
Brotherhood Trilogy**
The Thunder Lord
The Thunder Warrior
The Thunder Knight

**The Great Knights of de Moray:**
Shield of Kronos
The Gorgon

**The House of De Nerra:**
The Promise
The Falls of Erith
Vestiges of Valor
Realm of Angels

**Highland Legion:**
Highland Born

**Highland Warriors of Munro:**
The Red Lion
Deep Into Darkness

**The House of de Garr:**
Lord of Light
Realm of Angels

**Saxon Lords of Hage:**
The Crusader
Kingdom Come

**High Warriors of Rohan:**
High Warrior
High King

**The House of Ashbourne:**
Upon a Midnight Dream

**The House of D'Aurilliac:**
Valiant Chaos

**The House of De Dere:**
Of Love and Legend

**St. John and de Gare Clans:**
The Warrior Poet

**The House of de Bretagne:**

The Questing

**The House of Summerlin:**
The Legend

**The Kingdom of Hendocia:**
Kingdom by the Sea

**The BlackChurch Guild: Shadow Knights:**
The Leviathan
The Protector

*Regency Historical Romance:*
Sin Like Flynn: A Regency
Historical Romance Duet
The Sin Commandments
Georgina and the Red Charger

*Gothic Regency Romance:*
Emma

*Contemporary Romance:*

**Kathlyn Trent/Marcus Burton Series:**
Valley of the Shadow
The Eden Factor
Canyon of the Sphinx

**The American Heroes Anthology Series:**
The Lucius Robe
Fires of Autumn
Evenshade
Sea of Dreams
Purgatory

**Other non-connected Contemporary Romance:**
Lady of Heaven
Darkling, I Listen

317

In the Dreaming Hour
River's End
The Fountain

**Sons of Poseidon:**
The Immortal Sea

**Pirates of Britannia Series (with**

**Eliza Knight):**
Savage of the Sea by Eliza Knight
Leader of Titans by Kathryn Le Veque
The Sea Devil by Eliza Knight
Sea Wolfe by Kathryn Le Veque

**Note:** All Kathryn's novels are designed to be read as stand-alones, although many have cross-over characters or cross-over family groups. Novels that are grouped together have related characters or family groups. You will notice that some series have the same books; that is because they are cross-overs. A hero in one book may be the secondary character in another.

There is NO reading order except by chronology, but even in that case, you can still read the books as stand-alones. No novel is connected to another by a cliff hanger, and every book has an HEA.

Series are clearly marked. All series contain the same characters or family groups except the American Heroes Series, which is an anthology with unrelated characters.

For more information, find it in **A Reader's Guide to the Medieval World of Le Veque**.

# ABOUT KATHRYN LE VEQUE

*Bringing the Medieval to Romance*

KATHRYN LE VEQUE is a critically acclaimed, multiple USA TODAY Bestselling author, an Indie Reader bestseller, a charter Amazon All-Star author, and a #1 bestselling, award-winning, multi-published author in Medieval Historical Romance with over 100 published novels.

Kathryn is a multiple award nominee and winner, including the winner of Uncaged Book Reviews Magazine 2017 and 2018 "Raven Award" for Favorite Medieval Romance. Kathryn is also a multiple RONE nominee (InD'Tale Magazine), holding a record for the number of nominations. In 2018, her novel WARWOLFE was the winner in the Romance category of the Book Excellence Award and in 2019, her novel A WOLFE AMONG DRAGONS won the prestigious RONE award for best pre-16th century romance.

Kathryn is considered one of the top Indie authors in the world with over 2M copies in circulation, and her novels have been translated into several languages. Kathryn recently signed with Sourcebooks Casablanca for a Medieval Fight Club series, first published in 2020.

In addition to her own published works, Kathryn is also the President/CEO of Dragonblade Publishing, a boutique publishing house specializing in Historical Romance. Dragonblade's success has seen it rise in the ranks to become Amazon's #1 e-book publisher of Historical Romance (K-Lytics report July 2020).

Kathryn loves to hear from her readers. Please find Kathryn on Facebook at Kathryn Le Veque, Author, or join her on Twitter @kathrynleveque. Sign up for Kathryn's blog at www.kathrynleveque.com for the latest news and sales.